LOVE YOU TILL TUESDAY

LOVE YOU TILL TUESDAY
by M.E. Proctor

"Beautifully written and crafted, **Love You Till Tuesday** weaves a story akin to a complex jazz rhythm. At the center, a compelling P.I. named Declan Shaw supplies the beat. Proctor's work sings with authenticity and grit."
> —**Craig Terlson**, author of the *Luke Fischer* series.

"M.E. Proctor is going to be the next BIG name in crime fiction. Her writing is intelligent, exciting, cool and slick as hell."
> —**Punk Noir Magazine**

"Strong narrative pulled me in, precision dialogue kept me tuned, and characters that surged from the page held me to the end."
> —**David Cranmer**, editor of *BEAT to a PULP*

"In a crime fiction universe overcrowded with cookie-cutter detectives, M.E. Proctor's **Love You Till Tuesday** shows how to breathe originality into an investigation of the seamy underside. You won't easily forget P.I. Declan Shaw's witty, often dark pursuit of a killer."
> —**Nick Kolakowski**, author of **Boise Longpig Hunting Club**

"M.E. Proctor writes crime fiction that sits aside the masters of the craft whilst also standing alone in its pure originality and innovation to an often hackneyed genre. Elegant, flowing prose that tugs at your heartstrings whilst ramping up your heart beat."
> —**Stephen J. Golds**, author of a **Say Goodbye When I'm Gone**

"Make way for Declan Shaw, sharp as the edge of a knife, tough as a bucket of nails, emotionally damaged and irrepressibly charming, searching for truth in the mean streets of the modern American South— the neo-noir hero we need in these trying times!"
> —**Douglas Lumsden**, author of **A Troll Walks into a Bar**

"For the numerous fans of M.E. Proctor's short fiction, this debut novel is sure to be a revelatory delight. A sleek entry into the pantheon of detective fiction, **Love You Till Tuesday** keeps you guessing and holding your breath until the very end. You won't look at other P.I. novels (or hammers for that matter) the same way again."
> —**Mike McHone,** crime fiction writer

M.E. PROCTOR

LOVE YOU TILL TUESDAY

A DECLAN SHAW MYSTERY

Published by **Shotgun Honey Books**

215 Loma Road
Charleston, WV 25314
www.ShotgunHoney.com

Cover by Bad Fido.

First Printing 2024.

ISBN-10: 1-956957-70-7
ISBN-13: 978-1-956957-70-9

9 8 7 6 5 4 3 2 1   24 23 22 21 20 19

For my father.
He would have liked this.

LOVE YOU TILL TUESDAY

ONE

IT DIDN'T LOOK LIKE A CRIME SCENE.

No cluster of light-flashing police cars, no uniforms swarming, no plainclothes kicking around pretending to have an important job to do, and no yellow tape.

Maybe, for once, Steve Robledo could have a look at a scene without officers wisecracking and experts pondering. An ambulance was parked in front of the apartment building with two EMTs leaning on it, having a smoke. A Precinct 5 cruiser was nearby. The official presence was low-key, with the drama index needle on benign.

"That the right place?" Eric "Bogs" Sorensen stepped out of the car. "Looks like a false alarm. Grandma fell out of bed and knocked herself out."

Robledo ignored him. "Where?" he asked the EMTs.

One of the guys pointed. Up. "The deputy didn't let us in. She told us to wait. Got things to do, man."

Robledo doubted they were in a hurry. Nice day, low humidity, shooting the shit with a buddy, what's not to like? "The deputy told you to wait. You wait." He took the steps two at a time, careful not to touch the railing. He could hear Bogs lumbering behind; his three hundred pounds strained the sturdiness of the steps. The front door of the apartment was ajar, no signs of a break-in. Robledo pushed the panel open with an elbow and stood to the side, hand near his holster. "Police. HPD."

"All clear." A female voice.

The smell hit Robledo the moment he stepped into the hallway.

"Fuck," Bogs said. "First thing in the morning. I hate that."

Robledo scanned the apartment. Furniture in disarray, a grand piano by the window, picture frames on the mantel, books on shelves.

A young woman stepped forward. "Constable Precinct 5," she said. "Sally Gomatam."

"Sergeant Robledo. This is Sergeant Sorensen. HPD Homicide. Who called it in?"

"The housekeeper found the body. She called 911. Said there was an accident and Ms. Easton was dead. I was first on the scene. The woman is mistaken, sir. It isn't an accident. I called with details."

Robledo stared at her young, serious face. "Where's the housekeeper?"

"On the terrace."

"I'll take her," Bogs said. "Name?"

"Maria Camacho," Gomatam said. "She comes every Tuesday."

The big detective crossed the living room, mindful to steer away from obstructions, eyes on the floor to make sure he didn't accidentally disturb evidence.

"You didn't tape the scene, Gomatam," Robledo said.

She colored slightly and straightened up. "I secured the scene, sir. I kept everybody out."

Robledo pulled on a pair of gloves before entering the bedroom. The violence of the attack was plain to see. A soiled comforter, a sham pillow pushed under a nightstand, large brownish stains on the bedside rugs.

The victim was in the bathroom, naked, on her side, knees drawn. A puddle of blood surrounded her head, dark on the gray tile. Blood spatter on the white towels stacked on a shelf under the sink. The sink was clear glass, broken. More blood streaks on the shower door and the floor.

Robledo sat on his heels on the threshold. He didn't have to go in. He could study the scene from there. "I see why the housekeeper thought it was an accident."

"She steps out of the shower, slips, and falls on the sink," Gomatam said. "Cuts her throat on the broken glass. The blood pattern doesn't support it, sir. And there's the mess in the bedroom."

The medical examiner and the crime scene team would be there soon. They had a little time. "What do you see?" Robledo said.

"Sir?"

"You heard me. Go." After ten years on the job, he felt much older than thirty-five. He could still put himself in the shoes of an eager recruit. He doubted this one planned to be on patrol for the rest of her life. He moved away from the door to give her a clear view.

"If she fell, there would be blood on the broken sink," Gomatam said. "On the mirror too I think, or at least on the countertop. All the blood is below the counter. And the cut on her throat is too straight, sir. No way falling on the sink could do that."

"She was on the floor when the killer slit her throat," Robledo said. "What else do you see?"

"Bruises, contusions. She was beaten." Gomatam retreated to the bedroom. "Sorry. Can't breathe."

"It's easier if you stay in it," Robledo said. "Observe her hands."

Sally Gomatam leaned on the doorjamb. "It looks like she was tied up at some point. At the wrists and ankles."

"She fought her attacker. Raw knuckles and torn nails. Hopefully, the blood's not all hers." Voices were coming from the living room. "Good observations, officer. Go put up that tape. Start at the bottom of the stairs."

Two techs stood by the front door with their gear, their faces already sweaty in their special suits, the photographer was ready to start shooting, and the medical examiner was adjusting his mask.

"We have a ripe one, Steve?" the ME said.

"Beaten up, probably raped, throat slit," Robledo said. "Past rigor. I'd say some time Sunday, but it's hot in here … your call, Doc. She's in the bathroom. Tight quarters and messy, but the scene looks undisturbed."

"That's something," the ME said.

Sally Gomatam was back, swinging a roll of tape. "What do you want me to do?"

Robledo smiled. She was a little big for a puppy but he could use her to fetch. "Ring bells and talk to the neighbors. You'll have to come back after working hours to get them all. Keep the time window wide. My gut says Sunday but we don't know when this happened." He gave her one of his cards. "Call me if you get anything and email your notes even if you *don't* get anything. Names, addresses, phone numbers of every person you talk to."

She sauntered to the front door.

"They're cute at that age," Bogs said. "Bright-eyed and bushy-tailed. She knows you're pitching for the other team, Latin lover?"

"Go fuck yourself. What you got?"

"Maria Camacho does half a dozen apartments in the complex. Here's the list. She has the gate code and a passkey. Been working here for years. From Guatemala, became a citizen eight years ago. Married, two kids born here. All on the up and up. We have her contact info and prints. Any objection in letting the señora go?"

"None," Robledo said. "What about the victim?"

"April Easton. Maria's been doing the apartment since April moved in four years ago. Maria has only good things to say about her. Soooo pretty and talented." He rolled his eyes. "A singer. Very clean and neat. Interesting, no?"

"Artists don't have to be slobs. That explains the big piano."

"Tons of pictures up there, from concerts and awards and such. And I found this. Never heard of them." Bogs held a trade magazine open on a profile page—"The Easton Trio, A Fresh Sound in Jazz."

Robledo repressed a smile. Bogs and jazz, that was a stretch. "I'll poke around but you can go. Find the rest of the trio."

"Greg and Jake North," Bogs said. "Brothers. The article says the band's local."

"You have the glamour job. Enjoy."

Bogs took a peek at the thermostat in the hallway. "Ninety. I had a feeling coming in. It's that motherfucker again."

Robledo knew what his colleague meant. Three young women were raped and murdered in Harris County over the past five months. "The Hothouse Rapist" as the media nicknamed the freak. He always jacked up the temperature on the scene. It was his signature and it messed up time of death. Bogs had been on the case since the beginning. He obsessed about it.

"This place is a big step above his usual targets," Robledo said. "And she was tied up. He never did that before. I don't know, Bogs. It looks and feels different."

"Whatever. The same puke or another one, I'll crush whoever. Mind if I take the car?"

"Go. I'll catch a ride."

Bogs strode out and the floor quaked. He wasn't Robledo's partner. Bogs usually teamed up with Fisher, a Houston PD veteran. Fisher didn't show up today for some reason. When the call came in, they were both available and got the assignment. It was the way Robledo worked. He went wherever he was needed, often solo. The arrangement suited him. Protracted investigations made him restless. His impatience had garnered him a few nicknames. "Flash," "Wham Bam Rob," "In & Out Stevie." He shrugged off the labels. He was a closer. No matter what head-scratchers his boss, Frank Murphy, threw at him, he cleared cases.

Robledo signaled one of the techs. "Can you process the sideboard and the secretary desk? I need to get in there."

The man worked fast. Robledo thanked him and took a stack of files, letters, and invoices to the terrace. Despite what he told Sally Gomatam he wasn't immune to the stench, and he craved a cigarette.

He gathered information on April's family. Parents: Tim and Vicky, living in Katy. One sister: Jill, married to Sam Koenig, also living in Katy. He was going through credit card statements when one of the crime scene guys interrupted his studious concentration.

"Something you should see in the bedroom before we haul off the bedding."

The comforter was in a large sealed bag, ready to be shipped to the lab. The sham pillows were wrapped and labeled.

"The bed's freshly made," the tech said. "There are no stains on these sheets and pillow cases. All the action took place on top of the comforter." He pointed at another sealed bag. "We found a set of sheets on top of the washing machine. Stains, but no blood."

"The bed was stripped and remade before the attack," Robledo said.

"That's what it looks like. Her clothes were shoved under the bed, torn, ripped off. Her purse was in the chair by the window.

Wallet with ID, credit cards, and cash." He pointed. "A laptop sat on that credenza. We bagged everything."

Robledo peeked into the bathroom. The body was gone.

Bogs wasn't the sharpest tool in the HPD toolbox but he was dogged and systematic. He called Robledo a little after noon.

"I found the jazz brothers," Bogs said. "And I scored a big burning lead. The band played Coombs bar Saturday night, and the lady singer hooked up with an interesting dude. As in *person of interest* interesting."

Robledo pulled out his cigarettes and lit one. The pack was depleted. He had lost count of how many sticks he incinerated. He blinked when an errant warm breeze blew smoke in his face.

"'The brothers had a good look at him. We have him. I can smell it."

Robledo hiked his shoulders. Bogs's hunches were less accurate than the *Houston Chronicle*'s daily horoscope. Bogs tended to rush head-on through open doors. He often landed on his face.

"Tall, fit, dark hair, good looking, mid-thirties, black jeans, leather jacket, high heeled western boots," Bogs said. "Detailed enough for you? He sat at the bar with the Easton woman, chatted her up, and they left together around eleven-thirty. One of the brothers said the guy was rocking like a lead guitar. What the fuck does that mean?"

"That he had all the moves," Robledo said, amused.

April Easton must have spent the night with the guy. His DNA would be on the sheets found on the washing machine. In theory, it could also be on the comforter, but that defied logic. Why make the bed before mucking it up again? Robledo sighed. Bogs was getting too excited too fast. Full speed through that open door. With a brick wall right behind it.

"I'm on my way to Coombs," Bogs said. "The owner was

behind the bar Saturday night. I'll let you know what she has to say."

"Hold on a minute, Bogs. Where were the musical brothers on Sunday?"

"They did a benefit at their old high school in Kemah. Fundraiser barbecue. There's photos and videos. When I told them about their singer … man … They were supposed to leave for a six-week tour tomorrow and then go into a recording studio in L.A., they just signed a two-record deal. Big breakthrough torpedoed."

"It might be interesting to know if their success stuck in somebody's craw. Professional envy and the like." Robledo had spent the past hour reading through contracts and legal documents. One of them was an annotated copy of the record deal Bogs mentioned.

"I have their manager's info," Bogs said. "I'll get to it, but it's low priority. I'll deliver the guy from the bar."

"She could have marked her attacker. And it won't look like cat scratches."

"Good to know."

"Yeah, keep in touch. Don't go half-cocked now. We just want to talk to this guy. *Talk*, Bogs."

Bogs snorted. "Best lead I've had in five months of chasing that hothouse freak. Don't tell me what to do." He hung up.

Robledo dropped his cigarette in a planter and went back inside.

A tech came toward him holding a baggie. "We found a phone in the kitchen, under a towel."

"Hers?"

"It's locked."

"You mind if I have a look at the kitchen?"

"We haven't packed the items yet," the man said.

Robledo went around the bar counter separating the kitchen from the sitting room. The dishwasher was open with the top rack pulled out. Two stubby cocktail glasses sat side by side in there. A wine glass was on the counter next to a towel; a plate, fork, and knife were in the sink. He pictured the scene like a film reel. April Easton standing at the sink, rinsing the utensils, about to place the wine glass in the dishwasher. The bell rings, interrupting her. She goes to open the door. Robledo thought about Bogs looking for the man who left the club with her. Two cocktail glasses. They had drinks before getting in the sack.

"Run the prints from the glasses in priority," Robledo said.

The ME was long gone but an assistant was still around, sitting on the steps, eating a plastic-wrapped sandwich. Robledo handed him the baggie with the phone. "It might be set up for Touch ID. It's worth a try."

"Gross," the guy said.

"You handle stiffs in and out of the freezer, dude."

Robledo jogged to the complex management office. He spotted Sally Gomatam by the pool, in conversation with an elderly lady. Doing her canvassing with diligence. She would not let a single tenant slip through. He should mention her to Frank Murphy. The Homicide Commander was always looking for new talent.

Robledo showed his badge to the receptionist. "I want to see your surveillance videos for Saturday night and all day Sunday."

The woman was curious but refrained from asking questions. She stood at the office door while Robledo talked to the gate security employee.

"Start around eleven-thirty p.m. on Saturday," he said.

The video wasn't movie quality but it was better than Robledo expected. He couldn't identify the passengers in the vehicles. The drivers' faces were lit up when they leaned out of their windows to enter the gate access code. License plates were slightly blurry, yet workable. Around midnight, traffic was reduced to a trickle.

The white pickup showed up at the gate at 11:54 p.m.

The light illuminated the driver's face.

The security guy froze the picture, as he had done for the other four vehicles that had gone through since 11:30 p.m. Robledo didn't have to wait for the printer to spit out the copy. He knew who drove that truck.

Declan Shaw, from Shaw Investigations, a PI and a good friend of Commander Murphy.

Shaw matched the description of the man who left Coombs with April Easton, down to the leather jacket. Murphy was going to throw a fit.

Robledo was leery of private investigators. They poached at the fringes and were more hindrance than help. Most of the time. Shaw wasn't the typical dark alley snoop. He was smarter than the rest of the breed and steered clear of police business. The few notable times he crossed paths with law enforcement, the cases were big, made a lot of noise, and went federal. The feds had taken a hard look at Shaw a few years back. The PI had been checked and re-checked, marrow-deep. This guy wasn't the type to beat and kill a woman. Robledo pulled out his phone to call Bogs before he caused a hurricane-size shit storm.

"Sir?" the security guy said. "Do you want me to keep going?"

Robledo pocketed his phone. "Yeah." He knew how April spent Saturday night, but what about Sunday?

Shaw's white pickup exited the complex at 6:32 a.m. Very early for a Sunday. Too early for a hot shag. Did she kick him out or was he planning to come back with the croissants?

Shaw didn't come back.

Robledo spent another half hour squinting at videos, long enough to realize that Sunday at the apartment complex was a clusterfuck.

"There was a big birthday party at the pool," the receptionist said. "With outside catering service. Residents had barbecues going. And there were cocktail get-togethers later. The place was a nuthouse." She made a face. "It's the same every weekend when school's out and it doesn't rain."

Meticulous tracking of the visitors would take forever. "Do you have cameras covering the perimeter fence?" Robledo said.

They didn't. With everything that was going on in the complex that day, hopping the fence unnoticed was a cinch. Robledo was in for a drawn-out investigation. He almost wished Shaw was reckless and dimwitted enough to have killed April Easton. He called Bogs who didn't pick up. He left a voice mail. "The guy from the bar is Declan Shaw. Careful with him. Doubtful he's our man. Call me." He doubled down with a similar text.

He arranged for the video surveillance files to be sent to his work email address and went back to the apartment for another walkthrough before taking a cab back to HQ to get his car. He had to deliver the bad news to the Easton family.

TWO

APRIL'S PARENTS' RESIDENCE IN KATY was in a new neighborhood of winding streets all named after a species of tree. The Eastons were on Patula Pine Lane. Robledo kept misreading it at every turn as Petulia. The houses were that cookie-cutter two-story mansion style that spread and replicated like kudzu—that was a good street name—all over the Houston suburbs.

The bell was an intricate carillon. No plain ding-dong at the Eastons. You shouldn't profile people based on their choice of ringtone but combined with the house style and Petulia-Patula, it gave off a snooty vibe. The moment Vicky Easton opened the door, Robledo knew his instincts were spot on. April's mother wore a long-sleeved, ankle-length, blue silk tunic with elaborate embroidery on the front. Something from Morocco, maybe. She was in full make-up and her blond hair was freshly done. Not a lock out of the arrangement. She was picture-ready for a cock-tail pool party circa 1960s Palm Springs. Unless Robledo had accidentally stumbled into a time warp, she was one generation off. He pinned her at a well-preserved and spa-pampered sixty.

"Ms. Easton? I'm Sergeant Robledo from the Houston Police

Department." He held out his badge that she glanced at, one penciled eyebrow lifted.

"I prefer Mrs. Easton," she said.

The voice was native Texan, and whoever said that the accent was warm and welcoming had never met April's mother. Robledo felt X-rayed, with special emphasis on his slicked-back black hair, not-so-crisp shirt collar, faded jeans, and scuffed boots. There was no service entrance or he would have been directed to it with a dismissive wave of a manicured hand. She leaned to the side to look at the street behind him and his unremarkable vehicle parked along the sidewalk. Steve Robledo didn't give a shit about her opinion. As far as he was concerned, his old dented Ford was the soul of America.

"I need to talk to you and your husband, Mrs. Easton. It's important."

"Show me that badge again."

This time he also gave her a glimpse of his sidearm. Two can play, lady. He had seldom felt such immediate antipathy for anyone. And she wasn't even a suspect.

She stepped aside to let him in, with another look at his footwear. Was he dragging dirt in by any chance? He wished he was. Give her something to pick up after him.

"My husband is in the conservatory."

She preceded him. He had to adjust his long stride to her prim little steps.

The so-called conservatory was a section of screened-in terrace, next to the pool. Tim Easton was in a recliner reading the *Financial Times*, a drink chockful of ice by his elbow.

"Tim, darling," Vicky drawled. "This is Sergeant, uh …"

"Robledo, HPD."

"Houston? This is Katy, boy."

Dios. One of those. Robledo blinked. "The murder was committed in Houston, sir." He let that sink in for a couple of heartbeats. "It is my sad duty, as case officer, to inform the family of

Ms. Easton's passing." He could have danced around it but as Vicky noticed, he wasn't wearing the right shoes. "I'm sorry, sir, Mrs. Easton. Please accept my condolences."

He heard a soft plop to his side. Vicky had dropped in an armchair, one hand clasped on her mouth, eyes wide. "Jill," she mumbled.

Her husband froze for a couple of seconds, then folded his paper with a decisive flick of the wrist. "What the hell are you talking about, boy? Get a grasp, Vicky. Jill hasn't been Miss Easton in years."

Robledo was caught wrong-footed. "Uh … it concerns April, sir."

Tim Easton leaned forward and the recliner's footrest slammed down with an ominous clack. He flushed red, raised a hand as if to strike, blurted, "That …"

Robledo reached for his phone. Violent emotions in the elderly. Coronary. Stroke. Call medical support. He shouldn't have worried. Tim Easton took a few sharp breaths and his face returned to its previous suntanned and healthy complexion.

"What happened to her?" he said.

Robledo glanced at the mother. She was patting her hair back in place. It was unnecessary, the helmet had not been disturbed. Her lips were pinched in a thin scornful line.

"April was found dead in her apartment this morning. Nothing appears to have been taken. That's all we know, for now."

Silence. Robledo waited for the questions that always came next. *How is it possible, it isn't possible, not my daughter, who did it, why*, and the hardest one: *how did she die* … He got none of that. Nobody offered him a seat either. He took a card from his breast pocket and put it on the coffee table.

"I'll call in a few days to make an appointment, for an interview," he said.

"Why?" said Tim Easton.

Robledo was briefly taken aback and decided Easton's

reaction was the result of shock. "In cases like these, when motive is unclear, we look for clues in the circumstances of the victim's life, her activities, her relationships. You can help me understand who your daughter was, sir."

"Ah. You don't need to make an appointment for *that*, boy. I'll tell you what my daughter was. It won't take long. There are words for the kind of woman she was. I am a religious man; these words will not pass my lips. I disapproved of her, of her degenerate lifestyle, of the dregs of humanity she consorted with. Drugs, alcohol, sex. She was no longer welcome in this house. That's all I have to say."

Vicky added her bucket of scorn to the trough. "She's an ungrateful child. We gave her everything." She separated the words for extra weight. "She graduated with a good degree. She could have gone to law school, but …" She shivered.

"We thought she had come to her senses when she went to work for Sloats & Archer. As a paralegal, mind you," Tim grumbled. "But last year, she dropped everything. I said to Vicky, enough, I'm done with her. She wants to destroy her life, fine."

"We were so disappointed," Vicky said. "She could have had a family, like Jill. Instead, there was this, uh, promiscuity."

A little color came to her cheeks. As she pictured what promiscuity meant, Robledo assumed. "I'll talk to Jill."

"She has nothing to say to you," Tim said.

"It's a different dynamic between sisters, sir." Robledo strained to remain polite.

"You would know, I suppose, lots of niños in Mexican families. Catholics." Tim Easton sniffled in contempt.

Vicky must have sensed that the situation was turning tense. She produced a semblance of a smile. "Do you have siblings, officer?"

Robledo was tempted to manufacture enough brothers and sisters for two soccer teams. Respect for his mother held him back. "A sister."

Vicky's smile tightened. "Is she also with the police?"

He wished he'd asked Sally Gomatam to tag along. "No. Could I have Jill's phone number, please?"

Vicky turned to her husband. To ask for permission? Tim shrugged.

"Follow me," Vicky said. Her phone was on a credenza in the foyer. She scrolled through her contacts and read the number to him. "What happens now, officer?"

For the first time, she behaved like a normal parent. Robledo welcomed her attempt at civility. He was still reluctant to ask her to come downtown to identify the body. An unpleasant formality in all cases. With the Eastons, it could turn ugly. April's sister might be more amenable. "The Medical Examiner hasn't turned in his report yet. It might take a few days. Then we will release the b …, uh, April. I doubt she made plans for a funeral. I don't know if she has a will. I haven't talked to her lawyer yet."

Vicky's eyes widened. "She has a lawyer?"

That didn't fit with the bohemian lifestyle, did it? The parents were clueless. They had no idea April's career was humming. "The lawyer can handle funeral arrangements, I'm sure. Unless you decide otherwise. Just let me know."

"There are family considerations," she said, pensive.

"Of course. I left my card in the conservatory."

They were almost at the door when she asked, "Will there be something on the news?"

"I'm afraid so," Robledo said. "We will be discreet but reporters are resourceful. I recommend staying away from them. Goodbye Mrs. Easton."

He heard the door close behind him. He could picture April performing at Coombs, he could picture her in the apartment playing the piano, he could not picture her sitting down for Thanksgiving dinner with her parents. Yet, she displayed family photos on her mantelpiece and kept letters. Families were rarely simple. Robledo decided he should call his sister. With his crazy hours and her medical practice, they didn't get together often enough. A dinner date was overdue.

Dinner. He was running on fumes. He pulled into the drive-in lane of a burger joint and ate while checking his messages. Nothing from Bogs. A long report from Sally Gomatam. She provided a management summary which he appreciated. April's neighbors described the hectic Sunday parties. Noise, children screams, loud music. If there were cries for help, they were lost in the general revelry. The downstairs neighbor said she hadn't heard the piano in a few days. She thought April was on tour. Robledo's burger didn't taste right. He threw it in a garbage bin and entered Jill's address in the navigation app. He shouldn't tell the woman, over the phone, that her sister was dead.

Jill's home had none of the crass in-your-face feel of the Easton residence. It was a small two-level Tudor with a garage to the side. The landscaping was neat. Whoever chose the plants didn't intend to spend a lot of time on them. Put the stuff in the ground and let it grow. A pink trike was on its side near the garage door, dangerously close to the front wheels of a gray Ford Expedition. The family was home; light slipped through the blinds.

Robledo parked in the street and walked to the door. He considered knocking and decided to ring the bell. A standard buzz sounded this time.

The young man who opened the door was of middle height and build, with a pleasant, round face and spiky brown hair. He smiled. "Hello, how can I help you?"

"Mr. Koenig? I need to talk to your wife. It's a family matter." Robledo realized he hadn't identified himself. "I'm Steve Robledo, with the Houston Police Department." He showed his badge.

A puzzled frown. "Don't tell me Jill ran a red light again."

"Can I come in, sir? It's important."

"Of course, I'm sorry." Sam Koenig showed him into the

sitting room and pointed at a loveseat. He took the matching sofa and waited, hands clasped between his knees.

I'm going to destroy this man's peace of mind, Robledo thought. "It would be better if your wife was here, sir."

A shade of worry crossed Koenig's face. He swallowed and his prominent Adam's apple bobbed. "If it's bad, I believe I should hear it first. Jill is giving Amelia her bath."

Robledo delivered the little speech he couldn't use at the Eastons. "We were called to Ms. Easton's apartment in the Energy Corridor this morning, Mr. Koenig. There wasn't anything we could do. I'm very sorry. We believe April was assaulted and died sometime on Sunday."

"April? April is dead?" Koenig slid to the edge of his seat and leaned forward closing the distance with Robledo. There was no denying the distress on his boyish features. All the love that was missing from the parents' reaction was on display here.

"I'm so sorry."

Koenig looked toward the back of the room. Worry overlaid grief. "Jill, my God." He rubbed his forehead as if trying to smoothen the lines that had formed there. "Jill is not, uh, very strong …" He straightened up. "I think it's better if I tell her." A tilt of the head. "Maybe later?"

Robledo looked at his hands flat on his jeans-clad knees. "She has to be told and the sooner the better. April's body also needs to be identified, officially I mean."

Koenig blinked. "I … uh, does it have to be Jill, can I do it?"

Robledo nodded. He put his card on a side table. "Call me and I'll go with you."

"You know … who?"

"No. And we don't know why either. Sometimes there's no why."

"Bullshit," Koenig said. "You know what I do for a living?"

Robledo was surprised at the sudden flash of iron from this mellow guy.

"I'm an engineer. I build computer systems. No room for error. You said April was found in her apartment. I know that apartment. It's in the middle of the complex. The killer didn't walk in there by accident."

Here was somebody Robledo could have an adult conversation with. "You're right, Mr. Koenig. I believe she was targeted and I have no fucking idea why."

Koenig nodded. "What do we tell Jill?"

"Intruder?"

"Let me do the talking," Koenig said. "I warn you, she'll flip."

"I saw the parents," Robledo said. "They were icy. "

Koenig let out a groan. "April got her stubbornness from somewhere. She's of the Never Surrender ilk, like Tim Easton. Jill and I remained close to April. Tim and Vicky don't know we kept in touch. We saw April a few weeks ago, in concert at the House of Blues. She worked hard, she earned her success. Despite her parents trying to crush her."

Robledo was about to ask if the struggle for control of April's life could have gone awry when Jill came into the room.

"Oh, hi," she said.

Robledo felt her swift assessment brush over him. A subtle evaluation of his potential as a mate. It was lightning quick. Like her mother, she dismissed him. For entirely different reasons.

Sam Koenig pulled his wife's arm to make her sit down. He delivered the news. He was gentle and caring. As he predicted, she went berserk.

Robledo made a beeline for the front door. The couple was clenched in a teary hug.

Back in the car, he checked his messages again. There was another note from Sally Gomatam with a list of the interviews she conducted, and a short text from the ME that mentioned "multiple blood types." The doc worked late, Robledo could catch him at the office. Nothing from Bogs. He called him. This time, the big guy picked up.

"What the fuck?" Robledo said. "I've been trying to get you for hours."

"I nailed the punk. I beat you to it."

Robledo didn't like the sound of Bogs's voice. Too much testosterone and glee, too adrenaline-soaked. "You didn't get my messages? Shaw's not a suspect."

"Oh yeah? He's your type? You're falling for his smiling Irish eyes? The motherfucking mick is as guilty as can be. He's in holding. Booked, tagged, deloused, and processed. Ain't that the fastest case ever, Flash? Maybe you should call me that from now on, unless it means you shoot your wad in two seconds flat."

Bogs's laughter was loud, Robledo pulled the phone away from his ear. "Did Shaw confess?"

Another deep sustained laugh. "He's a tough one, all right. I'll get him. I'll break him."

Meaning Shaw kept his mouth shut. "Does Murphy know?"

"I'm waiting for him to come back from a meeting with the Chief."

"Meet me in the squad room and we'll go together. I have crime scene evidence."

A pause, then, "Fuck you."

THREE

THE DOOR OF THE INTERVIEW ROOM opened and Vince Wallace walked in. "They kept turning me around. I thought you were still at the Joint Processing Center. How long have you been here?"

"Don't know, there's no clock," Declan Shaw said.

"You look ragged. What did they do to you?"

"I'm just tired, Vince. I was on a surveillance gig all last night." The lawyer extracted a legal pad and a pen from his briefcase and sat next to Declan.

"After working hours, it takes a crane to lift the prison gates. You're out because Frank Murphy pulled rank. He wants to question you. I don't know how much time we have." Wallace checked that the camera in the corner of the room wasn't switched on and that the recording equipment on the table was off. "I had a deposition or I would have come sooner. Moira told me cops barged into the office, arrested you for the murder of one April Easton, and read you your rights. She said they roughed you up."

Declan shrugged and the handcuffs jingled. "Ever met Bogs

Sorensen? He's a cross between a rhino and a bulldozer." He stretched his long legs, leaned back in the metal chair, and closed his eyes. The chaos of the jail had kept him keyed up. Quiet put him to sleep.

"What's the story?" Wallace said. "They must believe they can make the charges stick or they wouldn't have arrested you."

Declan chuckled. "I'm a placeholder, a shining object, a just-in-case dude. I don't know what they have, Vince. From my perspective, it's simple. I met April Saturday evening. I spent the night at her place. She was asleep when I left."

"They can place you with the victim. Who is she? A girl-friend, a hooker, what?"

"Neither."

"A casual hook-up?"

"I resent that," Declan said.

Wallace put down his pen. "You're not helping."

"Not everything fits in a nice Q&A format, Vince. She was alive when I left Sunday morning. That's a fact."

"The cops don't know that or we wouldn't be here," Wallace said. "Let's backtrack. I gave you the Wilmer brief Saturday morning. You had to prep for a case in Florida but you said you would look at my file over the weekend."

Shaw Investigations was a two-person enterprise. Moira Perkins, Declan's associate, managed the office and handled background research. She assembled documents that he needed to go through before his conference with the Florida case prospect. Declan's top floor loft in an old warehouse was also the firm's office. Vince Wallace's law practice was in the same building, one floor below. They often worked together.

"I read your notes right away. I pegged it as a two-day job, with Moira on the online checks and me working the phones. I planned to deliver the report to you tonight."

"What about Saturday afternoon?"

"I worked on the Florida documents. By eight, I was running

out of steam. I decided to go to Coombs. The music's always good and the drinks are decent. I bumped into a friend from way back. He was about to leave and I inherited his bar stool."

"Name?"

"Stanley Borelli," Declan said. "He's a freelance photographer. I had no idea he'd moved to Houston. Last I heard, he was in New Mexico."

"What did you have to drink and how much?"

Wallace wasn't going to like the answer. "Scotch and soda. Doubles. Maybe four. Or five. The police will know. I used my credit card."

"You were well over the limit. Technically drunk."

"It takes more than that to make me keel over, buddy."

Wallace grunted. "Murphy & Co. will say you were impaired. How does the woman enter the picture?"

"I asked the bartender about the musical act and she pointed at a woman sitting at the end of the bar. They had a jazz trio that night and she was the singer and piano player. She looked interesting. A brunette in tight black leather, somewhere in her thirties, with that bright red pin-up style lipstick. I thought, okay, fun, maybe."

"Was she drinking?"

"Perrier and lime. I offered to buy her a drink and she said she never had anything before a show. She had the most amazing blue eyes, like arctic pools." The image was vivid and Declan's breath caught. He cleared his throat.

Wallace didn't press. He was taking notes.

"Introductions. Declan Shaw, April Easton. I told her what I did for a living. That lit a little something in her eyes." He flashed a thin smile. "It always does." Wallace's flat look made him wish he could retract the words. "She used to work as a paralegal at Sloats & Archer, but quit a year ago when the band started touring in earnest and they landed a record deal. We shared a chuckle. We both had a reluctant foot in the world of law. I felt that little click, you know. The possibility. The more I saw, the more I liked. She said that if I was still there after the show, I could buy her a drink."

"Do you often pick up girls in bars?" Wallace said.

"No, I usually troll PTA meetings. Come on, Vince! Don't look at me as if I flunked Bible Studies. I don't go out to get laid. It happens or not. It was like that with April. No pressure either way."

"You don't invest a lot in these little sex games."

"You gonna point the error of my ways, Reverend Wallace?"

"Forget it. Was she a good singer?"

"What the fuck does that have to do with anything?" Declan rubbed his eyes. He was fading fast. "She was brilliant. The set was a mix of classics and originals. For encores, they took requests. Anything, as long as the songs had something to do with streets. 'On the sunny side of the street,' 'Penny Lane,' 'Baker Street,' 'Walk on the Wild Side.' Nothing the audience threw at them stumped them. I was impressed."

"Did she have that drink with you after the show?"

"A jumbo Margarita on the rocks, with chicken quesadillas, and guac. She said she was hungry. She had lunch and nothing since. Horrendous stage fright. It vanished as soon as she started singing."

"What happened next?"

"She was going to call an Uber. I said I could drop her home. It went from there."

"Time?" Wallace said.

"It must have been close to midnight."

"She invited you to her apartment."

The implied judgment bothered Declan. Wallace was married with two young kids. Good for him. He didn't have to navigate the tricky dating obstacle course anymore. "She offered me a drink. I had a scotch, she had a G&T. We cuddled on the sofa and eventually made it to the bedroom."

"Anything out of the ordinary?"

Declan couldn't hide a smile. "Your ordinary might not be mine, Vince."

"Knock it off. I'm thinking of the medical examiner. Marks on the body, drug use."

"Nothing like that. We f … made love. They'll find my DNA. Not that it matters. I can't deny I was there. I left a note."

"Okay, keep going."

"I woke up at twelve after six. Saw the alarm clock. I thought it's Sunday, I can sleep in, and then I remembered the Zoom call with Harold Carlyle—he's the Florida case guy. I had to be online at seven. I rolled out of bed and gathered my stuff. April was asleep. I kissed her without waking her up, and I wrote the note."

"You had a business meeting at seven, on a Sunday?"

"Carlyle is in the UK and he's a fucking workaholic."

"I thought he was in Florida."

"The property he wants me to look at and his lawyer are in Florida."

Wallace acknowledged the clarification. "What did your note say?"

"I loved the music, the songs, and everything else. Will you play the piano for me? Call me." The words sounded trite now, pleading, and yet conceited. "We'd exchanged phone numbers but I wrote mine anyway. I hoped she would call or text. She didn't. I called her twice. I left a message the first time."

"When she didn't respond, what did you think?"

"That I blew it. That she woke up thinking she didn't need the complication. I don't know, Vince. I thought we had the beginning of something, and it bugged me that I misread the entire thing. A scratch on the glossy veneer of my ego. Damn stupid."

"You made your Zoom call?"

"With five minutes to spare. I even had time for a shower."

"You didn't use her bathroom?"

"To splash water on my face and take a piss. I flushed the toilet. Noisy but it didn't wake her up."

"Did you record the Zoom meeting?" Wallace said.

"Yes, and the client's lawyer recorded it too. We ended a little after nine-thirty. Carlyle gave me the job. Two hours plus on a Zoom is a brain melt. I went for a run in Memorial Park to clear my head and I had a burger over there. Then, back home and work all afternoon."

"Witnesses?"

"No, but I put the burger on my credit card. I shot off emails and wrote a bunch of memos, and left voice messages to a couple of realtors in Florida. It was almost five when I called April the first time."

"She didn't pick up."

"I told you, I left a message. Bjorn came up at six. We had a few drinks, ordered a pizza from Julio's, and watched *Miller's Crossing*. Bjorn left around eleven and I called April again. I felt like a fool. Monday morning, I went to the gym before Moira showed up. We finalized the client contract and booked my trip to Florida. I spent Monday night guzzling coffee and watching a warehouse in the Port of Houston area. A client tired of being told stuff fell off the back of his trucks. I have a nice photo portfolio for his perusal. Today was business as usual until the cops showed up."

Declan hadn't slept worth a wink, hadn't had anything to eat since breakfast, and could smell the funk of the holding cell on his clothes. Not to mention the greasy crud from the fingerprinting that he'd had no opportunity to scrub off. "It's Tuesday evening. April must have been killed Sunday and they found the body today."

"And you know that how?" Wallace said.

"They would have come for me earlier otherwise. I left a landslide of evidence of my passage."

Wallace didn't have an opportunity to comment because the

door swung open. A tall young man came in. He carried two paper sacks and three coffees in a cup holder tray. He put everything on the table and offloaded the tray.

"Steve Robledo, Homicide. Mr. Shaw, Mr. Wallace. Am I interrupting?"

Of course, he was interrupting. That was the whole point.

"I thought creature comforts were in order." Robledo pushed a cup toward Declan.

The cop's slow, low-pitched voice must have given countless suspects a false sense of security. It had the opposite effect on Declan. It put him on full alert. "I'd love a coffee, but I need to take a leak."

Robledo stared at him. He came to Declan's side of the table and produced a key to unlock the handcuffs. "I can't let you walk the corridors on your own." He gave Vince Wallace a little ironic bow. "We'll be right back."

The restroom was down the hall. Robledo walked in with Declan and stood discreetly to the side, near the row of sinks. He watched Declan wash the ink off his fingers. "I don't know why they still use that stuff. They could do the pads, like at the airport or the DPS."

"Theatrics," Declan said. "It's The Man saying *I marked you, you belong to me now*."

Robledo pulled out a pack of cigarettes and lit one. "I doubt the screws are that philosophical." He inhaled deeply and blew smoke in the sink. He opened the faucet and let water run.

"You've done this before," Declan said.

"Addicts. We learn to cope." Robledo took a couple more drags and went into a stall to flush the butt down the toilet. "How long have you known April Easton?"

Declan grinned. "My lawyer is five doors down. You can't wait that long?"

"Just trying to save time." Robledo motioned at the door. "After you."

One of the paper bags in the interview room contained Declan's wallet, phone, cigar case, and lighter. The other sack held sandwiches. Wallace passed. Declan was starving. The coffee tasted good and the tuna on wheat hit the spot.

Robledo wolfed down his chicken club. The handcuffs had been pushed to the side. "So, how long have you known Ms. Easton?"

Wallace pointed at the recording equipment. "Shouldn't …?"

Robledo gave him an if-you-insist-whatever roll of the eyes. He reached up to start the camera and knocked on the microphone to verify that the recorder was live. He stated the date and time, and the names of the people in the room then repeated his question. For the third time.

"I met April Saturday evening," Declan said.

"I wish you knew her better. Did she say anything indicating she might be threatened?"

Declan leaned forward with both elbows on the table. "Can I ask a question?" Robledo made a vague hand gesture. "An hour ago I was in holding looking at an indictment. Why the sudden change of heart?" From the corner of his eye, he saw Wallace twitch in his chair.

"What's your blood type, Shaw?" Robledo said.

Did all investigators answer a question with a question? Declan was guilty of the habit. "O negative."

"We collected three different blood types at the scene. You're in luck. None of them is O negative."

Declan felt the release of tension in his neck. He wasn't aware he had seized up. "I'm free to go?"

Robledo's smile lit up his thin, vulpine face. He draped an arm over the back of his chair and pushed Declan's personal items across the table. He kept the wallet. "I was hoping you might want to help." He flipped the wallet open and retrieved the private investigator license. He held it between his index and middle finger. "Don't you want to know what happened to April?"

FOUR

FRANK MURPHY PULLED OUT one of his desk drawers, tilted his chair back as far as it would go, and put his feet up on the drawer. Robledo and Wallace claimed the visitor chairs, and Declan made do with a dingy armchair from a neighboring office.

"I'm not going to apologize for putting you in the clinker for a couple of hours, Dek," Murphy said. "Bogs Sorensen rushed to conclusions, which is his default setting. He ignored Steve's input and I tore him a new one for that, but in all fairness, he was following a pretty good lead."

"A lead as wide as a runway," Declan said.

Murphy didn't argue. "You had to come in to clarify your role anyway. So, here we are. You ever been in holding before?"

"Not as a guest."

"Live and learn," Murphy said. "You got what you need, Steve?"

"Mr. Shaw gave me a blow-by-blow account of his weekend. The evidence supports his statements. We haven't found the note Mr. Shaw says he left behind, but the crime scene team isn't done. It might still surface." Robledo slouched loose-limbed in the comfortable chair, as relaxed as a drowsy cat on a sunny porch. "I wonder if Mr. Shaw noticed anything out of the ordinary in the jazz club, around April Easton's apartment when he got there, or when he left in the morning."

Declan thought Robledo was overdoing it with the Mr. Shaws. "April's outfit attracted attention. Guys stared. Once I started talking to her, they lost interest. When she came to the bar afterward, nobody noticed her. She had changed clothes and looked like the girl next door."

"And around her place?"

"I didn't see anything suspicious. I heard footsteps around the corner. A couple."

"Would you recognize them?"

"No."

"How do you know it was a couple?"

"I heard laughter. It was a man and a woman. I didn't see anybody when I left in the morning."

"Okay, all that's left is a DNA swab and a body exam," Robledo said.

Declan swung in his chair to face the cop. "A what?"

"We'd like an up-close and personal look at your body," Robledo said.

"You gotta be kidding." Wallace jumped to his feet. "You have no grounds for such an examination and no right to request it. My client has been forthcoming and candid. Crime scene evidence clears him."

"It's voluntary, Mr. Wallace," Robledo said. "Tightening the bolts, so to speak."

"You're a smooth bullshitter, Robledo. My advice, Declan, is to disregard these entreaties."

Declan still didn't know anything about the crime scene but he thought he knew where this was going. "Let's get it over with."

The DNA swab was a formality; the lab examination took

twenty minutes. Declan stood naked on a sheet of paper while two experts in white coats, armed with penlights and magnifying glasses, took pictures and inspected every square inch of his body as if he was a masterpiece being authenticated. Robledo waited in the hallway, sent out after a stern admonition from a flustered Vince Wallace.

"It's a denial of your rights." Wallace seethed. "It's humiliating."

After his passage through booking and processing, Declan was unruffled. This was white glove treatment in comparison. "Calm down, Vince. They'll save me a visit to the dermatologist. I hope they'll tell me if they find anything I should worry about."

The white coat in charge chuckled. His colleague didn't react. He was busy taking pictures. "Raise your right arm." Pictures. "Spread out your fingers." Pictures. "Make a fist." Pictures.

They were interested in Declan's knuckles. Left arm, left hand. All around, top to bottom.

"Please remove your hand from your genitals."

"Good Lord." Wallace moaned. The ordeal taxed his sense of propriety.

The senior guy crouched down to look at Declan's left leg. He examined the long thin scar going from ankle to groin. "Do you have metal implants?"

"A few."

"Fantastic job. The scarring is minimal. Motorcycle accident?"

"I fell down a flight of stairs. Bad landing."

"Does it still hurt, do you take something for the pain?"

Cops. They had to ask the questions, they couldn't help themselves. Looking for pill poppers. "No more Christmases in Canada," Declan said.

"Weather's a bitch. You a runner?"

"I try to get the miles in."

"Stick to tracks and gravel paths. Hard surfaces wreak havoc on the joints."

What was Declan supposed to say? *Thank you, doctor*?

The man pulled himself up with a loud knee crack. *His* joints needed lubrication. "You can get dressed. And to answer your question: there isn't anything you should worry about."

The two men exited.

"They leave when I put my pants on. I'm not exciting anymore."

"This is ridiculous," Wallace said. "I should …" He froze. He had been too wrapped up in his objections to arrive at the conclusion Declan reached well ahead of him. "She marked her attacker, is that it?"

"Unless the doc runs an underground market in kinky pics."

A knock on the door. Robledo peeked in. He glanced at Wallace and shot a quick look at the corridor.

"Can you wait for me in Murphy's office, Vince?" Declan said.

"You're sure?"

"I'll be fine." He buttoned his shirt and sat down to pull on his boots.

Robledo closed the door behind Wallace and leaned on it. "The lab guy says that for a man in your line of work, you're relatively unmarked. A bullet wound, a bum leg, not too bad." A rueful smile. One hand went to a shirt pocket for the pack of cigarettes that poked out. He stopped midway and scratched his nose instead.

"I stopped boxing without gloves and I don't have a feisty cat," Declan said.

"I wanted to get this out of the way. In case questions are asked down the road." The apology sounded false and the falseness was deliberate. Robledo was amused.

"That's how you get your kicks, *Steve*? If I'd known I would have asked you to stay in the room. Anything to entertain the police." Declan grabbed his jacket.

Robledo was still at the door, showing no intention to move. "I almost wish you were a suspect, *Declan*."

They sized each other up. It was silly, juvenile. Declan didn't give an inch of the three he had over the detective. Robledo reached for his pack of smokes. This time he went as far as putting one in his mouth. He didn't light up. Declan watched, fascinated. Was it a test of will, penance, Robledo's version of self-flagellation?

"She broke her nails in the struggle. More than enough for DNA," Robledo said.

The image was raw, a disturbing close-up from a yet unseen crime scene picture. "You cleared me. I'm out of here."

"Not yet. We have three open cases in Harris County with a somewhat similar M.O.—professional, independent women in their late twenties-early thirties raped and beaten to death. Murphy liked this avenue of research."

Declan was tempted to get his cigar case but Robledo would take it as a mockery. "Liked. Past tense."

"The lab identified three blood types at the Easton apartment. We're dealing with two attackers. That doesn't fit with our serial's profile. Unless he decided to mentor an acolyte and it's unlikely."

Declan stamped his feet to adjust the boots.

Robledo inserted the cigarette back in the pack. "I believe April's murder was a hit."

The sounds of the city reached Murphy's office muted and muffled, a low din over the rumble of the distant freeways. A car honk cut through, an aggravated bleat, an admission of animal helplessness. Night had fallen. Police HQ slumbered. Soon the place would kick back to rough life again.

Murphy opened a file and selected large photo prints. He slid them over to Declan. They were shots of the sitting room and kitchen of April's apartment.

"What do you see?" Robledo dragged his chair close to Declan's. Their knees knocked.

Declan dropped the kitchen pic on Murphy's desk. "I was never in there." He examined the sitting room photographs. The chairs were pushed to the side, the couch was out of alignment. "Nothing's broken. It looks like she was overpowered quickly."

"What about the bedroom?" Wallace said.

Murphy exhumed more prints.

Declan put a hand over the photograph of the stained comforter. April had been tortured and maybe she died there, on that bed where they slept together, entangled and love spent. "Was she found in the bedroom?"

"In the bathroom." Murphy hesitated. "It's hard to look at."

"Please, Murph."

Robledo's knees bumped Declan's again as he leaned closer. "She fought, she was beaten and raped, and she was tied up. It started in the sitting room, moved to the bedroom, and ended in the bathroom."

The pictures looked like art photographs, in stark contrast, abstract. Man Ray came to mind. The paleness of the body against the gray tiles, the white towels on the shelves, the broken sink, the dull glow of the faucet.

"Three blood types. Two killers." Declan was out of breath as if he'd run a mile all out. He swallowed the nausea that closed his throat, and pressed on his windpipe. Up to now, the murder had been disincarnate, a concept thrown at him. It had been all about him. The arrest, Wallace and Robledo's questions, the lab exam. April had been in the shadows. Now, she was in the spotlights. Declan put the pictures on Murphy's desk. His hands shook and he stuck them in his jacket pockets. He clutched the cigar case. The cool silver of the case felt good.

"Are you planning to leave town in the coming days?" Robledo said.

"I'm supposed to fly to Tampa tomorrow afternoon. Back Friday. Do I need to stay in town?"

"No, but be available if we call," Murphy said.

Robledo held out his hand. Declan shook it. He was surprised at how smooth the detective's hand was.

The doorbell rang, insistent. Declan rolled on his side to look at his phone on the nightstand. Three in the morning.

It was Murphy, gray-skinned and worse for wear.

"Don't you have a wife and a mortgage-free house to go back to?" Declan said.

"Bess is in Dallas for the week. Her sister's eldest just had a baby." Murphy dropped on the sofa. "Mind if I take my shoes off? I have the preliminary report from the ME."

Declan dragged an armchair closer and settled down. It was the darkest time of night.

"I've worked an ungodly number of murder cases, Dek. This is the worst I've seen in a long time. I could use your help."

Declan often proclaimed that he didn't *do murder*. His cases were misplaced spouses, wayward children, and stolen property. "Robledo seems solid."

"He's a cop; he has cop instincts. This case might need an infusion of quirk. I'm surprised you're not jumping on it. What happened to that ravenous curiosity?"

"I had a whiff of the other side of the justice system, Murph. It was disturbing."

"So you got a little shook, a little roughed up. Big deal, you can handle it. For God's sake, Dek, you had sex with the woman. Doesn't that mean anything to you?"

Now Murphy was after him for his less-than-perfect private life. Yet another indictment after Vince Wallace's morality-infused pronouncements. Declan had no patience for it in daylight. At three in the morning, it was unbearable. "Are you suggesting I have a responsibility to go after the killer, out of some sentimental obligation?" His irritation increased in sync with his discomfort, because his emotional bond with April was so flimsy, a one-night stand that he hoped might turn into something else, and now he would never know because she was gone. Investigating the murder would not answer the question that kept pinballing in his head. She didn't call back … It was self-centered, despicable.

Murphy backpedaled. "You're an excellent investigator and you're involved. Or is that the problem? You think you can't do the job because you're too close. You're having cold feet?"

Very clever. Nice pivot. Poking at his professional pride while implying he was a sucker for letting feelings override his brains. A lose-lose proposition. Either he didn't care what happened to April and he was a callous cad looking for a quick fuck, or he was a scaredy-cat that couldn't handle the pressure of a violent crime investigation. Murphy's move deserved applause.

"Does HPD approve of PIs moonlighting? Don't you hang a 'No Trespassing' sign on murder? You should order me to keep my sticky paws off your buffet, Murph, not dangle a moral carrot in front of me."

Murphy wasn't fazed. "I know you. No matter what I say, you will poke. You're on the fence right now because of the arrest or because the case hasn't sunk in yet, but you'll start thinking about it and with thinking comes sniffing. I'm not going to beat around the bush, Dek. I want to corral you. Keep you inside instead of out there, where I won't know what you're doing. I believe you could work well with Steve. He's not used to sharing. He's a lone wolf, same as you."

"Does Robledo know you're playing matchmaker?" Declan said.

"I haven't told him yet." Murphy smiled. "I'm his boss. He can't say no."

"And that's supposed to make him positively inclined toward me? You're out of your freaking mind."

"Fireworks are fun. Do you want the ME report?"

Murphy skimmed through the document. Stomach contents

indicated April had a light lunch—chicken and pasta with marinara sauce. She also had a glass of red wine and a chocolate bar. "Puts the time of the attack after noon. Judging from the extent of her injuries, the assault went on for a long time."

This was worse than the photographs. Declan's imagination supplied the visuals to Murphy's soundtrack. He was glad the lights were low in the loft and his friend couldn't see his face. "What else did you get from the scene? Fibers, tracks, prints?"

"The attackers wore gloves. One was torn and we found the shred of latex. There might be a workable partial somewhere. Steve is going back to the apartment tomorrow. I'd like you to meet him there. Something might jump at you that you didn't catch in the photographs. When are you flying out to Florida?"

FIVE

THE SHORT WALK UP THE STEPS of the apartment was a long journey toward pain. Declan closed his eyes when he reached the door and immediately regretted it. Darkness brought everything back in a rush. Holding April's waist, feeling the warmth of her skin under the t-shirt, feeling her heart beating, tasting the salt of the margarita on her lips.

"I don't know if I can do this," he muttered.

"The tech team isn't in yet," Robledo said. "We have the place to ourselves."

April's door was crisscrossed by yellow tape. It could have said "area closed for construction." The cold impersonality of the police procedure helped. It communicated seriousness of purpose and clinical logic.

"Anything out of kilter here?" Robledo said.

"Not that I can see."

Robledo had brought booties and gloves. They both geared up and slipped through the tape.

The small hallway was familiar. Clothes on the coat rack, keys on the hooks, and pictures on the walls. Standing in the middle of the sitting room gave off a different vibe than look-ing at the photos. The smell wasn't the blunt and sickening reek of death but an unpleasant mix of organic secretions. The air was musty. Stale breath, acrid sweat, dirty clothes, rot. As if too many people had been confined in the apartment and had left food out to spoil. The warm stickiness was cloying.

"Is the air conditioning out?"

"The thermostat is set at ninety," Robledo said. "We didn't touch it. It's one of the reasons why we suspected the serial. He always raises the temp at the scene."

Declan went around the room. He ended at the fireplace. "Has anything been removed for identification purposes?"

"No, we took shots of the picture frames and the team finger-printed them."

"April described the pictures to me." Declan pointed. "Her sister's baby, her sister's husband, her parents, vacation trips. One of the group photos is missing."

"There's a bunch of those. Are you sure?"

"It's a picture from a gangster-themed party. She looked cute in her Bonnie Parker beret, just like in the movie. I asked what happened to Clyde Barrow and she laughed. She said he had gone the way of the Hispano-Suiza."

"Clever girl," Robledo muttered.

"If you didn't take the picture …"

"Yeah. I'm with you. It means the killers did. It's a group shot. Other people know about it and have copies. I can work with that."

Declan remained silent. His voice would have betrayed him. He went to the bedroom. Robledo was right behind and banged into him when he stopped short of the king-size bed. The mat-tress was gone, the empty frame was a skeletal witness.

"Everything is at the lab," Robledo said.

Declan turned on his heels and took a step toward the bathroom.

"You don't have to go in there." Robledo held his arm to stop him but didn't insist when Declan pried his fingers loose.

There was a lot of blood. More than Declan gathered from the pictures. The photographer's bright lights had blunted the horror of the crime scene. Blood smeared the tiles, the walls, the glass door of the shower, the pristine white towels that hadn't been hauled away yet. It had turned a dirty dark brown and Declan's stomach cramped. Even after all the police traffic, the cloying smell of death still hung in there, caught in the mundane objects of April's life. The stains of violence were forever captured in the grout between the gray tiles.

"We'll get them," Robledo said.

Declan felt the cop's hand pressing his shoulder and the gesture broke his fragile hold on himself. He turned so abruptly that he unbalanced Robledo who stumbled. He crossed the bedroom in a few strides, went through the sitting room, and yanked the front door open. He tore through the crime scene tape. He let out a string of curses, fumbled for his cigar case, and lit a cheroot with a trembling hand. He inhaled too much and too fast; it hurt his throat and his eyes watered.

"Declan?"

"Sorry I broke your crime tape." He tore off the gloves and the booties. "I'm going home."

Robledo didn't try to stop him.

SIX

THE BIG OVERWEIGHT MAN in the green shirt with the yellow palm trees studied his putt. A seven-footer that looked straight and wasn't. A wrinkle would break the path of the ball. The man aimed right of the hole. The greens played fast today. The ball rolled in a perfect curve, and dropped in the hole as if it had been pulled in by an invisible thread.

"Nice shot," the man's partner said. He was about the same age, brushing seventy, but didn't carry the same kind of ballast. His waistline didn't stretch the blue polo shirt with the little green reptile on the left side, and the legs protruding from the tan shorts didn't look like country hams. Yet, the fat man was the better golfer of the two.

"I know this course like the back of my hand." Palm tree shirt pulled a bandana from the pocket of his shorts and wiped his bull-size neck. "I don't know about you but nine holes is all I can slog through today. And it's not summer yet."

"It'll be in a few days. I'll be in Colorado."

"I wish. Can't stand the altitude. I need these fucking oxygen cans."

They returned to the golf cart. It pitched on the right side. The lighter man drove and he was careful in the curves. Didn't want to tip over. He stopped the cart under a big oak tree. They were alone on that part of the course.

"It could have been a major mess, Buddy."

Palm tree shirt, Buddy Pagett, sniffed. "It turned out purty good, Wade my man. Happy accidents happen."

"The intelligence was incomplete."

Pagett turned in his seat and the cart rocked. "You asked me to put eyes on the lawyer and I did. I did more than that. I took care of the family. That was fucking risky. When you mess with the elderly and the children anything can happen. They don't bruise like the rest of us and you didn't pay me enough to cover mishaps."

"I didn't involve you in the last play. I know how far your conscience will stretch."

"Much appreciated. I told you the lawyer was having an affair, I gave you the address of the fuck pad and the description of the broad. I completed my part of the deal. Your people took over from there and they made a mistake." He chuckled and the rolls of fat under the tent-like shirt wobbled. "Damn lucky mistake. The lawyer still got the message and the cops have no fucking clue what it's all about. That's a home run in my book. What are you complaining about?"

Wade Benning gripped the cart's steering wheel. He shouldn't lash at Pagett. The repulsive oaf had done the job he was paid to do. The mistake wasn't his and he was right, it turned out to be a damn lucky blunder. Benning's agents got the wrong woman and still managed to hit a bull's eye.

Benning's problem wasn't Pagett, it was the big man south of the border, Gonzago, who wasn't happy anymore with *the lawyer getting the message.* Gonzago had finally realized that owning the prosecutor wasn't enough to guarantee the verdict. It was frustrating because Benning had told Gonzago early on that the only way to get the trial result he wanted was to buy a juror, or two, or three. The case was so revolting—sixteen people left to die in an overheated truck—even the lamest prosecutor couldn't lose it. It didn't matter the truck drivers that *forgot* to open the doors when they abandoned their conked-out vehicle were kids. That Gonzago didn't grasp the concept of depraved indifference said a lot about his regard for human life. Now Benning had to scramble to do what he should have done from the beginning, if Gonzago hadn't told him to shut up and follow orders, and a woman was dead, for no reason whatsoever. No matter how wealthy or prominent Benning was in the Texas business community, for Gonzago he was still a *tool*. Just like Pagett. With more to lose.

"You buying me a beer or should I put it on my expense statement?" Pagett said.

Wade Benning started the cart again. He despised Pagett. He couldn't wait to offload him at the clubhouse.

Pagett's unexpected burst of merriment gave Benning a start and the cart ran off the path through the crispy sunbaked grass.

"I'm going to screw him over this," Pagett said. "It's long overdue."

"What?" Benning steered the cart back on the path.

"You know who was banging that chick Saturday night? You'll never guess. Not a dull moment in that apartment."

Benning shrugged. He didn't care. Pagett got on his nerves. The morning golf outing was a routine debriefing, not a friendly get-together. He was relieved it would only last nine holes.

"Declan fucking Shaw!"

Benning slammed on the brakes. Pagett lurched forward and smashed into the dashboard. Without serious harm, he was padded. Benning felt a sharp pain in the pit of his stomach. It had nothing to do with his sternum connecting with the steering wheel. "What do you mean? Shaw is involved?"

Pagett laughed so hard tears ran down his wide cheeks

and mixed with the rivulets of sweat. "Ain't it a riot. I can see the headlines: 'Singer and Private Dick in Deadly Embrace!' 'Houston Sleuth Jazzing it up!'" He shook with hilarity. "With side by side pictures of the couple, all over the web and the rags. He can kiss his clients goodbye. And I have more in store. See how he crawls out from under the slimy rock I'm gonna lob at him." Pagett made as if he was throwing a football. He was turning poppy red. He pressed a hand on his chest to help catch his breath. "Ah. It's gonna kill me."

If only. "For God's sake, stay away from Shaw," Benning said. "He's dangerous." Declan Shaw was a better investigator than Pagett by a mile, and he had connections in places that spelled trouble. Federal places. Like Washington D.C. "Go to a church, Buddy, light a dozen candles and pray Shaw doesn't take an interest in the case."

Wishful thinking. Of course, Shaw would be interested in the case. He slept with the woman. It didn't get more personal. Protective measures were in order. To be handled with care. Sometimes trying to fix a problem ended making it worse.

Pagett was oblivious. "I know how to do it, Wade." The bandana was out again to wipe sweat off the shiny moon face. "I'll see that motherfucker's balls in a slow-cooker."

"You had an opportunity to get rid of him. Why didn't your guy put a bullet through his head instead of pushing him down a staircase?" Benning had to think and couldn't do it with this babbling barrel of lard by his side.

"In retrospect, it was a mistake. I'll bury him, Wade."

"Let it sit, damn it. The less waves, the better." Benning glanced at his dripping passenger and doubted his pleas for restraint penetrated Pagett's gristle-encrusted brain. "The cops questioned Shaw?"

"Arrested him yesterday. He didn't spend the night. Murphy sprung him loose." Pagett shrugged. "There was an interview, with Shaw's mouthpiece, that fucking sleaze Wallace, in attendance. They didn't sweat him, whaddya expect? He's flying out today, spic-and-span, clean as a whistle."

"Where is he going?"

"Tampa. My source says he's coming back Friday. I'll get him a nice homecoming present." Pagett guffawed.

"You have a screw loose, Buddy. I know I'm blowing in the wind, but here it is again: Stay clear of Shaw. And keep an eye on the cops. That's what your retainer is for. Who's lead at HPD?"

"Mexican by the name of Robledo." Pagett sneered. "Greasy fruitcake." He made an obscene gesture. "Pretty boy Shaw must have sent his junk all aflutter."

Benning had heard enough. "Why don't you have that beer? On my tab."

He'd done what he could. Pagett had a score to settle and like crazed cattle, he would go full speed ahead over the edge of the canyon. Benning had to take care of Shaw himself. He might be overreacting but it couldn't hurt to put a backstop in place. Shaw was going to Tampa. Out of Frank Murphy's and Houston police's sphere of influence. Something could be done. It would take money. These things always took money.

There wasn't much time to set up a trap, but improvisation wasn't always a bad thing. The plan to ensnare the lawyer had required weeks of surveillance, reams of documentation, careful timing, and, still, a mistake had been made. Benning shivered in the stifling heat. He couldn't afford another hiccup. Gonzago was neither patient nor forgiving.

SEVEN

MOIRA PERKINS COULD HAVE GONE to Tampa, or Declan could have called Daisy Diamond—affectionately known as Double D in PI circles—and asked her to sub for him. She was based in Miami; she was a close friend, a fantastic investigator, and he trusted her. His presence wasn't required on a first exploratory visit. If the case had legs, more trips to Florida would be needed and he would call on Daisy for help with logistics anyway.

Declan flew to Tampa because he couldn't face remaining in Houston, waiting for the police to dispense actionable information, fretting about Robledo shutting him off, and getting on Moira's nerves in the process.

He met Rowena Dowling, Harold Carlyle's lawyer, to get the keys to the top floor penthouse in the brand-new Artemis building that was giving her client searing heartburn. Carlyle left Florida at the end of April and wouldn't be back before mid-October. Declan was welcome to use the guest bedroom for his two-night stay. Rowena said: "Don't be surprised if you find out it's a storm in a cup of English Breakfast tea." Declan already knew the client was a picky perfectionist. The overlong Zoom meeting on Sunday made that clear. That a man of Carlyle's exacting disposition would invest in Florida real estate—he bought a block of ten condos, keeping the penthouse for himself—was a suit waiting to happen. Rowena visited the condos and noticed a few cracks here and there. Nothing she found alarming. She was a native Floridian and between the hurricanes, the storm surges, the drenching tropical storms, and the state's affinity for sinkholes, she had developed a *que sera, sera* attitude that was the polar opposite of Carlyle's British fussiness.

Declan's job was to figure out if Carlyle had reasons, beyond buyer's remorse, for wanting his money back.

He drove to Clearwater Beach and dropped his backpack in Carlyle's sprawling penthouse. He helped himself to the well-appointed bar, mixed a stiff drink, went to the terrace, and smoked a cigarillo contemplating the wide expanse of the Gulf of Mexico. He downed his drink and made another, with even less soda. He took a steaming shower, munched on two aspirins, went to bed, and dreamed of massive tidal waves and uprooted palm trees. The soundtrack was free jazz.

In the morning, after half a pot of strong coffee, he set to work.

Harold Carlyle's concerns seemed minor. A few hairline cracks zigzagged where the crown moldings met the sheetrock. One of the kitchen cabinet doors wasn't straight, a case of a weak hinge. A terrace planter leaked. There was no sign of structural damage. Doors didn't swing close on their own and picture frames didn't hang cockeyed. Harold Carlyle overreacted. This was a wasted trip.

Declan took a cup of coffee to the terrace. He leaned on the balustrade and watched the pelicans swoop and line back in strict squad formation, in groups of five or seven. Always odd numbers. The big birds had a destination in mind and traveled to it with calm and poised determination. Declan wished he could borrow a fraction of their confidence.

He sat in the rattan chair he had dragged out the night before and let his sight drift to the blue of the sea. The water wasn't that enticing color in Galveston. Too much Mississippi mud drifted west.

The view from the balcony, for all its flawlessness, was bland. A few sailboats, a line of tankers and container ships way out, birds and bathers. Declan, that much was clear, wasn't in the market for a condo in a Florida high-rise. Three days of this and he would go up the cheerful aqua walls.

Then he saw it. The disturbing discrepancy, the malevolent misalignment.

Maybe his chair was crooked. To make sure, he sat on the terrace floor with his back straight against the penthouse wall. He looked at the line of the railing. He looked at the line of the horizon.

They were off. The two lines crossed. On the left corner of the balcony, the railing was an inch above the line of the horizon. On the right side, it was an inch below. Declan went to the kitchen and found a tape measure. The balcony railing wasn't crooked. He took pictures. Now that he was aware of the slant, he wondered why he wasn't pitching to the side, like a kid in a carnival funhouse. The incline must be too slight to affect his balance. He decided to take a look at another condo.

The manager of the company handling the rentals was unctuous and accommodating. One of Mr. Carlyle's condos, on the fifth floor, was unoccupied and Mr. Shaw was welcome to visit it. Was he considering a purchase, by any chance, or a season rental? Artemis was the most prestigious residence in Clearwater Beach.

The tilt on the fifth floor was minimal, but if the building had been forty floors instead of twenty-two, nobody could have denied that Artemis, goddess of the Moon and chastity, was leaning. Declan had a case.

EIGHT

AFTER A LIGHT LUNCH at a seafood restaurant, Declan met with Evan Z. Hollander—Z for Zachary—who dragged him from one condo to another. They weren't comparable to Artemis. They were cheaper and they all looked the same; the decorative schemes were in a nautical color palette that was repetitive and irritating. A profitable segment of industry cranked out millions of wooden lighthouses and pictures of soaring seagulls, not to mention the inevitable blue and white striped throw pillows with rope accents.

Declan collected price lists, maintenance agreements, and contracts that were tortuous about fees and monthly charges. Secrecy surrounded the calculation of owners' costs for pools, fitness club usage, parking garages, and other amenities. Buyers were retired Northerners fleeing winter harshness and investors looking for quick returns. They bought batches of new condos and offloaded them as fast as they could because a newer, swankier project was always being built somewhere. Declan's client was one of those investors lured in by clever marketing. Living in the land of fog, he was a patsy for sea, sun, and sand.

"He's a smart investor," Declan mulled. "Maybe this is too far from his comfort zone."

"Every building that goes up is the best," Hollander said. "The epitome of seafront living, never to be outmatched. Until the next one emerges from the ground. Somebody gets a permit to build where nothing could be built before, and there you have it. The new super-exclusive abode. It's all politics. One elected official makes promises and then he's replaced. The out-of-bounds properties turn out to be in scope, or the in-bounds turn out to be out."

"There has to be a limit to how much more you can build on this coast." Declan was stunned by the wall of concrete fronting the shore. Could they squeeze another tower in between the existing ones?

"You've seen what they did in Dubai with those artificial islands," Hollander said. "I can see our developers do the same. You think you have seafront property and a few years later you're two streets inland. It's biblical. The first will be last." He extracted a handkerchief from his khakis and mopped his bald pate.

"Let's get out of the sun, Mr. Hollander."

Daiquiris were served in big hurricane glasses. Just looking at the condensation was refreshing.

"There's more to this case than meets the eye, Evan. May I call you Evan?"

"We're not much for formalities over here, son. We don't dress for it. What's on your mind?"

"You're a walking encyclopedia of Tampa Bay real estate. You've been at it for fifty years."

"And my father before me. When he started Hollander Properties after the war, none of this was here. Dad was involved with the first residential communities. Bungalows and ranch houses. He also dabbled in commercial properties."

"You weren't a listed agent for the Artemis building," Declan said. "All other major realtors had it in their portfolio."

Hollander chuckled. "I stayed out of it."

"Why?"

"I didn't like it. The Cassino people tried to convince me to change my mind. Big Ricardo Cassino himself called. We've done many deals together over the years. I gave him my reasons. He didn't want to hear them."

"Cassino Builders. Their reputation is excellent."

"They started shaky, but they evolved beyond that. Or so I thought." Hollander waved at the waiter and ordered refills. "You're not in a hurry, are you?"

"Too hot for that." Declan smiled.

The story was Floridian lore. Giuseppe "Peppe" Cassino arrived in Tampa in the late fifties. He ran various businesses in Cuba, sensed trouble, and disposed of his assets before Castro seized power. He had loads of cash and interesting contacts in certain circles. He started a construction company. His timing was perfect; the area was ripe for development.

"He contacted my father and offered him a partnership. Cassino builds, Hollander sells. My father didn't like the man and the company he kept. He passed on the offer. Peppe was offended. He decided to teach Dad a lesson. Nobody had ever dared say no to Peppe before. One afternoon, two heavies came to the office. They molested the secretary, beat up Dad, and pissed on the files. They threw typewriters through the windows. Maybe that worked for Cassino in Cuba. It didn't work with Dad. When he could talk again, he called old war buddies. One of them was with the FBI, another was with the Chamber of Commerce. Pressure was applied. Peppe never apologized or paid for the damage but he left Dad in peace. After Ricardo, Peppe's son, got involved, the business changed. Ricardo moved the company into luxury projects and made more money than his old man ever did. I worked with Ricardo and never regretted it." Hollander wiped his sunglasses on his untucked Hawaiian shirt.

The fresh daiquiris arrived, condensation and all.

"What changed?" Declan said.

"Ricardo is expanding all over the Caribbean. He's delegated building around here to project managers. Most of them are competent. Jason isn't." Hollander frowned. "No, that's not correct. Jason *is* competent, but he's greedy. He's cutting corners. That's why I stay away from his projects."

"Wouldn't Ricardo want to know if somebody hurts the brand?"

"His own son? That cuts too close to the bone."

"What kind of corner-cutting are we talking about?"

"Defects the buyer won't notice, not at the time of purchase anyway. Jason's projects look good, but it's builder-grade underneath and his contractors are sloppy. After ten years, the buildings will start to look shabby. Hurricanes, humidity, and the sea air age stuff fast. When you scrimp on the fundamentals, it shows. Investors that buy and sell right away won't end carrying the bag. The retirees that bought a so-called slice of paradise won't be so lucky."

Declan opened his cigar case and offered one to Hollander who passed.

"What did your client complain about?" Hollander said.

"Cracks in the moldings, leaky planters, electric outlets that don't work. He's convinced he paid too much for what he got." Declan didn't mention the sloping railing. "What about collusion with contractors, pay-offs for building permits, corrupt officials?"

"Cassino Builders would be in trouble," Hollander said. "Any number of government agencies would swoop in. Ricardo has the kind of deep pockets they salivate over. If you find something iffy, keep it sub rosa and negotiate a settlement for your client. When the tax guys and the tort lawyers get their teeth in, all they leave behind is a carcass. Your client wouldn't see a cent." He played piano on the arm of his chair, pensive. "If there's a serious construction defect, even the kind that won't show up for years, Cassino might be amenable to an arrangement." Hollander winked. "A competent engineer will be able to tell."

Declan smiled. "And you happen to know one."

"I know several."

After an email to Moira Perkins at the office to let her know that the Carlyle case showed promise, Declan called Daisy Diamond. He could change his flight and leave from Miami instead of Tampa. A convenient shuttle landed in Miami around 8 a.m. Daisy suggested they meet at the airport Hilton.

The debriefing with Rowena over dinner in Clearwater was quick. Declan told her the building was pitching but they needed expert analyses. She agreed to keep the client on ice until they had more data.

Declan tried to lose himself in the minutiae of a regular investigation but the return flight to Houston weighed on his mind. He didn't feel like going back to the penthouse right away and took the coast road north to Tarpon Springs. He wandered through neighborhoods looking for an access to the Saint Joseph Sound. When he found a place to park near an apartment complex with a view of the water, he got out of the car and lit a cigar.

April had been dead five days, and he couldn't make more sense of it now than when the cops arrested him. A hit, Robledo said. But why? She wasn't wealthy and she wasn't famous enough to have made enemies. Did he put April in danger somehow? Not all the cases he worked on in the past ten years were run-of-the-mill. He managed to piss off an array of powerful people. Some harbored lasting resentment. Could they have gone after April?

But he'd just met her.

He threw away the cigar and was about to drive back to Clearwater Beach and Harold Carlyle's penthouse when the lights of a police cruiser swept over him. He stepped away from the car, lit another cheroot, and waited.

The cop took his time. He must be checking the license plate. When he came out of the cruiser, he had one hand on the butt of his gun and a flashlight in the other.

"This is private property. What are you doing here?"

Declan kept his hands in plain view. "I drove along the coast, looking for a place with a view. I'm having a smoke, pondering life."

"Hands on the roof of the car. ID?"

"In my wallet. Back pocket."

"Hand it over. Slowly."

The cop went through the documents and pulled out Declan's Texas PI license. "You on a case, trying to catch somebody cheating?"

Declan chuckled. "I don't even know where I am exactly."

"Where are you staying?"

"A friend's condo in Clearwater Beach." He gave the address. The cop wrote it down. "I'm flying out tomorrow. I mean, today."

"Back to Texas?"

"Yeah."

The cop shone his flashlight into the car. Declan's jacket was on the back seat, his phone in the cupholder. "All right. This is a quiet neighborhood, Mr. Shaw. We don't care much for strangers hanging around at night." He returned the wallet. "Better be on your way now." He watched as Declan slipped behind the wheel, and didn't get back in the cruiser until Declan's car started rolling.

A white cruiser. Tarpon Springs Police. Declan made a mental note of the tag number. It was an ingrained habit.

He was back at the penthouse around two in the morning.

The encounter with the cop troubled him. For the second time in a week, his actions and behavior were examined and mistrusted. As a PI, he was used to being an outsider. Sometimes his motives were deemed questionable. This flip side of his chosen profession, the ragged fringe of the private detective aura, never bothered him. He took wicked pride in it. It was different now. A woman was dead. A woman he barely knew. A singer with a lovely voice.

The promise of April Easton. Murphy was right. He couldn't walk away.

Sleep would be elusive.

Fuck the shuttle to Miami. He took a shower, shaved, and packed.

Focusing on the road helped clear his head. It was a four-and-a-half-hour drive to Miami. At this time of night, there was no traffic. He texted Daisy. "Can we meet at 7? I'm driving over." She was an early riser and if she couldn't make it, he didn't mind waiting for her.

NINE

DAISY DIAMOND WATCHED DECLAN walk into the breakfast area of the Miami Airport Hilton. The tall, lanky silhouette was familiar, down to the slight limp from an old injury. He favored the left leg more than usual this morning. He wore black jeans with a dress shirt under a light jacket. And his inevitable high-heeled western boots. His dark hair was, as usual, just a little too long. How he kept it just there was a mystery Daisy hadn't solved yet. A backpack was slung over a shoulder. The reactions of the females in attendance amused her. An executive type in a couture skirt suit gave him a long, lingering, appreciative up and down, and the young woman replenishing the buffet stopped what she was doing and stared with a *who is this guy* look on her pretty face. It was understandable. He was as criminally handsome as ever.

But something was wrong. A lack of bounce, an out-of-character touch of wistfulness. Daisy knew him very well indeed.

"Morning, sweetie." He unslung the backpack and leaned over to kiss her on the lips. "Sorry for changing our meeting. I couldn't sleep; I figured I might as well drive."

"Hey, seven instead of eight. No big deal. A couple cups of coffee and I'm ready to roll."

The table was set for two and she filled his cup. He took it black, without sugar, the same way she did. He had a sip and kept silent, eyes on the silverware.

"You didn't tell me much last night," Daisy said. "The Carlyle case looks interesting."

He extracted a cigar case from his jeans front pocket, opened it, and put it on the table.

"Something's wrong with the building. Like that high-rise in San Francisco that's going sideways." He made a little hand gesture to show the exaggerated angle. "It's not that bad but Artemis isn't planted straight. I want engineers to have a look at it. I have names."

"You're all set then. Where do I come in?"

"I can't stay in Florida. I have to go back to Houston and I'm not sure when I'll be able to return." He looked away, played with the cigar case, closed it.

Something was definitely not right. Declan was a lot of things—complicated, funny, arrogant, charming, cynical—but he wasn't bashful. "You better tell me what's going on."

He ran the fingers of both hands through his hair.

"Come on, spit it out."

Her outburst gave him a jolt. "I met a woman."

Oh dear, the harder they fall. Daisy was suddenly, insanely, jealous of the harpy that buried her talons in this man, *her* man despite all the occasional semi-boyfriends on her side, and ex-girlfriends on his. Their last meeting was two months ago. A lot can happen in two months. "Tell me." She hoped she looked composed. She felt queasy inside.

His eyes were a little too bright. *Blood for every drop,* Daisy thought.

"I spent the night with her." He frowned. "I had a video

conference with Carlyle, so I left early in the morning. I thought, maybe there's more to this."

This? Daisy pushed away from the table. Was that how he described sex? This? Without a qualifier, without bothering to find a word to situate the relationship. Whoever this woman was, she held the wrong end of the stick. Daisy shouldn't be jealous of her. Hell no.

Declan made a sound, something between a sigh and a groan. He opened the case and got a cigarillo, lit it up with a brusque flick of the lighter, and took a deep drag that ended in a cough. Daisy had never seen him like that. She never imagined he could *be* like that. Her heart broke for him. When she agreed to meet, impromptu, at the airport she didn't expect this whirlwind of raw emotions.

"The cops arrested me."

He rubbed his eyes with the back of his hands, a boyish gesture that made Daisy's heart quiver. Arrest, what for? This had to be more than love trouble.

"She's dead, DD."

Daisy's hand flew to her throat. No wonder he looked rattled. But he wasn't a suspect or the police wouldn't have allowed him to leave town.

Declan said he met the woman Saturday and she was murdered Sunday; the police didn't have anybody in custody. They didn't even have a suspect. He was biting his lower lip, another childish reaction that sent Daisy's emotions up the flagpole. This is what he must have looked like when the doctors told him his parents both died in the car accident that he survived with minor injuries. He was eleven. He blurted out the story to her, one night on a beach, after too many rum punches.

Daisy spotted the buffet girl coming their way, embarrassment painted all over her face. The restaurant was non-smoking. Daisy plucked the cheroot from Declan's fingers and killed it in the saucer of her coffee cup. She made a shooing-off gesture.

The girl's eyes went wide in surprise. "Fuck off," Daisy mouthed. The girl retreated, blushing.

"The cop in charge of the investigation thinks it's a hit. I know in my gut that he's right. What if I'm responsible, DD?"

Daisy breathed easier. If he juggled theories, even with guilt mixed into them, he was on the mend.

"What should I do?"

On any good or bad day, Declan never asked anybody for any kind of advice whatsoever. Daisy gathered both his hands in hers. He didn't resist. "You're going to complete the Carlyle investigation, buy a boat with the proceeds, and take me to a remote island."

He looked at her. His eyes—green, light brown, somewhere in between, she could never tell—were uncertain. "I might have caused her death, DD."

"I hate to disappoint you, darling, but the entire world doesn't revolve around you." She let go of his hands. "Have you been contacted, have you received threatening messages? What's the point of a revenge killing if the target doesn't know it's a revenge killing."

He took a sharp intake of air. The eyes—green, definitely—were focused now. "I'm a fucking idiot."

She smiled. "Yeah. Are you involved in the investigation?"

"The case is in Frank Murphy's shop. You know how he is. He wants to do the right thing. He asked me to help, but I don't know what I can do." He shrugged, played with the cigar case. "Maybe Murphy feels obligated because we're friends and he roughed me up a bit."

"Does it matter what Murphy wants? How many cases are the cops working on at any given time?" They both knew the answer to the question. Too many. "She was killed Sunday. When did they find her?" He gave her the timeline. "Tuesday, okay. This is Friday. For a couple more days, she will be top of mind, and the investigators will fire on all cylinders. Then she will take her place in the queue." Declan tensed and she grabbed his hands again to give them a firm squeeze. "Unless there's fresh evidence, the case will go dormant. The cops will pull the file out to refresh their memory, hoping something will surface that they missed before. Then, when the DNA comes in, there will be a flurry of activity. They'll get the databases going. In three weeks?"

"The lab backlog is staggering. Murphy will push."

"He can't do much," Daisy said. "Think about what *you* could do in three weeks, answering to nobody." She smiled. "With your usual disregard for rules, laws, and your own safety."

He switched the grip, held her hands to kiss her knuckles. "Buy a boat with the Carlyle fee, eh? Boats are a hassle. Better to charter one for a month."

His impish smile was back. Daisy was both pleased and disturbed. He was back in searching mode, but this newfangled insecurity was still there, in the set of the eyes and the fever burning behind them.

"You should have breakfast, Dek. Something more substantial than coffee."

"I'll have a bite before the flight. Can you take a chunk of the Carlyle case?"

"I can take as much as you need me to take. Do you want me to handle the engineers?"

She knew they were on safe ground now. In the four years they'd known each other, their relationship had gone through high and low tides. It had traveled across the entire spectrum of feelings and the rainbow of yearnings, but all through the turmoil, the working partnership had remained on an even keel. Even when he slammed the door on his way out and she cursed him to hell, the work never suffered.

He briefed her thoroughly, told her what he needed, and promised to email the entire stack of background material. He was precise and to the point, and it was freaky how fast he'd regained control.

"Don't get in touch with Rowena Dowling or the client," Declan said. "I have to remain their primary contact. Carlyle is paranoid and Rowena is fidgety. I'm not trying to screw you. You know I'll cover the expenses and the fee, fair and square. And I'll be back as soon as I can."

Meaning what?

As soon as he was over the woman, as soon as he solved the murder?

Daisy didn't ask. "I'll handle it," she said.

TEN

WADE BENNING LISTENED to the voice repeating the account number for the bank transfer. The amount was what they'd agreed upon.

"How did it go?" Benning shouldn't have asked. It was a breach of protocol, and the silence on the line made him cringe. He was too nervous about Shaw and it showed. It was never smart to let operatives know you were insecure.

"I can give you a summary."

Benning detected contempt. Damn it, he paid these people enough to be entitled to a report. "Think about repeat business," he said.

The pause on the phone was shorter this time. "We confirmed the target's arrival in Tampa and followed him to Clearwater. We had eyes on him all day Thursday, using multiple cars and on foot operators. He didn't spot us. We experienced a slight hiccup when he changed his flight reservation."

Benning's heart missed a couple of beats. A hiccup. Was that what happened with the Easton woman?

"Instead of taking the Tampa to Houston flight, he booked

a seat on the shuttle to Miami and flew out of there. It didn't change our timeline. We ascertained that he was tucked in for the night in Clearwater and completed the assignment. We couldn't replicate the exact pattern as this was an outdoors mission, but we stuck as close as possible to the previous event."

Benning was impressed by the language manipulation, how it sanitized the deed. Assignment, pattern, event. He wanted to say: *so you found a woman, beat the crap out of her, raped and killed her, and did it in such a way Shaw will be in the crosshairs.* No doubt the reluctant conversationalist would cut the call in disgust.

"Let us know when you want to spring the trap," the voice said.

That was refreshingly straightforward. "I will." Benning hung up.

It was just a precaution. Maybe unnecessary.

Benning went to the sideboard and fixed a drink. Insurances made you feel good. Nice, warm, prepared, protected. He pushed away the thought that when the time came to collect on the claim, insurance companies always stuck you with a ridiculous deductible.

ELEVEN

BY EARLY AFTERNOON FRIDAY, Declan was back in Houston. Moira Perkins was putting files away and tidying up as she always did before the weekend.

"Any news?" Declan said.

"The case is no longer on the front page of the *Chronicle*. A Stanley Borelli called this morning. He sounded nervous. I told him you were out of town on business. He left his number and address." She handed him a pink post-it. "How do you feel?"

"Fine."

"Stay in tonight, please."

Moira was only a year older but she treated him like a teenager. "I bet Vince will also order me to stay put."

Vince Wallace did. Being a lawyer he used more words than Moira. "It's a miracle your name hasn't popped up in the news. One of the articles mentioned April was dropped home after the show by *a friend*. Police departments leak like sieves but it looks like Murphy managed to plug the holes. And it helps that reporters are too obsessed with politics to spend much time on a murder case. Mind you, you're not out of the woods yet."

Declan was reminded of Daisy's grim timeline. A couple days more and the police would turn their attention to fresher matters. "I'll let you know if I hear anything."

"Stay away from the cops," Wallace said. "Lay low."

Declan didn't tell him Murphy asked him to work with Robledo. The lawyer would go ballistic.

He called Stanley Borelli. The photographer didn't pick up and Declan left a message. He stretched out on the sofa with a spy novel and a vodka martini. It didn't work. His thoughts kept veering off the page, and he didn't taste the cocktail.

Daisy called in the morning. Declan sounded foggy from the heavy drinking of the night before. Her ear was a finetuned instrument. "Bad night?"

"I remember nothing about the night."

"You answered the phone, so I assume you are willing to raise from the bottom of the tank."

"I rolled out of the gutter," Declan said. "Shoot."

"I talked to Uncle Kevin."

Kevin Diamond founded the detective agency Daisy ran. When she looked for a job after a short disastrous marriage straight out of college, Kevin offered her to join his team. She showed natural dispositions for the trade.

"He told me enough colorful stories on Peppe Cassino to guarantee a bestseller that will never be written. Whoever attempts to write it would be made to eat their computer hard drive and it would be ruled an accident."

"Are the Cassinos still mob-connected?" Declan said.

"Not like in the fifties and sixties, but they have contacts they can go to when they need recommendations."

"Like what?"

"Specialized services. Reliable muscle, bagmen, flexible

contractors. It's smart. The best plans often founder because people use cheap amateurs to save a buck."

"Isn't Uncle Kevin retired?" Declan said.

"His memory is in fine working order, thank you. I use some of the same sources as the Cassinos when I need discreet professional services."

"DD, I'm shocked."

"Because you are so spotless, honey?"

"What does your intelligence network say?"

"Jason, Ricardo's son, is Peppe's true grandson. He's in bed with unscrupulous contractors and he's skimming. He has expensive habits that his dad won't pay for. I'll be in Clearwater Monday with the engineers. We'll take a look at Artemis." The tone of her voice changed. "Are you planning to crash again tonight? I can fly over and pull you up by your suspenders."

"I don't wear suspenders and my bootstraps are worn out. I'm caught in a snag, DD. I want to push the cop in charge of the investigation to give me something to do but it might piss him off, and I don't want to go over his head to Murphy."

"Try something new, babe. It's called patience." She hung up.

Declan didn't have to be patient for long. Robledo called a bit later.

"We released April Easton's body to the family. Nothing to do now but wait for the lab."

His lazy tone irked Declan. "What about the neighbors and the missing Bonnie Parker picture?"

"We interviewed the neighbors. They were busy partying. Nobody noticed or heard a thing. Nothing on the photo yet. I've been digging through contacts in the musical industry and former law firm colleagues."

"You could give me part of the dig," Declan said.

Robledo was silent for so long that Declan thought he'd hung up.

"You could do the lawyers," he said.

Declan swallowed a moan. April left Sloats & Archer over a year ago. Talk about stale leads. "Okay, email the stuff."

"I'd rather bring it. Are you home?"

It reeked of snooping. Robledo wanted to see where Declan lived. In what kind of squalid haunts he carried out his disreputable commerce. "Scuttle over."

The front doorbell rang half an hour later and Declan buzzed Robledo in. He waited on the landing, curious to see the cop's reaction to the antique clanging elevator, a beloved remnant of the building's warehouse past. Robledo's worst suspicions must be confirmed. Murphy had saddled him with a shady PI who lived in a dump.

The elevator stopped with an ominous teeth-aching screech. Declan pulled the metal curtain open and flashed Robledo his most charming smile. The expression on his visitor's face told him all he needed to know. Utter dismay.

"If I'd known I would have taken the stairs."

"You get used to it." Declan stepped away from the door. "After you."

Robledo walked in and stopped dead. With all the blinds up, the loft was so bright it seemed to be floating in air. The tall metal columns that Bjorn Gonzalez designed and carved to replace the original drab concrete pillars were the trunks of magical trees with the high ceiling as canopy.

"Madre de Dios," Robledo whispered. "You live here?"

"I used to be on the floor below. It's Vince Wallace's office now. Lunch? Moira made meatloaf."

Robledo wandered around, amazed. The large abstract seascape on the back wall held his rapt attention.

Declan set plates on the kitchen counter and opened a bottle of wine.

"I didn't expect this," Robledo said. "Are the other floors the same?"

"Bjorn Gonzalez is on the ground floor. He has double the

ceiling height. He needs it for his work. He's a sculptor, massive pieces. He made the support columns and the sculptures scattered around. That's how he used to pay his rent. The second floor is laid out as a four-bedroom apartment, and Vince's office is open plan like this one but with smaller windows. I have to fend off people who want to buy the place. I can't imagine living anywhere else."

"I see why."

Declan got a bottle of sparkling water and poured a glass of wine for Robledo. They sat down at the counter to eat, elbow to elbow.

"How was Florida?"

"Promising." Declan described the case without naming names, except Daisy's.

"Daisy Diamond," Robledo said. "That's a stripper's name."

Declan grinned. "She was born with it and didn't change it when she married. Daisy Gad didn't have the same in-your-face kick. Smart move, as it turned out. Gad was a goner. You'd like DD. She's spunky."

"You seem to like her a lot."

Declan cleaned the dishes and had a glass of wine, good resolutions be damned. "We connect and we collide. Sparks fly, it's enjoyable, and then we run off in diverging directions. Maybe one day we'll be too tired to run." He opened the floor-to-ceiling sliding doors to the terrace. "You must be dying for a smoke."

Robledo went to stand next to Declan at the balustrade. He changed his mind and dropped in a deck chair. The pack of cigarettes was out. Declan gave him a light and sat on the tiled floor with his back to the view of the city.

"April's funeral service is Monday afternoon in Katy." Robledo sounded melancholic. "I'd like you to go. The family knows me. I can't go inside. It would be bad form."

This wasn't witness cooperation or checking off a list of

contacts. It was real case work. "What should I look for at the funeral?"

"The parents give me a weird vibe," Robledo said.

"They're grieving."

"Not exactly. The parents broke all contact with April a year ago. The sister remained close. She collapsed when she heard the news. There's murder and then there's … this obscenity. It's hard. It was hard for you. You managed to hold it together until you saw the bathroom."

Declan couldn't deny it; the echo of the violence done to April sent him over the edge. The cop studied him through the smoke curtain of his cigarette. Declan went on a tangent.

"April came face to face with evil. It's a word I don't use often because it's too easy. It's a convenient box to stick things in we don't understand. Things we don't want to look at because they burn the soul and the only way we can erase them is by burning something on top of them, like ranch brands camouflaged by cattle rustlers. Burn after burn, until the mark is blurry and there's no more pain because all the nerve endings are shot."

Robledo drew deep on his cigarette. It crackled. "I know cops like that. The walking dead. They're toxic."

"I want a chunk of the investigation, Steve. I need your okay to poke around without you hovering over my shoulder or having to get approval for every move I make two days in advance and in triplicate." Declan's glass was empty. He was tempted to get a refill. He lit a cigar instead. "April was in my life for an eyewink. The length of a song. She's vanishing from my memory already. Who'll tell her story if we don't? I need to understand what happened. The murder served a purpose. I need to believe there's logic in the world, even if it's twisted."

Robledo smiled. "Is that why you became a PI, to bring order to the universe?"

"A minuscule universe. Finding people, things, truths. There are worse occupations."

"You could wear a badge," Robledo said.

"Murphy asked me, years ago. I don't respond well to rules. I go out of my way to avoid them." He crushed his cheroot on the tiles. "Tell me about the people I'll see at the funeral."

Robledo described his visit with April's parents, Tim and Vicky. "April is the bad daughter, Jill is the good one." He recalled the conversation with Jill's husband, Sam Koenig. "I believe he has more to say. He implied the parents tried to sabotage April's career. You'd think her success would have turned them around. A record deal is nothing to spit at."

"If they pictured April climbing the corporate ladder or raising a family, her success is their failure."

"And now, a murder. Like cause and consequence."

"April could have come in contact with all kinds of people. How far have you progressed on the music angle?"

"Her manager couldn't string two sentences together without crying. I interviewed local artists. April was well-liked. She wasn't a flash in the pan, she paid her dues. I have a call scheduled with the record producer."

"If there's a hitch in April's life, somebody in her inner circle must have an inkling," Declan said. "Any insight from the band?"

"Bogs Sorensen did the legwork. The guys are both married, two kids each. In-demand session musicians. No drugs, no priors. A couple of traffic citations, paid. We also got into her phone and laptop. Nothing icky."

Robledo seemed in no hurry to leave. He looked comfortable on the terrace, out of the sun, chain-smoking. Declan didn't mind having him around. He didn't need another day alone, ruminating.

"We found the note you left for April. It was stuck in a volume of George Bernard Shaw's letters. Is there a hidden message?"

Declan smiled. "Imagine where she would have put me if my name had been King."

"A *Cujo* paperback?"

They talked about their hardscrabble college years. Declan in New Orleans, Robledo in Austin. The cop said he was lucky to report to Frank Murphy who was upright and worked harder than any officer on his team.

"I'm spoiled. If they move me, I'll be a pain in the ass for my supervisor. I'll have to resign. I might try to get that law degree I couldn't afford earlier, become a nuisance for lazy prosecutors and half-assed cops."

"You could come work with me," Declan said.

"And learn to bend the rules a tad?"

"For a deserving cause."

"That is a slippery slope. What are you doing tomorrow?"

"Detox," Declan said. "Talking about a slippery slope. I'll sweat the booze out, drink gallons of water and work on your law contacts list. We need to find the missing Bonnie Parker picture. The killers didn't take it because April was cute."

TWELVE

DECLAN'S SUNDAY PROGRAM UNFOLDED as planned. He ran in Memorial Park till he couldn't lift his feet anymore, drank enough water to drown in, fixed a massive salad, and hit Robledo's list of April's former colleagues. The professional websites and social media platforms gave him names to attach to the pictures from April's fireplace. One of the names stood out: Amy Corrigan. A redhead with freckles. She was in several group shots.

Mid-afternoon, Declan called Stanley Borelli and hit voice-mail again. It worried him that Stan hadn't called back. He decided to pay him a visit.

Stan rented an apartment in Montrose. He had gone up in the world since his juvenile delinquent days. Declan pressed the buzzer at the gate and a female voice answered.

"Hi there. I'm a friend of Stan's. Declan Shaw. He called me and I can't get him on the phone."

"Wait a minute." The intercom clicked off. She was back soon. "What did Stan drive when he left New Orleans?"

She was checking his credentials? "A battered brown Pinto."

The buzzer whirred and the gate slid open. "Make sure it closes behind you," she said.

The woman who opened the door was molded in the tightest white jeans Declan had ever seen.

"You wanna beer? Stan is out on the patio."

She walked, stiff as a plank, toward the kitchen. Declan stared open-mouthed. The sound of the patio sliding door broke his fascinated contemplation.

"Your assistant didn't say when you would be back," Stan said.

Assistant. Moira would be livid. "I got home Friday afternoon. I called you and left messages."

"I turned the damn thing off."

Declan couldn't see his friend's face with the light behind him but the voice was strained.

"What's going on, Stan?"

Stan pointed at a chair near a large portable fan. The patio was in the shadow of the building. Sounds of kids splashing and squealing issued from the pool behind the fence.

The woman brought two ice-cold cans in koozies, set them on the table, and disappeared inside to go lie down flat or stand against a wall. Stan closed the door behind her. He took a sip of the beer. He used to be a chatterbox and inclined to get into long rambling philosophical dissertations. Reticence was not in character. Declan was about to grab him and shake the words out of him when he muttered, "It's, uh, about the singer at the club."

Declan leaned forward and his chair almost tipped over. "You know something?"

Stan's eyes went wide and he looked confused. "No, no … I …"

"What? For God's sake." Panic flashed on Stan's face and Declan brought his voice down. "Tell me. Please. I was with her, you understand? The night before."

"Ah." It came out in a long exhale.

"If you know something and you're in danger, there are ways to protect you," Declan said.

Stan pulled out a fat joint from his shorts' pocket. "Wanna share?" Declan passed. "Yes, I remember, you were never a fan."

"Messes with my head. Don't string me along, Stan."

Stan inhaled deeply. "A man called, Thursday. He didn't give a name. He said—exact words—'Declan Shaw is an old friend of yours. You were at Coombs with him Saturday'—that wasn't true, we met by accident. He didn't give me time to correct him. 'Your friend fucked that singer all night long. It got out of hand and he lost it. In a bad way.' I turned cold, Dek. I stopped breathing. Then he said 'There are other women. You know him, Borelli, you know what happened in New Orleans.' I didn't want to hear more, I cut the call." Stan grabbed his beer and drained it. He took a puff from the joint.

"Why didn't you call me right away?"

"Because I thought it over. The New Orleans bit. Nobody knows. So I thought, he's fishing."

"But you believed him about April."

Stan twitched. "I had that feeling … I always sensed when stuff went sideways around you. I always knew when you got yourself in a pickle and you would do whatever was needed to get out of it."

Declan remembered. Can you remember something you never forgot? Stan was too pale and the kid showed through the adult's face, frightened. Just like then, in the hostile nights of the New Orleans streets, when nothing the world had in store for them was fair or even half-decent.

"I didn't hurt her, Stan. She was asleep when I left. She was attacked later that day. The police cleared me."

Stan blinked in the cloud of smoke. "That's good." He coughed.

His eyes bounced all over the place. It was unsettling. What was in that joint? Declan reached for his friend's hand in an effort to rope him in and bring him down from the cloud. Stan looked at their joined hands and slowly pulled his hand back.

"What can you tell me about the man who called, what did he sound like?"

Stan crushed the beer can. The action seemed to steady him. "I saw him. I went to my studio, Friday morning. The guy walked in and threw questions at me. Where did we hang out in New Orleans, with whom, what gigs did we pull. And on and on. He dropped little bits of information in the middle of it. The accident at your grandmother's house, your broken hands, the study grant. He had the facts right."

Standard technique. Cloak your ignorance in shreds of truth. "The police investigated the accident at the house," Declan said. "The hospital and the college have my records. The information is easy to find. Did he drop other factoids?"

Stan's voice was firmer now but he still avoided looking at Declan. "He had nothing else. I told him to go to hell."

The fan whirred. It made a small click when it changed direction, like a timer measuring the progress of Declan's thoughts. "Could he have been a cop?"

"He didn't show a badge. You know a cop who asks questions and doesn't show his badge to focus your attention?"

"What did he look like?"

"Short, pale, balding on top, hooded eyes, a beer drinker belly, dressed like a schlub." Stan had the practiced eye of the shutterbug on the lookout for the perfect light, angle, and facial expression. "A small-time crook. A common type."

"Cheap newshound?"

"Could be. After I left my message for you, a reporter came after me. He bugged me all day yesterday. That's why I turned off my phone."

"Interested in the same subject?" Declan said.

"Yep. He dropped a card in my mailbox at the studio." Stan fished the business card out of his pocket.

Dirksen A. Loomis. Senior Blogger. Zeta Wire Service. Declan had never heard of them. Plenty of mudslingers infested the web.

"How did they get my name?" Stan said. "Before last Saturday, I hadn't talked to you in over a year."

"They know you at Coombs?"

Stan's pallor deepened. Declan took a page out of Robledo's playbook. He slumped in the deck chair and relaxed. Stan used to have no secrets for him, but that was twenty years ago. He took time lighting one of his cheroots. He pointed it at Stan. "You remember when I decided cigarettes were a bad habit?"

The sidestepping move earned him a shaky smile. "A bench in Jackson Square. You crumpled the pack and threw it in a bin, underhand if I recall correctly."

"It was a lucky shot. I suggested you do the same with your weed." Declan chuckled.

The haunted look slipped off Stan's face. "What do you do as a PI, Dek?"

"People hire me to find answers."

"What kind? Like ... who killed April?"

Declan stiffened when the thrill ran down his spine. It was difficult to remain loose. Steve Robledo had this thing down to an art. "Cops build fences around murder cases."

"But you knew her."

The longing in Stan's voice couldn't be missed. "I wish I knew her more. I might be able to help the police if I did."

Stan stared at the ground. "Would you help the police?"

Trick question. Stan was a functioning junkie. He figured long ago how to manage his addiction. He mastered the balancing act but it was a precarious equation. Cops were disrupters. To be avoided. Which side would he lean if Declan told him he worked with the police? He might clam up. Yet, Stan had been rattled by Declan's possible connection with the murder.

"I saw the crime scene photographs."

It landed like a well-aimed punch. Stan's head dropped between his knees and he sobbed.

Good ole Stan releasing the waterworks. Weed always made him emotional but this was more than chemically-induced pathos. Declan dropped the stub of his cigar in the beer can. He was getting the hang of that false Zen-like detachment. Cool on the outside, wired on the inside. The sun slipped toward the horizon.

"How did you meet her, Stan?"

Stan reacted to the sting of the whip. He used the koozie to wipe his eyes. "What if the cops come for me?" Declan knew that sheepish look well. Stan believed he had done something stupid. "It was only a few times, I swear."

That's at least one more than me, Declan thought. "The cops are looking into April's private life. What will they find?"

Stan sighed. "She came for a studio shoot. Promo pictures. She photographed well. We had fun with glamour shots." He bit his lower lip, looked away.

"How long did it last?"

"A few weeks last year, when she was in town between tour dates. Then she met a guy." He let out a short laugh. "You can't lasso April."

"Who's the guy?" Declan said.

"Gordon something. She said he was a sports agent. He must not be around anymore if she left Coombs with you."

Declan didn't like the sound of that. Out with the old, in with the new. It didn't fit with what he imagined—what he wanted— April to be. "Where were you last Sunday?"

"Here. We had friends over for a potluck."

Declan motioned at the sliding door. "Who's she?"

"Gloria. We've been together a long time. She's patient with me and when I get tired of a place, I find out she's already packed her bag." Stan searched his shorts for another smoke. All he could find was a bent cigarette. He put his lighter to it. "It's bugging me, Dek." He tapped the side of his head. "Taking all the space in there. And then that snoop asking questions about you." He looked at Declan like he used to when he expected to be told what to do. "I love you man. I wouldn't be here today if you hadn't … I want to know about April. Should I hire you?"

"Don't be silly." Declan stood up, peered over the fence at the swimming pool and the screaming kids. April's apartment complex must have looked like that a week ago. A week already. "I'll find who did it, Stan."

As much for him as for his old friend.

Instead of going home, Declan made a detour to visit Frank Murphy. The HPD commander lived on the west side of town, in a quiet neighborhood of ranch houses with tended unfenced lawns in front. Declan pulled into the driveway. It always struck him how out of place his old pickup truck was among the glossy Lexus, roomy SUVs, and freshly car-washed sedans.

He rang the bell. It wouldn't do to bang on a cop's front door. Very rude.

"I can't believe this thing is still on the road," Murphy said.

"It runs better than it looks and I stay under the radar."

As soon as Declan crossed the threshold, the smell of cooking engulfed him. As did Bess Murphy, flushed pink by the stove heat.

"You should put some meat on these bones," she said. "Single men have terrible feeding habits. You're staying for dinner."

The first time Declan had dinner at the Murphys, he was sleuthing on the fringes without a PI license. A teen gang burglarized cell phone shops. Long hours of surveillance paid off. Murphy complimented him on a job well done and brought him home. Declan must have looked like he could use a meal. Murphy also lectured him. Get legit or I'll bust your ass. He called it career advice.

"Bess, dear." Declan kissed her on both cheeks. "What's cooking?"

"A pot roast. Frank, fix the boy a drink."

Murphy was already in the sitting room, rummaging among bottles and glasses. "Pick your poison."

Declan spotted a Bushmills Black Bush that spoke to his ancestry. To Murphy's too, but Declan's connection to the old country was closer, one generation remote from the bog.

They went to the patio. The late afternoon heat was bearable. Beltway 8 rumbled low a few miles out, smothered by the thick foliage of old oaks. A dog barked a few houses down the street, excited by a squirrel or a cat.

"You live in a nice part of town."

"The commute is reasonable and Bess knows everybody. Maybe when I retire …"

Bess poked her head out to announce it would be thirty minutes to dinner.

"What are you doing around here? Did you have another look at April's place?"

Her apartment was ten minutes away. "I went to see an old friend, Stan Borelli."

Murphy squinted. "And you're telling me that why?"

"Two guys contacted him to ask a lot of questions about my time in New Orleans. Stan was at Coombs Saturday. He was leaving when I got there."

Murphy took his time extinguishing his cigar in a clay pot that didn't house a plant anymore. "You didn't mention this tidbit at the office."

"I told Vince Wallace. It was a one-minute conversation." Declan whipped out the blogger's business card. "Might be a made-up name."

"Dirksen Loomis. You want me to look into it?"

"I'll ask Moira," Declan said. "If he's real, we'll see something online soon."

"Anything in that New Orleans stuff that could come back and bite you in the behind?"

"I was a kid, Murph. I did my share of stupid stunts. I don't have a record."

"All that proves is that you were smart enough to avoid getting caught." Murphy sighed. "You came to Houston after college. Nothing has surfaced in all these years and the feds took a long hard look at you after that sex trafficking case you stuck your nose into. Any reason why something might emerge?"

"I don't talk in my sleep."

"Deflection is a fucking tell. Let's try another angle. Who'd want to mess with you?"

"I've ruffled a considerable packet of fluffy feathers over the past few years. The more I made you and the FBI happy, the more I inconvenienced connivers big and small. People I don't even know. I believe it's opportunistic. Linking me with April to embarrass me, scare away clients, and generate clicks."

"You don't think it's about your role in the investigation?"

"Robledo visited yesterday. I haven't even dipped a toe in the case yet."

THIRTEEN

THE RIVER OAKS MANSION sounded hollow. The cook and the butler were still there, the gardeners still came once a week, the same day as the housekeeping crew, but Elida was gone and it made all the difference. Wade Benning realized how much space his wife occupied in the big house. The air smelled different. He missed the clack of her heels in the marble hallway. He even missed the piercing laughter that used to irritate him. He wished he was in cool Colorado with Elida instead of being stuck in sweaty Houston doing the bidding of dubious associates. The business had changed over time, and got nastier as the stakes increased. He wished he could pull out. Gonzago made it clear that it wasn't an option. Benning had to see this trial mess to the end. After the verdict, maybe he could negotiate some sort of retirement. The commitments you make when you're in your thirties, running hot, with business opportunities left and right, seem light. You never think they'll come calling years later, with interest.

And there was Elida to think about. Gonzago was family. There was a lot of history there, to be proud of. Elida's people were more Texan than Stephen Austin and Sam Houston. It used to fill Benning with glee, that he was connected to all that. It helped getting a foot in the door. It helped with making money. Gonzago didn't ask for much in the beginning. A word here and there, facilitation, introductions. Benning's involvement with Gonzago's activities had grown so gradually he hadn't noticed until about five years ago how much of his business was closely connected to the big man's ventures.

Many of these ventures were sensitive. And insanely profitable.

The money flowing in was exhilarating and nasty problems were handled at a safe distance. Strangers dealing with strangers.

This trial business was different. Gonzago called in a personal favor. There were family considerations. The kids on trial were second or third cousins, or nephews maybe, something vague like that. In retrospect, Benning suspected a power play. Gonzago couldn't rely on his usual intermediaries and came to him as a last resort. It wasn't a big deal. Sure, Benning would take care of it.

He lined up reliable operators and set the wheels in motion. His agents put pressure on the lawyer to steer the trial toward a desirable outcome. The Easton woman was the wrong target. It was unfortunate for the woman but the problem was minor and manageable, from a business perspective. Until Shaw's name popped up.

Maybe he should have hired a cheap punk to put a bullet in Shaw's head. Right there and then, on a street corner, a gas station, make it look random. Gonzago would have done it and the hell with kicking a hornets' nest of cops and feds.

Benning typed his password in the computer to access the documents sent by his surveillance team. He scrolled through transcripts and audio files. The vehicle data was dull. Shaw didn't call anybody from his truck and he had no passengers. The bug recorded engine and traffic noises. The specialists did a good job identifying the places and people Shaw visited over the weekend. He went to Memorial Park for a run. Benning had a fleeting thought for Buddy Pagett. The fat fuck couldn't run to save his life. Shaw visited a friend in the Montrose area. Stanley Borelli, a photographer. A brief audio snippet pointed at a New Orleans connection. Benning made a note saying "Research Shaw's activities in New Orleans." More interesting was Shaw's visit to Frank Murphy, the HPD Homicide Commander, in West Houston. They must have talked about the murder. No way to know what they said. This was useless crap. Benning didn't want to think of how much he spent to bug Shaw's apartment and truck.

He set aside the vehicle surveillance and went to the office recordings. It troubled him that Shaw's office was also his residence. At least there was no video. He couldn't have tolerated that. Spying on somebody's private life was sleazy.

Shaw didn't have any romantic entanglements over the weekend and that was a relief. He discussed business with his partner, Moira Perkins. Benning knew Moira was married to Roger Perkins, an HPD officer. Her pleasant voice reminded him of Elida's. He listened to recordings of Moira answering phone calls, contacting clients, and managing fees and timesheets. He could use an assistant like that, precise and professional. Did Pagett have anybody of that caliber? He doubted it.

Benning scribbled a name. Daisy Diamond. She had something to do with Shaw's Florida case. Shaw sounded unsure when he talked to her. Under his New Orleans note, he wrote "Get information on Daisy Diamond."

Shaw seemed interested in the Easton murder case, but he wasn't working it and that was good news. Maybe Benning wouldn't need to activate the Tampa insurance. It didn't trouble him that a woman had died in a Tampa back alley, just as a precaution. Collateral damage was part of the cost of doing business.

The conversation with Steve Robledo delivered another

interesting piece of information. Benning wrote, "Missing Bonnie Parker picture?" And underlined the words twice. He reclined his desk chair and closed his eyes, hands folded on his stomach. A photograph was taken from the woman's apartment. His agents were under strict orders not to remove anything. Did they disobey and grab a souvenir, or did somebody from the investigation team snatch it?

He should ask Buddy Pagett for a copy of Shaw's police interview. See what was said about this picture. Anything out of the ordinary was important.

He focused on the transcript of Robledo's visit. The conversation was innocuous. Yet, he felt a chill. The cop stayed for hours. They sat on the terrace. Where there were no bugs. What a ridiculous oversight. His guys were supposed to be the best. For what he paid them, they ought to be fucking perfect.

Benning's thoughts took a turn. Should he use the Tampa insurance now?

He went to the sideboard and mixed a cocktail.

It was better to wait. Shaw didn't know he was an inch from the jaws of a snapping trap. Benning might not have to strike at all. The trial was in the defense phase and the stopgap with the jury was in place. It could all be over before any action was needed.

That was the right way to handle it.

And he would check the surveillance reports as they came in. He shouldn't let them stack up. Benning turned his attention to the lawyer. He wasn't as concerned about him as he was about Shaw but the boy prosecutor couldn't be ignored. He had shown a stronger backbone than expected. If he had been compliant, the Easton thing and the Tampa remediation would not have been necessary.

Benning switched off the computer. His eyes rested on the wood paneling of his office. Cedar. The smell was long gone, erased by smoke and alcohol vapors. Aged. A concept alien to

Houston where almost everything was perennially new, built with glass, concrete, and metal. Benning felt aged. He was aged. Even if his mind was as sharp as ever.

FOURTEEN

A GIRL STANDING AT THE ENTRANCE of the funeral home handed out leaflets with April's picture on the cover. The photo was atrocious.

"Please sign the book," the girl said, pointing at a register. "Use the door in the back to get to the chapel."

Declan had donned a suit and tie for the occasion and given a shine to his boots. He pretended to write his name and leafed through previous pages. A big contingent from Sloats & Archer had come to pay their respects. He recognized names from Robledo's list, including Amy Corrigan's.

Fragile-looking chairs had been placed in tight rows in the plain space they called a chapel. There weren't enough to accommodate everybody. Flower arrangements surrounded the casket. More wreaths and bouquets were placed along the sides of the room. Poster boards covered with pictures of April and her family lined the walls. Declan looked for the group photo missing from the apartment. The photographs weren't in any particular order. April as a baby was next to April on a sailboat. She was once a pigtailed girl, a moody teenager, a perky student, and a tennis player, but nowhere was she Bonnie Parker. Declan stood transfixed in front of a striking shot of April on a windy beach in a flowing dress and straw hat. He tore himself away from it with regret and turned his attention to the front of the room where family members stood in line like dignitaries welcoming VIPs. The parents were first, the father granite-rigid, the mother pale and thin-lipped. They didn't speak, they just nodded. No kisses and no hugs. The sister was a couple of steps to the side, with her back to Declan. When she turned around, he thought he was seeing double. The siblings were much more alike than the pictures on the fireplace led him to believe. Jill was shorter and curvier, but the hair color was the same and the facial features came out of the same mold, softer and more filled in. If he had seen Jill from a distance, or in passing, he could have mistaken her for April. The spell broke when she reached for her husband. Her body language had none of April's easy fluidity. She was awkward, stiff, a girl afraid of messing her freshly laundered Sunday clothes. If April had once been that body-conscious, she had shaken it off. Her stage presence was sensual, a come-on with a sense of humor.

The husband, Sam Koenig, exhibited a boatload more empathy than the rest of the family. He gave his full attention to visitors, patted people's shoulders, kissed an elderly lady on the cheek. His smile was appropriate, yet natural. A few minutes later, the preacher walked in and talked to April's parents. The service was about to begin.

All the chairs were taken and Declan stood in the back, near the door. The service was short. The preacher read a passage from the book of Revelation and one of April's former law firm colleagues gave a fond and moving tribute that made the entire audience reach for tissues. April's father walked to the front. He started with a passage from Isaiah that made Declan cringe. "The righteous are taken away to be spared from evil."

The preacher concluded the service with a blessing. People

started leaving, some gathered around the family. Declan spotted a vibrant redhead. Amy Corrigan. He would try to catch her in the corridor. He turned on his heels and found himself nose to nose with April's band.

"Greg and Jake." He was amused to see the musicians take a couple of synchronized steps back. "I'm Declan Shaw. Who's Greg and who's Jake?"

They pointed at each other.

"I'm Jake. You were with April, after the show." He was the bravest of the two but his voice wasn't too steady. His brother was looking around. Where was a uniform when you needed one?

"Relax. The cops cut me loose." Declan handed one of his Shaw Investigations cards to Jake.

"You left the club with her," Greg said.

"I gave her a ride home."

The brothers exchanged glances. "She has a car," Jake said.

"She didn't have it on Saturday," Declan said.

"She drove Friday," Greg countered.

"She wouldn't have driven to the show if she planned to go home with him," Jake said. "Sorry we gave you the eye, man. We described you to the cops."

"No biggie. Many people saw me."

"Any idea who did it?" Jake said.

"Not yet. Are you guys still playing?"

"Trying to sound halfway decent. We have to find a singer." Greg shrugged. "Can't imagine auditioning anybody right now."

"It's raw, man," Jake said.

The brothers shook Declan's hand and left. Amy Corrigan was in deep conversation with a tall dark-haired woman in an elegant business suit. Declan didn't remember her from the pictures in the apartment. When Amy adjusted her purse's shoulder strap and said goodbye, Declan preceded her into the hallway. People were making their way to the exit. Amy appeared, searching in her purse. He let her pass in front of him.

"Ms. Corrigan?"

She turned around, with her glasses and keys in one hand. "Yes?"

"I'm Declan Shaw. You have a minute? I'm a friend of April's."

She blinked and gave him a quick once over. "Ah … of course you are." She blushed. The color lit up her delicate complexion.

"I'm working with the police."

"I'm sorry. I … uh, I misunderstood. Forgive me. How can I help you?"

This wasn't the place for a conversation. Too many eaves-droppers. One fellow, in particular, was far too interested in them. Small, shabby, so neutral he could disappear into the beige walls. He fit Stanley Borelli's description of his pesky anonymous questioner.

"We can't talk here. Do you mind if I give you a call?" Declan gave her one of his cards and a pen. He kept an eye on the gray guy while she wrote her number.

"I'm in meetings tomorrow morning. Call me in the afternoon."

The snoop in the corridor had retreated behind a potted ficus tree. Amy Corrigan gave Declan his card back, smiled, and walked away. He waited a beat, pretending to search his pockets for his smokes. When the little bald man went to the exit, right behind Amy, he followed suit.

Declan was at the door in time to see the guy cross the parking lot and get into a red Explorer. Too far for the tag number but the funeral home had surveillance cameras. With a little luck, and a little help from his cop friends … Where was Robledo?

The parking lot was emptying. Declan moved away from the door and lit a cigarillo. The detective came trotting from the back of the parking lot when Declan was about halfway through.

"Where have you been?"

"I came early," Robledo said. "I took pictures of the flower arrangements and the poster boards before people arrived. I found a spot with a good view of the cars coming in. It felt like the cops at the beginning of *The Godfather.* Their ratio of gangsters versus bystanders was way better than mine. I'll put somebody on the license plates."

"I'm interested in a particular vehicle," Declan said. "A red SUV. An Explorer, I think." He pointed at the corner of the parking lot. "It was parked over there, next to that hulking white pickup."

"What about it?"

"The guy who drives it was too interested in my conversation with Amy Corrigan."

"I remember seeing that name," Robledo said.

"She was in three of the group photos. I have a call set up with her tomorrow. What did you gather?"

"Nothing on these posters looked like Bonnie Parker."

Declan pulled out the leaflet with the ghastly picture of April. "What do you think of this?"

"I've seen better mugshots."

"They had plenty of photos to choose from."

"I bet it's the parents," Robledo said. "It reeks of petty resentment."

"You were right about them. I could feel the chill waft across the room. The sister was a shock. She's an April look alike. Until she moves. Have you gone back to the brother-in-law, Sam Koenig?"

"Not yet. What else you got?"

"I chatted with the band members. They were surprised April didn't use her car Saturday. They said she drove to the show the night before." Declan crushed what was left of his cigar under a bootheel. "Have you processed her car?"

"I can think of a dozen reasons why she decided to leave the car at home."

"It's worth a check," Declan said.

"Right. Thanks for the assignment."

"Hey, you asked me to come. If you don't want to hear what I have to say …"

Robledo threw both hands in the air. "Fine, I'll have a look at the fucking car." He extracted a cigarette from a battered pack. Declan was ready with the lighter. Robledo grunted a vague thank you. "I'll let you know about the red SUV."

Moira stood in the middle of the loft holding a sheaf of paper.

"You're getting ready to start a bonfire?" Declan said.

"I wish burning this crap would be the end of it. I printed that off the internet. It's all about you and April Easton, and it stinks."

The article headlines screamed. In bold and all caps. "Sex." "Singer Slaughtered." "Seedy Dives." "Booze." "Drugs." "Bondage."

"Gross exaggeration," Declan said.

"It's all you have to say?" Moira was flustered. She seemed more upset by his cool reaction than by the salacious postings.

"Some of it is correct. Give or take semi-literary hyperbole."

"This stuff is spreading so fast I can't keep up with the online searches. I'm deluged with social media messages and the email box imploded. I put our main number on voicemail, the phone was driving me nuts. How can they do this so quickly?"

"Bots, algorithms, digital trickery." Declan dug into the bottom drawer of her desk where they kept the burner phones. He gave her one, and pocketed another. "From now on, we use these for calls. I'll keep the tablet to access the server. Go home. On the way down, warn our tenants they might get spam calls. Tell them not to let strangers in. I'll take care of Vince."

Wallace didn't need a detailed briefing. "Murphy should issue a statement. Something about protecting the privacy of people that are outside the scope of the investigation."

"Let's not overreact. They're trolls. No legitimate media outlet has picked it up. If we start screaming, they'll think there's fire under the smokescreen and we'll have a real problem."

Declan used the burner phone as soon as he was in his truck. He called his go-to computer wizard, Leyla Kareem. Her services were expensive and worth every penny. Declan couldn't do what she did.

"I have a request, Leyla."

"That's not your usual number."

"Burner. Do a search on me and you'll know why. Call me back."

The phone rang a few minutes later. "I can handle it," she said

Leyla's preferred modus operandi was minimal physical contact. "There's more to it than blocking, sweetie. I need a face-to-face."

Declan picked up Leyla on the corner of Sul Ross and Mandell thirty minutes later. They went to a sports bar with a big garden. It was a favorite watering hole for young professionals. A table was occupied by a couple and two big labs. The place was dog-friendly. Guys played bocce ball in the back. They were beer-loud.

"You realize you might be blowing this out of proportion," Leyla said. "Were you in love with that singer?"

"That's got nothing to do with the job at hand. I want to know who's behind the web storm."

Leyla spun Dirksen Loomis's business card around her fingers. "It's a decoy. I doubt anybody live would answer calls. I can fake a message and leave a number with a tracer. The email is bound to return an undeliverable. I'll initiate name searches, with variations. We'll get a lot of fluff that'll take a lot of time to screen through. Do you want to pay for fluff?"

Declan waved the question away. "What can we do about the postings and the emails?"

"Cancel your social media accounts. I will adjust the spam filters on your email accounts and harden the firewall on your server. Although that one is already so solid, they would have to clone me to get through."

"I want a trace, Leyla. Can't you get an IP address?"

"That's a wild goose chase. If these people are halfway able, the signal will bounce all over. Good luck in fixing a location."

She wasn't giving him much hope. "How do the police nail online sex predators? Don't they get IPs?"

"Most of these perverts are not sophisticated. They use the family laptop at night from the kitchen nook. The cops build traps in chat rooms. For a trap to work, you need interaction. The noseeums that buzz around you don't want to interact. It's bite and go."

He told Leyla about the goons that harassed Stan Borelli. "These guys didn't seem clever."

Leyla sat cross-legged on the picnic bench. She was a small woman, thin-boned, pale, bird-like. From the back, she looked fourteen. With her skinny black jeans, black t-shirt, and pixie haircut she gave off a teenage goth vibe. When you looked into her dark eyes, you understood your mistake. Declan was impatient with stupidity but he had all the time in the world for Leyla Kareem.

"It would be easier if they were after something in particular," she said.

"They want my New Orleans secrets. Stan knows a lot but even he doesn't know everything."

She hummed something unidentifiable. She always did that when she was mulling things over. Declan remembered sitting next to her an entire afternoon while she hacked into the records of a secretive company. She never stopped humming. It put him to sleep.

"Are those the kinds of secrets you would keep on your server? Encrypted, of course."

"They're not anywhere." He tapped his head. "Even in here, they make me nervous." He lit a cigar and blew the smoke away from Leyla.

"Did your name ever appear in a police file? Apart from a week ago, I mean."

"I was interviewed once. A friend of mine was killed."

"Tell me about it."

"Three kids found dead in an abandoned house. One of them was my friend Maurice Silverberg. Maury. They had a gun. The police said the kids fought over it. Bullets went everywhere."

"Who owned the gun?"

"Probably stolen. The owner never came forward."

"They knew the kids fought for the gun from the injuries?"

Declan nodded. "And the fingerprints on the gun. Maury's and those of the older kid, Patch Mitchell. Maury was fifteen. I loved him."

"Did you know the other two?"

"Yeah, big bullies. They got their kicks from beating up the younger kids."

She looked up. "I know how we can do it."

"Don't drag Maury into it, please."

"No need. But maybe you have an enemy, a bully, like that Patch kid. The kind of asshole that still chews on his resentment, no matter how much time has passed. He hates you. When he sees the ruckus online, he smells an opportunity to fuck you sideways. How does that sound?"

"Terrifying."

"I'll build a fiction. A bot to lure other bots. We get a contact, we snap the trap. You need to give me something fragrant to work with. Something that smells like pralines, gumbo, and boudin."

"So cliché. When this is over, I'll take you to *La Nouvelle Orléans* and I'll show you what fine dining means." Declan's voice had taken the cadences of his adoptive hometown. "*Au champagne, bien entendu.*"

She giggled. Now she looked fifteen, back *and* front. "We'll watch your enemies scramble to take the bait." She clinked her glass against his. "You know that movie *North by Northwest*? I love it."

Declan had homework to do. Create, out of thin air, juvenile offenses that were believable yet as far as possible from those he committed. It wouldn't be easy. He had experimented widely.

He closed the blinds on all the floor-to-ceiling windows. He loved his tall panes of glass but right now they made him feel naked. He checked the agency's email box and was stunned at the pile that accumulated in the last couple of hours. He read a few messages. They looked computer-generated. He didn't bother deleting them; Leyla would wipe the box clean and zap all new incoming. The agency's social media accounts were clogged. Declan canceled them. They were pure PR and not needed for day-to-day operations. Moira used fake accounts for investigations; he didn't touch those.

He switched on the TV because he found the silence ominous. People were trying to hurt him and they zeroed in on the most opaque period of his life—the eleven years he spent in New Orleans after his parents died.

FIFTEEN

IF HE HAD BEEN WELCOMED with open arms into his grand-mother's house to live happy and content among uncles, aunts, and cousins, the buzzards wouldn't have anything to peck at. But Declan's stay at *La Maison Dunoit*, as it was known across town, was everything but blissful.

The attention he received from family members was the wrong kind. He had to protect himself, and the best protection was not being there. He spent as little time as possible in the big house. He depended on friends, some he made at school, some he made on the streets. By the time he turned fifteen, he was battle-hardened, and he had learned a panoply of tricks, none of them of the kind suitable for polite conversation.

All in all, it was excellent training for a private dick.

"Can you get in?"

Stan breathed down Declan's neck. "Shut up. I can't hear a thing with you babbling."

Declan had opened safes like this one before. They were

ticklish and challenging. He enjoyed them. Man against machine. The final click gave him a surge of heat. He stepped away from the opening door, raised his hands.

Stan and Maury rushed in with the bag. How much was in there? Declan didn't care.

"Don't touch the door or the shelves, you idiots. You'll leave fingerprints, you're not wearing gloves."

They did as they were told. Loyal soldiers who needed constant reminders. Perfection is a struggle. Declan grinned. This was pretty damn close to perfect.

Back in the abandoned house they used as their HQ, they looked at the loot. The piles of banded banknotes and the gun stared at Declan as if trying to hypnotize him. He knocked the gun off the money and Maury swooped for it.

"How much is there?" Stan said. He had popped a couple of pills as he always did after a job and his eyes were too bright.

"Fifty thousand," Declan said, "Give or take."

"Half for you," Stan said. "Maury and I share the rest."

They always did thirds. "We go equal," Declan said.

"Maury and I talked it out. Without you, we'd be staring at that safe like dummies. We decided to split this way before we knew what was in the safe." Stan smiled.

"I want the gun," Maury said.

"All right, but it's our last safe-cracking job," Declan said. "Done and out. I also decided that before tonight."

They both looked at him as if he'd gone crazy. Stan was first to react. "What about the plan? We decided to go after these bastards. Screw them. Strike a blow for the kids they messed with. This one's my choice. Last week we did Maury's. What about yours? Don't you want to kick these guys where it hurts?"

"There are other ways, Stan. You know how I feel when we do the same thing over and over. I start thinking our luck will run out. It's been two months. It's time we do something else."

"But you're so good," Stan wailed.

Declan took his share and went upstairs. He had a cache in one of the corner bedrooms. In a few days he would take the money out, and hide it somewhere else. He had several places around town. Downstairs, Stan was telling Maury to put the money in his backpack and "stop playing with that fucking gun, you're gonna shoot yourself!" Declan shook his head. Stan loved dope and Maury loved guns. It took a strong hand to keep them in line.

He still wore the soft leather gloves he pulled on before breaking into the man's house. The gloves were like a second skin and he often forgot he had them on. He was superstitious about them. He never took them off until the job was completed. He often kept them on until he went to bed. Stan said he was a compulsive freak.

"I'm not going to change my process because you mock me, buddy," Declan muttered. Just like Stan wouldn't stop self-medicating *to relax*, as he said. Declan put the money away, keeping the gloves on.

The gunshot startled him. He cursed. He should have taken the damn gun from Maury. Did the fool drop the piece and shoot himself? He ran down the steps four at a time, using the creaky banister to swing around the corners. He reached the first landing as two more shots rang accompanied by shouts and screams. He came to a dead stop. This wasn't Stan and Maury. Other people were down there. The light from the candles Maury lit when they arrived flickered on the ceiling of the foyer. The beam of a flashlight drew a circle on one of the walls. Stan yelled, "Get off him." More screams, then a crash as the light dimmed. Declan reached the bottom of the stairs and peered around the corner. Maury was on the floor, a large shape loomed over him. Stan was on the side, held in a chokehold by a guy spewing out a stream of high-pitched curses. The light of the remaining candle caught a metallic reflection in the guy's hand. Knife. When Maury's attacker straightened up, the flashlight showed him holding the gun. Declan pushed away from the wall and ran, head down, to the shape with the gun. He hit the guy in the stomach at full speed and they both fell, Declan on top. They thrashed. The gun went off. The sound was deafening. The gun went off again and Declan managed to grab the guy's wrist. Another gunshot. Declan's adversary bucked. From the corner of his eye, Declan spotted movement to his left. He rolled to his right, reached for the gun, and pulled the trigger, no time to aim. Then nothing moved anymore.

Heart thumping, Declan rushed to Maury's side. His friend was dead, a bullet had blown off the right side of his head. Declan stepped back, on unsteady legs. His thoughts were like his vision, clear. All the blood was behind and under Maury's head, Declan hadn't stepped into anything. He turned his attention to the two strangers. One of them was Patch Mitchell. He was the shape Declan struggled with. Patch was a neighborhood bully and juvie graduate who hung around the high school selling dope. Patch had taken a bullet in the chest. If not in the heart, near enough to end his sorry career. Declan's gloves were sticky with blood. His stomach flipped over. Not now. He couldn't puke now. Stan. Where the hell was Stan?

"Stan?" His voice died in his cotton-filled ears.

A moan came from a dark corner in the back of the foyer. Declan circled the man with the knife. A bullet had ripped through his throat, blood poured from the wound, his dead eyes stared at the ceiling. Declan considered his lucky shot. A fraction of an inch to the right and he would have four inches of steel inside of him.

Stan sat on the floor with his back to the wall, knees drawn to his chest and his head on them.

"Come on, Stan, we have to get out of here." Declan pulled his friend up and Stan fell against him. "Okay, it's okay." As he adjusted his grip on Stan, he tried to remember what they did when they got to the house.

He had picked the lock and opened the door. Then Maury lit the candles he carried in his backpack, and they sat on the floor to split the money. Part of the money was in the cache upstairs. The rest was in Maury's backpack. Supporting Stan with one arm, Declan reached for the bag. He resisted grabbing the flashlight to inspect the room. He took a long and nerve-racking minute to scan the foyer and didn't see anything that would indicate two more people were there tonight. He shouldered Maury's backpack and half carried Stan to the door.

Then he almost fucked it all up. His bloody gloved hand was a hair from the door handle. He jerked back as if the handle was a live wire.

"Fuck me," he muttered.

He used Maury's backpack to press on the handle and pull the door open. His hearing was starting to clear. Sirens wailed in the distance. Maybe they were coming this way, maybe not. New Orleans nights were always full of sirens.

"Don't go." Stan's voice was tinny.

Declan couldn't take Stan to his parents' house, not in this state, not before prepping him for the police questioning to come. They were a known trio, Maury, Stan, and him, hanging together after school. They never left together for their nocturnal adventures, always met at a prearranged location, but Stan and he would be interviewed and Stan was in no shape to handle the pressure.

A year before, after an embarrassing family scandal, Declan had been exiled to a garret above the detached garage. The place wasn't luxurious but better than the bedroom under the eaves that he had been confined to earlier. It had a decent bathroom with a proper shower, a double bed, and a small stove. A battered armchair, table, two kitchen chairs, a chest of drawers, and shelves for his books completed the set-up. Many people in town had to make do with much less. The biggest advantage of the arrangement was that Declan was free to come and go without having to navigate the corridors of the big family house.

He avoided the house's gated entrance and climbed the garden wall. Stan had recovered somewhat and managed to follow him. At sixteen, even doped and shaken, you're still limber.

"Empty your pockets and take your clothes off," Declan said. He removed the money from the backpack and put it on the table. He stripped and his blood-stained clothes joined Stan's on the pile. "Get in the shower."

"You have blood on your face," Stan said.

Declan wiped the stains off with alcohol and cotton swabs. The cotton balls joined the clothes on the floor. While Stan was in the shower, Declan stashed all the discarded stuff in the backpack. He rifled through his drawers for clothes that would fit Stan. A pair of jeans he had outgrown should work. Sneakers would be tight. Stan had big feet.

Stan appeared, wrapped in a towel. "I can't go home."

"You're staying here tonight."

His relief was heartwarming. "Where do I sleep?"

Declan pointed to the bed. He showered, put on fresh clothes, and left with the backpack. He had picked the big house's back door lock so many times it opened when he whispered. He went through the utility room into the furnace room. He mouthed a silent thank you to whoever arranged for a cold January spell. The backpack and its contents went up in flames. Thanks were also in order for his grandmother who resisted modernizing the house. It didn't often freeze in New Orleans, why the hell would she waste money to replace a furnace that had served generations of Dunoits so faithfully. Declan waited till the entire load was consumed and took the extra precaution of raking the ashes. Where these instincts came from, he didn't know. Maybe Grandma was right when she declared in righteous fury that Declan came from a long line of good-for-nothing parasites and grifters, with some highwaymen thrown in for good measure.

Stan was in bed when Declan got back to the apartment above the garage.

"I haven't been much help tonight." Stan was still pale.

"There wasn't much you could do with a knife on your throat."

"They came in from the back. Maury was playing with the gun and … I tried to take it from him, but I wasn't seeing too straight." He frowned. "Where are you going to sleep?"

"You could scoot over a bit. I have to whisper a few lies in your ear."

The script was short. They were together all night. They walked, they sat in Jackson Square, they talked. Then Stan said he didn't want to go home. And here they were.

"It's thin."

"We're kids," Declan said. "How deep are we supposed to be?"

"What about being in the house?"

"We've been there, just not recently."

"A little guilt would help." Stan turned to face Declan and kissed him on the mouth. A warm kiss, not creepy. "What if we have a big secret?" He chuckled. "I love you, man."

"Stan, you're a genius." Declan raised on an elbow. "Can you stay off the pills? You run off at the mouth when you're high."

Stan flopped on his back. "If word goes around that we're doing it, you'll lose Suzy. That's a bigger sacrifice than me staying off the dope."

If he was suspected of shooting two guys, even in self-defense, Suzy would be lost anyway. Two lucky shots, no fingerprints, and a run in the night. What else are you hiding, Declan Shaw?

"Sleep now."

The shooting was top of the news Saturday evening. Declan and Stan didn't see the TV segment because they were at the movies. Suzy Caswell was with them. They saw *Fallen*. All three enjoyed the thrilling ride, even if Declan didn't care much for the super-natural thing. He liked his whodunits realistic.

Stan smirked. "Reality is real enough. Bye, lovebirds." He walked away. He was stone-cold sober.

"Why don't you come watch the game with us tomorrow," Suzy said. "We'll throw a football at half-time."

"Will you let me tackle you?"

"I'll be on your team. You throw long."

"I love you, Suzy," Declan said. "Will you marry me?"

She punched him in the chest. "This time next year, we'll be writing college essays. None of that eloping for me, buster. I want a degree and a job. Then I'll marry you. In that order."

"Providing I have a degree too."

"Oh, you will." She kissed him. "Have you figured out what you want to do?"

He hadn't. "I like to find things."

"You should be an archeologist. A discoverer of lost civiliza-tions. It's cool. And while you're on your expeditions, I'll make money building bridges and dams."

"Deal. I'll watch the game with you if you come pick me up. An hour before kick-off?"

"Just one hour?"

Suzy broke the news to him Sunday afternoon. She brought the paper. "Maury was killed Friday night," she said. "It's a horrible story. Look."

Declan bent over the article, hair falling over his eyes, hid-ing them from Suzy. The story started on the front page, one column, and continued inside for a half-page, with a picture of the Colvin house in all its dilapidated glory. Three boys shot dead. Riley "Patch" Mitchell, 19, Clement Gordon, 18, and Maurice Silverberg, 15. Mitchell and Gordon were in posses-sion of drugs. Autopsies were being conducted. Crime scene evidence indicated a violent struggle with multiple shots fired. A hunting knife was recovered. Mitchell's and Silverberg's fingerprints were on the gun. Gordon's were on the knife. Motive was unclear. Several hypotheses were considered: a drug meet, a gun purchase, a sexual assault attempt. The article went on to say that Mitchell had a long criminal record and Gordon had been arrested multiple times on drug-related charges. Silverberg was a minor and his record was sealed. Investigation ongoing. The article ended with a plea to the authorities to tackle the problem of youth violence and gang-related activities in New Orleans.

Declan folded the paper and sat on the bed.

"You were with Stan and Maury after school Friday," Suzy said.

He took a deep breath. "We talked about getting together Saturday. I said it would have to be late because Jerry asked me to help out at the shop. He received the parts for that old Mustang and he's in a hurry to get going on it." He ran his hands through his floppy hair. "What were they doing in that house? Maury was scared shitless of Patch."

"We all are," Suzy said.

"Always picking on the small ones. And that shit he peddles …"

Suzy sat on the bed next to him. "I'm going to say something terrible, but I hope Maury shot him."

Declan held her in his arms. He felt disconnected, watching himself comforting Suzy, yet misleading the one person that knew him best. She was more dangerous to him than an entire police squad. She was smart, she could spot a faker, and love didn't blind her. He shouldn't ever try to lie to her. The secret was to be true, in the moment, in the world that she lived in. It just wasn't *his* entire world.

"I'd like to close my eyes and lie down for a while. You mind, Suze?"

The principal gave a short speech before classes started on Monday. By then, most students knew what happened Friday night. Boys exchanged nervous glances; girls sported red eyes. Sensitive souls mourned Maury's passing. Declan and Stan listened to the embarrassed "it sucks, bud" pronouncements that were the teenage equivalent of the adults' "so sorry for your loss." Students and faculty were united in common discomfort. At lunch, the principal called Declan and Stan to his office.

"You were close friends with Maurice. Detectives from the New Orleans police department want to talk to you. I'm not happy with this request. Minors should not be interviewed without a parent present. I am aware of your respective family circumstances. Borelli, do you want to call your mother?"

Stan's mother was in no condition to sit on a police interview. And his father …

Declan intervened. "Does it have to be a parent, sir? Could an adult stand in? You, maybe, or a teacher …"

The principal's face lit up. "That is an excellent idea. What about Miss Delgado?"

Stan smiled in relief. Carolina Delgado was the guidance counselor and art teacher.

"I'll see with the detectives and Miss Delgado if that is acceptable. What about you, Shaw?"

"If I could call Mr. Caswell, sir, Suzy's father. He's helping me with my college plans."

The principal pointed at the desk phone. "Call him. I'll talk to the police."

Because Paul Caswell was a half-hour away, Stan and Miss Delgado went first. It suited Declan. Hopefully, the cops came to the interview without an agenda. If they pressed Stan, he would create confusion. Carolina Delgado, who was aware of Stan's fondness for weed would plead for leniency. The kid's family was unreliable. His trust in adults was non-existent. The ball would be in Declan's court.

"What do they want from you?" Paul Caswell said.

They were in the corridor waiting for Stan to be released from the vice principal's office. The interview lasted longer than Declan expected. It had been going on for almost forty-five minutes.

"Stan and I were Maury's best friends. They think we know what he was doing Friday night."

"Do you?"

"You think I would have let him go meet these ghouls on his own?" Declan said. He tended to answer a question with a question. He had to watch it.

The office door swung open. Carolina Delgado had an arm around Stan's shoulders. His face was buried in his hands and he sobbed. Carolina's eyes were red.

Declan jumped to his feet. "Stan, you okay, what happened?"

Carolina Delgado raised a hand. "It was emotional. Stan needed to get all that stuff out. It would have been better in a psychologist's office, but the detectives are good men, they understand."

Declan swallowed his anger. It would have been better if the cops had hit Stan on the head with a phone book. He wouldn't have been sobbing then—well, not like this anyway.

"Please, come in." A deep voice, a slight southern drawl. "I'm Alvin Compton and this is my colleague, Thompson Cross."

"Paul Caswell. Declan asked me to be here today."

Declan tore his eyes away from the closing door and Stan going down the corridor, Miss Delgado by his side. He looked at his opponents. Compton was white, tall, and bald. Cross was Black, athletic, and younger. Horn-rimmed spectacles were perched on the tip of his nose. Both cops looked competent.

"What did you do to Stan?" He bit on the words. Let them believe he was angry, one emotion to hide another.

"These gentlemen have a job to do, Declan," Paul Caswell intervened. "They're not here to harm children."

Compton smiled. "Coming to the defense of your friend, eh? Sit down."

The two cops were behind the vice principal's desk. Paul Caswell and Declan had the visitors' chairs.

"Let's start with identification," Cross said. "You're Declan Shaw, you turned sixteen last July, you live with your grandmother Emilie Dunoit in the Garden District. You're an A student and you've never been interviewed by the police. Correct?"

"Yes."

"What's your relationship with Maurice Silverberg?"

"He's a friend." He should have used the past tense. He shrugged and looked away.

"How did you meet him?"

"Here, in school. The day I started."

"Maury is a year younger than you."

Softball questions. Declan told them he arrived in New Orleans in December, five years ago, after missing four months of school. He was enrolled in fifth grade, where he became friends with Maury. "By January, they figured they made a mistake and I went to sixth with Stan and Suzy, Mr. Caswell's daughter. But I stayed friends with Maury."

Compton leafed through school transcripts. "They reserved the right to hold you back if it didn't work."

"Yes."

Compton leaned forward. "When did you last see Maury?"

"Friday."

"You were with Stanley."

"Yes."

"That was at the end of the school day. Then what?"

"I went to work at Gracie's Market." Declan rattled off his schedule. Monday at the library, Tuesday and Wednesday at Bordeaux Gardens, Friday at Gracie's, and Saturday at Jerry's garage.

"Sunday you rest." Cross grinned.

"I catch up on stuff. I hang out with Suzy."

"You have a full plate," Compton said. "When do you sleep?"

"The places I work at aren't open at night." Now wait for it.

"Which gives you time for your other activities."

"Movies, the mall, a burger, or a pizza. There's a place where they let us shoot pool for free if it's not busy. Stan's a fantastic photographer. I go with him, Maury comes too sometimes." He blinked. Wrong tense again. "It's safer to hang out as a group."

"We have Declan over for dinner a few times a week," Paul Caswell said. "The boy needs healthy home-cooked food."

The diversion came at the best possible moment.

"Describe where you live," Cross said.

Declan kept the domestic details to a minimum. "I don't have a phone. People who want to reach me call Mr. Caswell's number. If we had a different ring for my calls, Suzy could answer with 'Mr. Shaw's office, how can I direct your call.' That would be funny." He smiled and caught himself. "Uh, sorry."

"What did you do Friday night, Declan?" Compton said.

"After Gracie's, I hung out with Stan. We talked about stuff. We didn't go far. Weekends are wild in the Quarter, it's too crowded."

"Did you go to the Colvin house?"

"No." Declan resisted adding a comment such as "I wish I had," or, "not that Friday."

Compton frowned. He expected a qualifier. "But you've been there before."

"Oh yes, many times. It's spooky. Stan took great pictures in there. Black and white."

"It'll be hard to look at them again," Compton said.

Cross shifted in his chair.

Declan could feel what these guys were thinking. He shouldn't get too comfortable with this knowledge. They brought Stan to tears. Stan had weaknesses, but he was hard to break. When his dad beat him, he didn't flinch. What had they done to Stan to push him over the edge?

"You know more than you're telling us, Declan," Cross said.

"I know Patch Mitchell is dealing. Everybody knows. He was arrested but he came back, and the kids, they buy his stuff. I broke his nose."

"After he banged your head into the sidewalk," Cross said. "Concussion. It could have been worse."

"I didn't see him coming. It's the streets, sir. I come from Texas. Big country, big sky, big sunsets. I'm used to looking in the distance. I had to adjust my eyesight." He gave something away, something that meant a lot to him, that was much too mature for his age. But this was a transaction and he could not afford to lose. Fuck, he couldn't afford a tie.

"The streets are hard, son," Compton said. "Patch Mitchell is far from the worst that can happen to you out there. Stanley was hurt on the streets."

Now Declan knew what route they took with Stan. They made him cry, but those were familiar tears from old wounds. Stan could water a magnolia tree with them, and shoot you the finger a minute later. Stan didn't analyze like Declan, but his instincts were impeccable. He gave the detectives something they weren't looking for and didn't expect, and they walked away from the dinner table sated.

"You've been hurt too, haven't you?"

"Stop this right now," Paul Caswell said. "You have no right to harass this boy."

After his cheeky Texas elegy, Declan couldn't dissolve in tears like Stan. "You said they had a job to do, Mr. Caswell." Suzy's father looked at him as if he was a creature from outer space. "You showed me how to block my door."

Caswell blanched. "I didn't do enough. I should have taken you in. Who hurt you, Declan?"

"It doesn't matter. It won't happen again. I know how to

protect myself." He also knew how much to let slip to the detectives who absorbed his words like believers at a revival.

"I'm sorry too, Declan," Compton said. "We're failing our kids big time."

Game, set, and match. Declan could be generous. Not too much. "I'll go to college and I'll get a fucking degree." He didn't say he considered becoming a lawyer. That would be too pat.

Compton gathered his papers. "That's great." He turned to his partner. "Let's go, Thom. Thank you for your help, Mr. Caswell. And thank you for what you're doing. How well do you know Declan's grandmother?"

With Compton occupied with Suzy's dad, Declan focused on Cross who was taking his sweet time to get out from behind the vice principal's desk.

"That was fucking impressive," Cross muttered.

Declan shouldered his backpack. The swing of the books inside was reassuring. English Lit. Geometry. Bradbury's *Martian Chronicles* that he had to return to the library. Real, solid. Not mind games.

"I'd like to talk to you again, Declan. In ten years, or twenty, whenever you feel like it."

It came from left field and Declan's eyes smarted. He turned away. "Won't you be retired by then, sir?"

"Once a cop, always a cop. Do you play chess?" Declan didn't. "But you know what a *sacrifice* means." The detective sat on the corner of the desk. "It's a simple and effective strategy. You can get carried away, however, and realize in the end that there isn't anything left to protect."

"The cost was too high," Declan said.

Cross nodded. "A Pyrrhic victory. You said you could protect yourself. I don't doubt it, but think about what it does to you, how it changes you. Remember to take the armor off from time to time. It can become so comfortable you'll forget you're wearing it." He picked up his briefcase. "I hope you find the big sky again, Declan. Call me if you want to talk. Thompson Elijah Cross. I shouldn't be hard to find." He held out his hand. They shook.

"I don't know if I'll be in the phone book but you have ways to locate people. Look for Declan Francis Philip Shaw." He smiled. "I'll try to stay out of trouble."

Cross winked and joined his colleague at the door.

SIXTEEN

DECLAN WROTE DOWN A FEW bullet points for Leyla's online trap before calling Robledo.

"You have a new phone?" Robledo said.

"Have you seen the online onslaught? I shelved my phone."

Robledo whistled. "Who have you upset since we last talked? Oh wait, that was today."

"Cut it out. Got anything for me?"

Robledo had worked fast. He had the tag number of the red SUV—a Ford Explorer leased to a Preston Macaulay Derring. "I'll text you his DL pic. He doesn't look anything like the description you gave me. The address on the DL is not the address on the lease. That's a company, MKA Trading, in Pasadena. I've sent you the address and phone number."

"Thanks."

"Do you think the online trolls have something to do with April's murder?"

The more Declan chewed on it, the more he doubted it. "It would be stupid. Why put a burr under my saddle if all it's going to do is motivate me to dig deeper."

"Most criminals *are* stupid," Robledo said. "I'm jealous you're getting all the attention. I'm in charge of the fucking investigation. Everybody thinks we're so dumb we can't find our dicks in the dark. I need a PI to unzip my fly."

"Whoever underestimates you is making a serious mistake."

"Yeah. April's car didn't start because the battery was dead," Robledo said.

"It worked fine the day before."

"She must have left the lights on."

"Lights switch off automatically, Steve."

Declan was already running hypotheses. Somebody disables April's car to force her to call a taxi. When she comes back home, the killer is waiting for her. She's attacked outside her apartment. A mugging. But it didn't unfold that way because Declan was with her. The plan had to change.

Robledo's thoughts were on the same track. "I've had faulty batteries."

"Me too."

"We'll look for prints and signs of tampering. On another note, I arranged an appointment with Sam Koenig, tomorrow, his office on Richmond. Meet me in front a little before ten."

Progress on the investigation and the relationship. Robledo was sharing.

Declan called Daisy in Miami. She also commented on the unfamiliar phone number.

"You're the third person to tell me that."

She hadn't been idle. Her trip to Clearwater to meet the engineers was productive. "I learned a lot on the geology of Florida and why we have sinkholes, among other curiosities. More research is needed but it looks like the building was not anchored properly, foundations not going deep enough. The engineers noticed hairline cracks in the pilings in the garage. A combination of load-bearing issues and quality of materials. I'll keep digging."

"Remember what Uncle Kevin said about the Cassino mob connections. Be careful."

"I need to look for blueprints and permits, and go poke at contractors and material purchases. Discrepancies in the books, bank accounts that get too fat too fast, you know what I mean. Do I have permission to acquire specialized talent?"

"No undue risk, DD."

"I won't do anything you wouldn't do yourself."

That was far from reassuring.

Robledo was stepping out of an old Ford as Declan parked his truck in the garage of Sam Koenig's building.

"How do you want to play it?" Robledo said.

Declan was surprised the detective asked for his opinion. "Either Koenig knows of the internet barrage, and there's no harm in saying I'm a friend of April's, or he doesn't, and I'm a consultant with connections in the music industry."

"Works for me. I hope Koenig can give us an insight into April's private life. I would prefer to talk to his wife but she's still under medical supervision."

Koenig met them in a conference room on the twentieth floor. Robledo introduced Declan as an investigator working with the police.

Koenig recognized the name. He had seen the web postings. "You're, uh … April's boyfriend?"

"April spent her last night with me, Mr. Koenig. The slanderous posts got that right. It's all they got right. If I were a suspect I wouldn't be here with Sergeant Robledo."

"I'm sorry. You took me by surprise. What can I do for you?"

Robledo jumped in. "We want to know if anything in April's life could have indicated she was in danger."

Koenig turned to Declan. "You were close to her, wouldn't you know?"

"She was immersed in her work," Declan said. "I asked about the pictures in her apartment and she gave me a few names. I didn't push. I thought she would tell me more when she felt like it."

Koenig sighed. "That was April, all right. The music always came first."

He told them how he met Jill. They were both in college. Jill needed a shoulder to cry on, she felt unloved. April was her parents' favorite. The talented one. April was the star, leaving Jill in the shadows. In school too April was the brighter of the two.

"It didn't go the way Tim and Vicky hoped," Koenig said. "They never imagined April's music could lead to a career. It was all decorative to them, social graces. April didn't see it that way. She played with various short-lived groups and decided music was what she wanted to do. The parents didn't take it well. When she joined Sloats & Archer they thought she had settled down."

"Back in the fold," Robledo said.

"It didn't last. Jill and I married right out of college. We got pregnant a few years later, and the dynamics shifted. All we heard was, 'why can't April be like Jill.'" Koenig shot a glance at Declan. "April's lifestyle became an irritant. She used to bring a friend for Thanksgiving dinner, but it got awkward."

"It was never the same friend," Declan said.

"It didn't sit well with Mama. April stopped coming to family gatherings. Jill and I still met her for dinner. I can't recall the names of the guys, they kept changing."

"Were you sexually attracted to April, Mr. Koenig?" Robledo said.

Koenig put his coffee mug down. He missed the coaster, and corrected his mistake. "I'm not her type. I'm a nerd with a boring job."

"Did she have any long-term relationships?" Declan said.

He thought of Stan Borelli and the guy named Gordon, and revolving doors.

The flush of color in Koenig's cheeks was noticeable. "I … don't know." He blinked. "Jill told me that six months was a record."

"Nasty break-ups, guys with grudges?" Robledo said.

"April wasn't serious about any of them and, forgive me, Mr. Shaw, I don't think her partners were serious about her either. She liked it that way."

"Do you think you could ask your wife for names?" Robledo said.

"I'll try."

"On a different note," Declan said. "When did the sisters become close?"

"Amelia's birth, maybe. Tim and Vicky were all over the baby, so much that I had to tell them to give us some space. After the baby, they became all nice and helpful, when they didn't give us the time of day before. Jill started to see more of April."

"Tim and Vicky changing gears. April's lost, let's switch to Amelia," Declan said.

Koenig stared at his coffee. "My in-laws are not nice people, Mr. Shaw."

"If I were you, I would take my wife and daughter on a trip," Declan said. "Load the car and get out of Dodge."

"That was light on the data," Robledo said. "Why did you cut me off when I asked for names?"

"He got it. No need to hammer it in. The entire conversation revolved around April's affairs."

For once, Robledo didn't reach for his cigarettes. "How did it feel learning that the woman played around?"

Declan hiked his shoulders. "She went for what she wanted and didn't make a fuss about it. I would have beaten the six-month mark, no sweat. She was leaving on tour three days later. Not enough time to get fed up with me."

"What makes you think she would have given you three days?"

"Wouldn't you?"

The detective shot him the finger, got in his car, and drove away.

It bugged Declan that April slept around. He didn't expect her to be pure and demure. She was attractive, single, and successful; potential partners were a dime a dozen. He had imagined a couple of relationships that hadn't panned out because she was focused on her career. He hadn't pictured her to be so much like him. Restless. He wished he could ask her how it worked out for her because it didn't work out that well for him. Vince Wallace quipped that he didn't invest much in his casual liaisons. Declan could hear Daisy's voice, just before she slammed the door shut after one of their clashes, "If you get into a relationship believing it isn't going to go anywhere, guess what, it won't go anywhere."

He felt a sudden urge to drop the entire ball of wax and run the hell to Daisy. The fee from the Carlyle case would cover a boat charter. She knew places to sail to that were way off the beaten track.

Then the memory of April singing at Coombs took the heretic notions away and dissolved them. He went in search of a restaurant with a terrace to have lunch before calling Amy Corrigan.

Amy had seen the online garbage. "I know a hatchet job when I see one."

"I'm glad you don't believe that crap."

"Oh, I believe some of it. I know April. You're catnip. Dinner tonight?"

"I'm not in the right mood to be nibbled at."

"Nothing of the kind, don't fool yourself. Be in front of the office at seven. Wear glasses or a hat, or something. My colleagues are the worst gossips. And they love trash bloggers."

With the entire afternoon to kill, Declan drove to Pasadena to have a look at MKA Trading, the company that the red Explorer he saw at April's funeral was registered to.

The office—two barred windows and a metal door—was in a strip mall with a tattoo parlor and vape shop on one side, a pizza takeaway place on the other, and a nail salon further down the row. The other shop fronts were boarded up with "For Lease" signs so old they were baked into the dirty windows. The red Ford Explorer was among the vehicles in the litter-strewn parking lot.

Declan went around the block. The back of the strip mall was as uninspiring as the front. Broken plastic furniture, two large dumpsters spilling their contents, metal barrels, and discarded building materials cluttered the alley. He parked a block over and walked back to have a look at the building. The tattoo parlor and the pizza joint would be busy late at night. MKA and the nail salon might have more regular hours. The pizza place had vents under the roofline. If he decided to go that way, it would be a tight fit and he would have to crawl in the rafters to reach MKA. Possible but unpleasant. The roof was the kind of flat, slapped-together construction that hurricanes loved to rip off. The electrical equipment was up there with the air conditioning. Judging from the condition of the walls, the roof must be one big rotting disaster waiting to happen. Nobody worried about roofs until they leaked. It wouldn't be a hard climb, with a little help from a dumpster. He needed tools. Bjorn Gonzalez, heavy-duty artist, had all kinds of implements that could cut, smash, and destroy.

Satisfied that he had some sort of plan, Declan drove to the museum district. The Butterfly Center at the Museum of Natural Science was open and teeming with children. They were quiet and as much in awe of the glass habitat as he was.

The place was calm-inducing. Where should he take Amy for dinner? A casual place, not too crowded. He knew a bar on the second floor of one of the downtown renovated lofts. It had a terrace where he could smoke, the drinks were generous, and they made a decent burger.

He hoped Amy Corrigan had seen the Bonnie Parker picture. Their only clue that was a clue *because* it was missing. Sometimes investigations hinged on what should be at a scene and wasn't, or on what a suspect didn't say. Declan could amuse himself endlessly with these kinds of puzzles.

It was still too early to go pick up Amy. He called Moira for a status report.

"Where are you?" she said.

"At the museum, killing time before my next appointment. I won't be home until late. What's new?"

"I had to tell two snoops to take a hike. Bjorn threw punches when a few excited pseudo-media hounds tried to block his truck. Our constable wrote citations. To the besiegers, not Bjorn. The coast should be clear tonight. These online clowns are too lazy to hit the pavement old style."

Lazy maybe, but increasing the pressure. "Some of the blogs were signed by a Dirksen A. Loomis, it's spelled the way it sounds," Declan said. "See if you can find anything on him. Don't call me back, email me. Do you think you could call in a favor with the constable and get the names of the fake reporters?"

"You think they were hired?" Moira said.

"It's a strong possibility. If they're professional troublemakers, they might have a record."

Amy Corrigan waited in front of the office when he pulled up. If she expected a more respectable vehicle than Declan's old pickup truck, she didn't show it.

"These people harassing you," she said, as soon as she was in the passenger seat, "what do they hope to gain from it?"

"Apart from click-throughs and ad revenue, I don't know. Scare my clients away? That would point toward my competition. The blogger has a source in HPD because my interview was leaked. I can't see why anybody would come after me because of the investigation. I'm nowhere."

"Maybe you found something without knowing it."

"That's a pleasant thought. Sadly, I don't know a shred more than the cops."

"They don't have trolls on their asses."

Her freckled face was all scrunched up in a pout. With the incandescent red hair, she looked like a creature from an Irish folk tale. A sprite or a petulant Tinkerbell.

"Why did you agree to see me, Amy?"

"April was my best friend and I loved her." She turned in the car seat to look straight at him. "I loved her a lot more than you did. I was with her Friday night and she didn't say a word about you. When she had a new man in her life she couldn't stop talking about him."

"I met her Saturday."

"Damn." She remained silent for a while. "Where are we going?"

"A bar downtown."

The patrons were inside, in the air-conditioned cool. Amy didn't mind sitting outside. The terrace was in the shade and a fan produced a sluggish breeze. She ordered a martini and he had a scotch, neat.

"You mind if I smoke?" Declan said.

"As long as I'm upwind. It's a pity, you're a perfect match for April."

"Sam Koenig implied as much." Her casual remark hurt.

"The brother-in-law, the gentle soul," Amy said.

The atmosphere was pleasant on the second floor of the old

building, with the setting sun painting flames in the windows of nearby office towers. A sudden burst of laughter from the street below pierced the din. Houston moved at a slower pace in summer when most of the foot traffic had retreated to the tunnels.

"Is that your opinion or April's?"

"Did I sound condescending?" Amy said. "I met the guy. I guess he's good for Jill."

"The cops haven't been able to talk to her. She's a mess."

Amy took a sip of her martini and pursed her lips. "Jill's always been a mess."

"She lived in April's shadow, but the sisters bonded, over time."

"Why do you care about this, Declan? You just met her. Is it the investigator's instinct, a murder is waved in front of you and you have to run and solve it?"

He took a long drag of his cigarillo. "I've never been so close …" He blinked in the smoke.

"To violent death?"

He contemplated the bottom of his glass. There were no tea leaves floating in there. "I've lost people before. It's the first time I might be able to do something about it. That doesn't make much sense, does it? I can't bring her back."

"There's a measure of control in action," Amy said. "When you move, the world doesn't weigh down so much on you. I'm also looking for sense. Random violence freaks me out, and I hate feeling helpless. It makes me angry."

"There's nothing random in April's murder. She was targeted."

"By whom?"

"Let's take it in order. How long have you known April?" He turned on his tablet. "Names and dates. Everything you remember."

The girls were college roommates in Austin. University of Texas. Both pre-law, intending to go to law school. Amy with more diligence than April who was too passionate about music to spend much energy on anything else.

"She was way smarter than me. I would sweat all night on material she absorbed in a couple of hours. I was the dogged student and she sailed through. When we moved to an apartment off-campus she had the bigger room because of her piano. She sang in local clubs."

Amy listed venues, some of them still in business, and various guitar players that were occasional boyfriends.

"Weed came with the territory and cheap liquor. None of these guys were violent. They all loved April."

"Was there room for you in all this?"

Amy sighed. "I was smitten with April. Pining. She wasted her time with these hopheads. I treasured a dark hope that she would one day have a major heartbreak and I would be there for her. But her heart was never broken, not by any boyfriend. Her parents took care of that."

Amy recalled the years after college when Tim and Vicky Easton did their best to abort April's musical hopes. They paid off club owners to deny her auditions and scared off bands that considered taking her on. For a while, April kept trying, working day jobs that left her evenings free to roam the club scene. Then the Eastons lined up business contacts for job interviews and April relented. She went to work for Sloats & Archer where Amy had been for a year already. The family pressure eased and April resumed her musical activities.

"The Eastons thought music was a harmless hobby and they stopped trying to shoot it down."

"Did April ever find out her parents screwed her?"

"A club owner told her he wished he'd hired her years ago. He was told she was a flake. April discovered the truth. There was a terrible scene at her parents' place. She resigned from the law firm a week later."

"Who was she seeing recently?"

"Before you? Sorry, that's uncalled for. Julian, I suppose, but it fizzled in May when she toured in California." Julian Waugh was an architect dividing his time between New York and Australia. "They tried to organize their agendas but it was complicated."

"I heard of a Gordon …"

"Last year. Gordon Beasley. I thought he was a keeper."

"What happened to him?"

"He asked her to move in with him and she said she needed more time. They might have made it, but April could be awfully single-minded."

"Let's have something to eat," Declan said.

They were given a corner table inside and didn't talk about April while eating. Amy said she considered leaving Sloats & Archer to join a firm in Austin that seemed willing to offer her a partnership after a reasonable work-in period. "S&A is stuffy. You have these middle-aged men hogging the top spots. It's a great place to learn but I won't wait thirty years for a seat at the table."

"You could start your own practice."

"It takes contacts and I'm not a social animal." She smiled. "I would freak out about the rent."

"It's been a pleasant evening, Amy."

She was lost in thought. "I can't think of a single event in April's life that could have led to this. She was too smart to get involved with dangerous people."

"Could you help me identify the people in April's photos?"

Amy went through the images on his tablet. She named several lawyers from S&A, a few college friends and family members, the more recent boyfriends, Julian and Gordon, and the band members.

"I noticed a picture from a themed party," Declan said, "but I don't have it here."

"They're all the rage at S&A. Casino nights. We all get a stack of chips. I always lose my bundle after a couple of plays. April was pretty good at it; she traded kisses for chips and ended the evening singing on top of the piano."

"That party looked like mobsters and gangsters. She went as Bonnie Parker."

"I remember one where we were flappers. We had fun making the dresses out of old table runners. Gangsters … I don't know. I'll look at my stack of souvenirs. It had to be at S&A, or maybe a conference or symposium. Something professional. It's the kind of thing that tickles lawyers. Why does that one matter more than the others?"

It wouldn't do any harm to tell her, yet Declan hesitated. "I wonder because I didn't see it on the boards at the funeral home. I recognized the other group shots."

"You remember that stuff? That's some talent."

"I spent a lot of time on the photos. Apart from you, who was close to April at S&A?"

"I'd say Keith Garland. April worked for him. He's a character. A fantastic trial lawyer, the criminal variety, in the mold of a Racehorse Haynes or DeGuerin. On his way to become a legend." She looked at him sideways. "You better bring your A-game."

Declan called Robledo after dropping Amy at her apartment. He gave him a summary of the evening with the names of April's most recent boyfriends knowing full well that the information was useless. He didn't mention Stan Borelli.

"She knew the Bonnie photo?" Robledo said.

"No, but she said she would look at her pictures. I didn't tell her that the photo was missing. Who else knows about it?"

"Murphy. We decided to keep it under wraps. We may want to spring it on somebody down the line."

"I plan to call on lawyers at Sloats & Archer tomorrow. See if somebody remembers Bonnie Parker. Amy said theme parties are a thing at the firm."

Robledo didn't say what he planned to do next. Declan suspected he had been given additional assignments.

"Okay, keep in touch." Robledo hung up.

Declan felt the release of the leash. He was on his own, with next steps lined up. He called Leyla Kareem.

"You have the legend?" she said.

"A synopsis, with one verifiable element that they already have."

"Good. I had a bite today." A hacker tried to breach the server firewall and was blocked. "If they're serious, they'll try again and give me more to work with. What do you want me to do, slam the door in their face?"

"There isn't anything sensitive on the server. Can you steer them to the legend? Feel free to improvise on what I'll send you."

"A bucket of chum? Sure."

SEVENTEEN

WADE BENNING WALKED IN CIRCLES around his polished desk. The transcript of Declan Shaw's Houston PD interview was in the middle of the green blotter. The document had been hand-delivered by one of Buddy Pagett's flunkies. Benning read the file four times. He grew more concerned with each reading.

There was no mention anywhere of the Bonnie Parker photograph.

It had to be deliberate. Shaw omitted that detail on purpose during the interview. Maybe it was that typical PI trick of concealing information that could be monetized or traded for later. Pagett did it all the time. But Shaw's behavior didn't fit the narrative. He talked with Robledo about the photograph; he even asked who else knew about it as if it was a major clue that they had to hide from prying eyes.

It made sense. There were roving eyes and ears at HPD, as the file on the desk proved.

Benning placed a call to his operatives and left a terse message. The conversation was overdue. He had to know why they took the picture from the apartment. He completed another circuit around the desk. This time he pulled his laptop from a drawer and set it on top of the file. He couldn't look at the document anymore. It disturbed him.

He was entering his password to look at the Shaw surveillance data when his phone rang.

"Another job?" the flat voice said without preamble.

"A question," Benning said. "Did you take anything from the apartment?"

"It's against procedure."

Benning bottled his impatience. "I know it's against the rules, but something is missing. The police are looking for it."

"What's missing?"

It was like talking to HAL, the computer from that movie that always put Benning to sleep. "A photograph."

"What kind of photograph?"

How the hell would he know? The fucking photo was missing. "Did you remove a photograph from the apartment?"

"No."

"What about your partner?"

"No."

Calm down, regroup, there had to be a logical explanation. The operative might be lying. If he did, this call would warn him to destroy the damn photograph. If he didn't lie …

"Thank you, I'll investigate," Benning said.

He didn't have the means to investigate unless he contracted with Pagett, and he wouldn't do it if he had a gun to his head. He wouldn't give a scrap of sensitive information to the fat lump. Pagett never saw data that he couldn't use to put the squeeze on you.

Maybe the answer was on the computer. What was Shaw up to?

The surveillance showed that Shaw was batting away the fleas that harassed him online. The attack might slow him down but it didn't seem to be crippling. Benning had to tip his hat to the man. Shaw had resources in place and people he could depend on to get him out of trouble.

Shaw's other focus was lawyers. He wasn't anywhere yet but he was inching closer to the heart of the scheme. The woman used to work for a law firm, she hung out with lawyers, she had friends in those circles. She might even know *the* lawyer.

That was the real danger, not some misplaced photograph.

Shaw's line of investigation had to be nipped in the bud. Tampa. Benning had tippy-toed long enough. Time to activate the trap. He picked up the phone again. He didn't have to check his contacts. He knew the number. He had just called it.

EIGHTEEN

DECLAN WORE HIS BEST SUIT—the handmade double-breasted Armani, not the more subdued version he chose for the funeral—for his attempt to see Keith Garland without an appointment. He called earlier, pretending to be from the local FBI office, and asked if Garland was available for a short meeting. The receptionist told him Mr. Garland was in conference all afternoon but would be in the office this morning. He ended the call without giving a name or a number. It always amazed him how helpful and trustworthy people were, even in a law firm.

Sloats & Archer's offices were in Uptown, not far from Sam Koenig's. Declan parked in the ground floor garage. The firm occupied four stories in the glass and metal skyscraper, above mid-level. High enough for a view but not in the clouds which might suggest to clients that their fees were of the same lofty nature.

He walked to the reception, without a briefcase, carrying only his tablet. On his six-foot-four frame, and the boots added some, the sharp tailoring never failed to make an impression. A couple of male lawyers turned to watch, their heads on a swivel, and their female colleague stopped in her tracks as she was about to enter a meeting room.

"Keith Garland, please," Declan said, unsmiling, to the receptionist who looked thunderstruck.

"Yes, sir." She put the phone to her ear, ready to punch the extension, then caught herself. "Do you have an appointment, sir?"

"No." A hint of a smile. "That won't be an issue."

"Mr. Garland is busy, sir." She was biting her lower lip, embarrassed at having to disappoint this handsome man, who was so much her type.

"Please call him." Declan leaned on the desk, lowered his voice. "It's important. Tell him it's about a murder." He detached the words and his eyes never left hers.

She picked up the phone. "Ginny? There's a, uh, gentleman here to see Keith." Her voice dropped an octave. "He says it's … about a murder." She listened. "No, he didn't give his name." She must have been reminded of the rules because she tightened her grip on the phone as she turned to Declan. "Ginny … Mr. Garland's assistant needs to know your name, sir."

"I will tell Mr. Garland in private, Ms. …" She wore a badge on a lanyard looped around her neck. "Ms. Patterson." He let his eyes linger a fraction too long on the dangling ID, the plastic card lifting with each of her breaths.

"I'll escort him, Ginny," the receptionist said and put the phone back in the cradle. "This way."

She teetered on her high heels, anxious to keep four hurried steps ahead of him, and was hyperventilating by the time they reached the end of the long corridor. She threw herself, with something akin to desperation, at the glass door of Garland's executive assistant's office.

"Susan, are you out of your mind?" The woman who stepped out from behind the desk was tall, middle-aged, and dressed for battle in court. Amy Corrigan said Keith Garland was a character. So was Virginia Chambers, according to the name on the door. She wouldn't be intimidated by anybody or anything.

Susan Patterson ran away. Declan prayed she wouldn't break an ankle.

"Who do you think you are?"

"I apologize, Ms. Chambers," Declan said. "I have reasons for wanting anonymity."

"Do you intend to ask Mr. Garland to represent you?" She examined him, head tilted, speculating. Murder. Was he the killer, was he a suspect, did he have valuable information pertaining to a case. Ginny Chambers was too professional to ask any of these questions.

"I already have a lawyer," Declan said. "He's excellent."

She smiled. "You dress to kill. We can be forgiven for jumping to the wrong conclusions."

"My usual laid-back attitude wouldn't get me past the front desk."

"Laid-back, my foot." She glanced at the lights on her desk phone. "Keith is busy right now. I'll go see how long he'll be." She was back quickly. "Five minutes. Coffee?"

She brought two cups on a tray and sat with Declan in the little waiting nook.

"How well did you know April Easton, Ms. Chambers?"

"How well did *you* know her?"

Sometimes truth is an asset. "I needed more time to fall in love with her and maybe she would have loved me back."

"So you have a personal interest in the case."

"And professional. April worked for Mr. Garland. I hope he can help me fill a few blanks."

The office door opened behind Declan. "Good luck," she muttered.

Keith Garland was in his fifties, medium height with a slight paunch stretching the vest of his three-piece suit. He reminded Declan of a hunting dog, affable yet capable of single-minded focus.

"Whatever you're selling, young man, I won't be able to afford it." The voice was pitched low to fit the size of the room. It had range to climb several registers if needed. "What's that anonymity thing about? The entire office will remember you, the way you look."

"They'll remember the suit," Declan said.

"You're familiar with the fallibility of eye witness testimony, I see. Very well, come in."

Garland's was a typical, old school lawyer's office, with leather-bound books. The blinds were half-closed to filter the morning light and the walls were bare of the usual ego-stroking pictures of the premise's occupant shaking hands with celebrities. An arrogant attitude of sorts. He didn't need the feel-good crutches.

Garland attacked as soon as the door closed. "Who are you?"

Declan handed him a business card. "I'm a friend of April Easton."

"Private investigator. The job must pay better than it used to." Garland contemplated the card. "Shaw. Wasn't there something, a while ago, a brutal abuse case involving a prominent local family? It went federal if I recall."

Declan nodded. "I made friends and enemies on that one."

Garland sat behind his cluttered desk. "Do you expect to make new ones?"

"I'm the target of a nasty blogosphere campaign. I didn't want to bring your firm into it. April died Sunday afternoon. I was with her Saturday night." Declan preempted the follow-up question. "Crime scene evidence clears me. I'm working with the police."

"Then you don't need me."

"Not as a lawyer. I'm talking to people in April's circle. One event, in particular, is of interest to me. A themed party. Amy

Corrigan doesn't have any recollection of it. I wondered if you could help."

Garland grunted. "Sol Archer loves these gimmicky celebrations. They bore me to death but the young ones seem to like them." He pressed a button on his phone. "Ginny? Come in, will you."

Garland told his assistant what he needed.

"Carol has the books." Ginny turned to Declan. "She works for Mr. Archer. She displays the pictures in the big meeting room for people who want copies and then she makes a photo album. Every year." She shot Declan a lopsided smile. "She might be a blackmailer in the making. I'll go get the last ten books."

"She'll want to know why," Garland said.

A shrug. "I'll invent something."

Garland questioned Declan while they waited. He could talk about his relationship with April and his activities that weekend, but not much else. Crime scene details shared by Murphy and Robledo were off-limits.

"April would have made an excellent lawyer," Garland said. "She was inquisitive and hardworking, with a quick mind. I was disappointed when she decided to leave but I never doubted she would succeed at whatever she decided to do."

Ginny was back with the photo albums. "I said we were thinking of a photo montage for S&A's 50th birthday." She chuckled. "It's in six years, we have time."

They looked at the group photos. Declan had copies of a few of them on his tablet. No trace of Bonnie Parker.

"Could it have been a family reunion?" Ginny said.

"I didn't recognize any of her relatives," Declan said. "And the people in the picture were April's age. Mid-twenties, early thirties. No scruffy beards or longish hair. They looked a lot like the people in your group photos, Ms. Chambers. Cub lawyers."

"Let's assume your profile is correct," Garland said. "Where could a party like that have taken place?"

"School reunion," Ginny said, "training class, professional retreat, conference."

Garland warmed to the chase. "Class reunions would be a mixed bag of looks. I lean toward a professional event."

"Meeting expenses would be on your tab," Declan said.

"Ginny, hit the books. We're stingy about these outings. I don't think we sent April to a lot of off-site meetings, she was more valuable to us here, toiling away in a broom closet on a pitcher of water and a chunk of dry bread."

"I'll go through the expense statements," Ginny said. "Are you going to wait, Mr.?"

Declan smiled. "Shaw. Declan Shaw."

"The private investigator. Pleased to meet you."

"Show him to a conference room, Ginny." Garland held out his hand. "Good luck in your search."

Declan used the waiting time to strategize with Leyla Kareem. She had read his synopsis and had comments.

"Why don't we use the real story? You were a kid and won big at a card game. The guy called you a cheater and smashed your hands with a tire iron to teach you a lesson. I like it. It fits the crooked detective narrative."

"I still hit tables in town, Leyla, and my poker buddies put enough money on display to have the right to be nervous."

"But you don't cheat."

"It doesn't matter. In a game of bluff appearances are everything."

"All right. It's your gig, but of all the possible offenses you could have committed, I would have chosen a less sleazy one."

Declan wasn't about to tell her that of *all the offenses* this was one he didn't commit. Even in a lie, truth mattered. He had to be able to look people in the eye and tell them that the accusations were total bullshit.

They agreed that Leyla would start planting gossip on social media platforms and chat rooms. The gist of the story was that

Declan hadn't latched on April because he admired her talent or her looks. He was after her money, the upcoming bounty of the record contract. He had done it before, in New Orleans, attaching himself to wealthy women. His medical record—the surgery on his hands—was supporting evidence. An angry relative had decided to get payback.

Declan's phone dinged while he was going through the details with Leyla. It was Moira. She would have to wait.

"I'll drop my line in the muddy waters of the web," Leyla said. "Don't be surprised if they bite like piranhas."

Declan hoped one of the bites would come from Dirksen Loomis and MKA Trading. If it didn't, he still had the shop front in Pasadena to turn the digital tomfoolery into reality. That reminded him to look at the satellite views of the Pasadena neighborhood. The images were blurry at high magnification but a roof feature intrigued him. Protuberances, bubbles? One for each shop. He couldn't tell what they were.

His coffee cup was empty but he didn't go next door to ask Ginny Chambers for a refill. Roaming the corridors of Sloats & Archer in search of a restroom wasn't recommended. He regretted frightening the receptionist. He should send her flowers. No, better not. Two dozen red roses would freak the hell out of her. He scrolled through his recent calls. Robledo had called twice. Declan didn't feel like talking to him right now.

He called Daisy.

"Carlyle should sell," she said. "Right now."

The experts didn't leave any room for doubt. The building was unsound and corrective measures would be so expensive they would never be implemented. Life expectancy estimates for Artemis ranged between ten and twenty years, depending on how much weather events stressed the area.

"I emailed you the report," Daisy said. "Once the cracks get wider, you won't need a measuring tape to figure out what's going on. I have a line on the official that pushed the building permit through. His lifestyle doesn't match his paycheck. A couple of inspectors might have their hands in the cookie jar too, and I've got the main contractor under surveillance."

She was a model of efficiency. "Thanks, DD, I'll talk to the client. Keep building the file."

"Aye, aye, sir."

She had completed the investigation faster than Declan expected. He called Rowena Dowling. Carlyle's lawyer didn't answer and he left a short message. "The building is a disaster. Call me back at this number."

He was deep into Daisy's report when Ginny Chambers walked in with a couple of typed sheets.

"April was with us for four years," she said. "We sent her to a couple of events every year. Some were training, others were seminars and trade conferences. Here's the list with dates, location, and organizing body. What's the deal with that photograph, Mr. Shaw?"

"I haven't been able to identify anybody in it." It was close enough to the truth.

"Like a slice of her life you know nothing about."

"There has to be a connection somewhere. It could be in that photo."

She pushed the chairs back under the meeting table. Everything in order, ready for business. "People don't function well when the world around them is incomprehensible. That's what you're doing, isn't it? You're searching for explanations to reassure us that we have a grasp on reality."

"The grasp is thin sometimes." It was thin in April's defiled bathroom. Declan folded the pages with the list of events and put them in his breast pocket. He didn't want to look at them now. Don't jinx it by being too eager.

Ginny Chambers opened the conference room door. "I'll take you to the lobby the back way. Do you have any idea how hard it is to find a good receptionist?"

NINETEEN

"WHAT'S THE MATTER, BUDDY? We can't be seen together these days. Murphy's on the warpath, sniffing for leaks. Your geeks weren't subtle. They quoted from the crime scene report and the Shaw interview."

The man slid into the booth, feet first, his flexible body curving in the space between the table and the leather-upholstered back. Buddy Pagett envied that agility, even if he didn't envy anything else in Fisher. The man oozed uncleanliness. It was a general attitude, a slinkiness from the tip of his pointed shoes to the tip of his rodent nose. And Fisher espoused it, reveled in the disquiet that bathed him like his cheap lavender-scented cologne. He dressed the part in a three-piece brown suit cut too tight, wore his thin blondish hair too long, and sported his fingernails grubby. A bravo, a knife for hire. It never ceased to amaze Pagett that Fisher was a cop. If Pagett had been an academy instructor, he would have shown him the door at first whisper. Unpleasant didn't begin to capture it. Warped was more adequate.

"Murphy suspects you?" Pagett said.

"He went after Bogs Sorensen, who swore on his mother's head he didn't do anything wrong." Fisher laughed, showing a row of small yellow uneven teeth. "Always truthful, Bogs. Can't be blamed for sharing with his loyal partner, can he?"

"You weren't his partner when the body was found," Pagett said. "How come?"

"I was busy."

Pagett knew better than asking Fisher why he was playing hooky. He sighed. "It's not going the way I hoped."

Fisher snapped his fingers at the waiter, muttered, "Dos Equis."

He didn't have to raise his voice. The waiter scurried away. There was something about the man that got people hopping.

"Maybe you didn't hope hard enough," Fisher said.

Pagett dipped a tortilla chip in the salsa bowl, munched without tasting anything, and pushed the bowl away. "That whole social media shit is overblown. Shaw didn't even blink."

"Whaddya expect? He was cleared." Fisher didn't bother acknowledging the waiter who brought the beer and drank half the glass in one long swallow. "Bring me another."

"I need you clear-headed, Fisher. What do you suggest?" It hurt Pagett to ask this lowlife for advice but he was running out of ideas. It was hard to shelve such a golden opportunity. How often would Shaw be entangled in a murder case, on a cunt to cock level? "I thought that New Orleans angle would deliver. There ain't anything on record over there? I can't believe he didn't step in anything smelly. The boy is fucking reckless."

Fisher drained his glass. He pulled a napkin out of the dispenser to wipe his mouth, balled the piece of paper, and dropped it on the floor as the waiter approached the table with his second beer. "I poked. Nothing official. Rumors. Illegal poker games. Nobody is naming names, but the kid found the seed money to get a seat at the table somewhere, and he didn't get it from his grandma. Dunoit is an old name in New Orleans, but that's all it is. Old. They're broke. Shaw went to college on a full scholarship." Fisher shrugged. "Scams, robbery's my guess. A bit of hustling too, probably, for quick cash. I've seen school pictures. Cute boy. Could swing his dick on both sides of the aisle. Smart, good grades. You won't catch him on a teenage rap." He smiled. "I might have something, though."

Pagett knew what that smile meant. Money. Fisher was fucking expensive. Getting the transcript of Shaw's HPD interview had come with a hefty tab. At least Pagett made his money back with Wade Benning, plus a juicy percentage. Fisher had thrown the New Orleans inquiries in for free because he didn't dig up any usable nuggets. If he had, he would have bled Pagett dry.

"I'm not buying sight unseen," Pagett said.

"That goes without saying. This place stinks, Buddy. Ever considered giving the great outdoors a try?"

Was that a veiled threat? Fisher made Pagett squirm. Sitting in a bar with him, even in the darkest corner, made his nerve endings tingle. For all his cons, Pagett was a traditionalist and considered himself straightforward. In a contorted business. He met in bars and cafés, discussed deals over a good meal, mistrusted email, and techie mumbo-jumbo. "What have you got?"

Fisher leaned in the corner of the booth, twisted to cross his legs under the table, and rearranged the condiments caddy. "We logged an anonymous phone call this morning. Something about a rape-murder in Tampa."

Pagett let out a long raggedy breath. "Tampa. Shaw was over there last week."

Fisher nodded and sucked his lips in. He looked feral. Hungry. "The caller said, 'Check out the PI who should be locked up for the Easton murder.'"

"Bullshit."

"Yeah," Fisher said, "but the dates correspond, and the description of the attacker fits. It's uncanny. I checked with Tampa. Now, you do what you want with that. Or maybe you want *me* to do something with that." The rodent smile was thin and sly.

"How many anonymous calls does HPD get and why do you know about this one?"

Fisher snorted. "Because it's my case. Bogs and I work the serial. We get pinged when something pops up that matches: women late twenties-early thirties, beaten, raped, and cut. Like the Easton chick and the three others in Harris County. Tampa wants to talk to Shaw. They got the same call we did." He tilted his head to the side, looking at Pagett. "I thought the calls came from you. Nifty frame job, I thought." He shrugged. "It looks like you don't know anything about it."

"Florida ain't my scene. I can't pull something like that at short notice." Pagett twirled the salsa bowl. "It won't go any-where. Murphy will nip it in the bud."

"He might not be able to. Tampa's angling for an extradition order."

"Would take Shaw out of contention for a while." Pagett liked the idea. His bloggers could milk the incident. "Murphy will ask Shaw to come in. Maybe he's already at HPD."

"He wasn't when I left. You should have seen Bogs. I thought he was going to come in his pants." Fisher's smile stretched and he showed his uneven teeth again. "The fucking moron has it stamped on his brain that Shaw is our killer." He tapped a finger on the side of his head. "When he's got an idea in there, it'd take a jackhammer to get it out. I should carry a muzzle. Next time he sees Shaw, he'll bite his head off."

Pagett leaned forward. His gut was in the way. The edge of the table pressed on his stomach, digging deep into the flesh. He didn't feel it. He closed his eyes. Points of light danced behind his eyelids. He exhaled slowly; his heart beat like mad. "Sorensen and Shaw … what could happen … if …"

Fisher whistled under his breath. He looked around for the

waiter. The man was behind the bar. "Oh, Buddy." He shook his head, raised his hands. "I'm not sticking my neck out."

"Imagine what it would be worth, Fisher." A light shine of sweat had formed on Pagett's forehead. "Not just to me, you understand." He was compiling a list of clients who would forever be in his debt if Shaw was no longer an irritant. His mouth was dry. The air in the bar was as sticky as clay.

Fisher broke his train of thoughts. "Bogs is a caveman. He'll throw punches." He shook his head. "He won't go all the way, Buddy."

"You're saying it can't be done?" Pagett said.

"I'm saying it's more complicated than poking Bogs with a cattle prod. And it'll have to be dressed up real good." Fisher's eyes were mere slits. His hands had clenched into fists.

"You'll find something," Pagett said. "We split fifty-fifty. On whatever I get."

Fisher's mouth twisted. "I'll be in touch. Dust off your Rolodex."

TWENTY

MOIRA'S MESSAGE WAS ON TOP of the list. In all caps with a cascade of exclamation points.

"CALL ME!!!!!!!"

Declan heeded the call. "What's the matter?"

"Where are you? Yesterday's pesky gnats have multiplied, Dek. There's a crowd in front of the building. They're not pretending to be reporters anymore. They're waving placards and there's a big bearded fellow shouting in a megaphone. It'll take more than a constable to disperse them this time. The back door is still clear but I don't know for how long."

The pressure had reached a peak. "I need a change of clothes and stuff from the office," Declan said.

"Tell me what you need. I'll pack a go-bag."

The instructions didn't take long. "There'll also be a few things to pick up at Bjorn's."

He hung up with Moira and gave a quick call to Bjorn Gonzalez.

"Should I drop something heavy on these idiots?" Bjorn said.

"They salivate over that kind of spectacle. Ignore them. I

need to borrow tools for a job. I don't know when you'll get them back."

"*Sin problema.* I have more gear than I know what to do with. *Ten cuidado*, eh?"

"Always. Thanks."

Declan was at Moira's house in the Heights ahead of her. He was about to call Robledo who had left a heap of messages, when Moira pulled in. She carried two backpacks and a duffel bag.

One of the backpacks contained a change of clothes.

"Two media vans arrived as I left," Moira said. "We'll be on TV."

Declan traded the fancy suit for his usual jeans and shirt combo. "What were they protesting, same nonsense?"

"Pretty much. *Justice for April. Arrest the murderer. Serial rapist. Corrupt cops.* Fifty people, at least. It didn't look at all spontaneous. I recognized the guys from yesterday. Rog said he would check if they were on file."

Roger Perkins, Moira's husband, was HPD. His beat was anti-terrorism.

Declan inventoried the contents of the other backpack. Burner phones with chargers, tracker bugs, camera, binoculars, gloves, a flashlight, and his lock picking set. The duffel bag contained Bjorn's tools.

"This is a list of events April attended when she worked at Sloats & Archer," Declan said. "Check if any of these conferences organized a themed party—gangsters and molls, Prohibition, Roaring Twenties, anything in that flavor. I need a list of speakers and attendees."

"Will do. What are you up to?"

"Going to pay a visit to an outfit that might be behind this smear operation. It'll be rocky for a few days, Moira. If we're on TV, clients will get fidgety."

"Don't worry," she said. "I can charm the scales off a cobra."

Rule number one when on the run: be anonymous. Declan couldn't be spotted in Pasadena, near the MKA office, and he assumed the trolls knew what vehicle he drove. A box in the back of the pickup contained a selection of decals. In fifteen minutes, the white truck became the workhorse of a plumbing company based in Cleveland, Texas, complete with a local phone number and a website address. Calls would go to voicemail and the URL brought up a bland page with boilerplate text and an email address. Leyla Kareem monitored these flimsy identities.

Declan complemented the truck's disguise with matching driver accessories—cheap sunglasses and a ratty ball cap from a sporting goods store. He kissed Moira goodbye and drove north on 59 into his fictional plumber's territory. He parked at a burger joint, ordered inside, and pulled out his tablet. He finished reading Daisy's report. Her investigation was rich in names and details, and listed an impressive catalog of construction flaws. Declan forwarded the report to Rowena Dowling with a short two-paragraph management summary. She called back right away.

"I didn't expect it to be that bad," she said. "The report from the engineers is damning, and I've only read the first page."

"The building is not going to crumble for a while. Carlyle has time to negotiate a deal."

"I don't think he will."

"He would be stupid to hang on to his condos."

"He's not a quitter. I know what he'll say. He'll clasp on his superhero cape and demand justice for all the owners."

Declan was dumbfounded. "Justice from whom?"

"The builder, of course."

Harold Carlyle taking on Cassino Builders and their mob connections? "It's a fantasy, Rowena. The only people who will see any money will be the lawyers. The case will be stuck in court for so many years that the building might be condemned before the proceedings end. That is if Cassino plays according to the rules, which I doubt."

"Are you suggesting Harold could be hurt?"

"And you, and other plaintiffs, if it gets nasty. The Cassino firm started rough. This could revive all their bad habits. Advise him to settle, Rowena. Once he's out, he can tell the other owners to do the same."

"There's a righteous bone behind Harold's British mustache and stiff upper lip. He'll want to wave the flag."

"Discuss it with him," Declan said, "but don't let him start anything before you talk with me again."

"What are you thinking?"

"A veteran realtor told me a story about his father and Peppe Cassino in the old days, and how they resolved their business disagreement. It could come in handy."

"Very well. I'll get back to you. In the meantime, send me your bill."

With several hours to kill, Declan drove to the Anahuac Wildlife Refuge, east of town and an easy one-hour drive to MKA's office in Pasadena. The odds he would run into anybody he knew at a nature preserve were minuscule. With binoculars and a professional camera, he hoped to blend in.

He shouldn't have bothered. There wasn't a birdwatcher in sight. He found a park bench in the shade and called Robledo.

The detective picked up immediately. "Where the fuck have you been? I've been trying to reach you all day."

"I was busy, Steve. What's going on?"

"When were you in Tampa?"

"You know when. I left last Wednesday and came back Friday. What's bugging you?"

"You still have your boarding passes, car rental agreement, restaurant bills, and all that stuff?"

"Sure, yeah, I have to itemize to charge the client. Now, will you stop with the questions and answer mine for a change? What the fuck is going on?"

"A concerned citizen left a message on the anonymous caller line. A woman was beaten, raped, and killed in Tampa, last Friday. The helpful caller said, and I quote 'Check out the PI who should be locked up for the Easton murder.'"

It punched all the air out of Declan's lungs.

"You still there?" Robledo said.

"Yeah. Bastards. I swear I'll nail them. You know it's bull."

The silence on the line was full of dread. A mallard crossed the path a few feet in front of Declan and never turned its head in his direction, he had gone that still.

"We contacted the Sheriff's Office in Tampa," Robledo said. "They got an anonymous call too, similar wording with a bonus, a description of the attacker. Tall, lean, dark hair, dark clothes, boots, wearing gloves, and a bandana over his nose and mouth. You have to come in, Declan."

No way. He had a job to do at MKA tonight. This Tampa bullshit was a crude framing attempt. What kind of caller could give a physical description and connect Houston and Tampa?

"And you'll hand me over to Bogs to process again, is that the plan, Steve? When did it happen, where in Tampa?"

"I am not at liberty to say. Come in, Declan, or we'll have to issue an APB. We have no choice. It's all over the web and the regular media is relaying the news."

"That's how police work is done these days? With anonymous calls and digital mob rule?" It was fortunate Declan was alone with the ducks. One look at the expression on his face and people would call 911.

"I'm sure you can explain." Robledo didn't sound convinced.

"Tomorrow. I'll turn myself in tomorrow. I've got stuff to do."

"Your ass is hanging out there, Declan. With the APB, every cop in the area will have your pic, truck description, and tag number. You don't want a confrontation. Tempers are running hot."

"Tomorrow."

Declan switched off the phone. One sacrificial burner. He stepped on it and dropped the pieces in a garbage can. He shut down his tablet. He would be out of touch for a while. Moira knew what to do: play for time and retreat behind client confidentiality. The trolls raised the stakes. Declan didn't doubt this latest scheme came from the same source as the web postings and protests. Getting into MKA's Pasadena office was more urgent than ever.

He left the Wildlife Refuge and got back on I-10, exiting in Baytown. He drove south and crossed the water toward La Porte, before aiming north again. The San Jacinto Monument was nearby. The landmark was about to close and the tour buses were leaving.

He carried a tripod and camera to a spot near the pedestal of the column and pretended to fiddle with settings. A few people had decided to stay for the sunset view but they gave him a wide berth.

By 8:30 p.m. the sky was on fire and Declan took pictures he could be proud of. A park ranger came to look and Declan showed him what he framed.

"You chose the perfect day," the ranger said.

"The wind looked good, for the clouds." Declan kept his face in shadow. He forced a tad on the Texas drawl.

"You sell these?"

"Hope to. It's a change from the weddings and such."

"I bet. Nice meeting you."

"Same. I'll go now. My moon shots aren't as good."

Declan gathered his gear and went back to the parking lot. The ranger disappeared around a corner. He would remember him but a description would be iffy.

The drive to Pasadena was short. Declan wasn't in a rush to

get there. He went down side streets and backtracked. When he approached the objective, he explored every street in the area to identify potential escape routes.

He parked two blocks from MKA, near a garage advertising retreads and hubcaps. A Mexican restaurant did brisk business on the corner. The gear from the backpack went in Bjorn's duffel bag with the camera and the tablet, and he shoved the backpack behind the driver's seat. There wasn't anything of value in there but windows had been smashed for less.

The stench in the strip mall back alley had gained strength. A combination of the day's heat and the relative coolness after the sun went down. The dumpsters were fuller than the day before. Declan scared away a squad of screeching cats and a platoon of rats. He fastened the bag to have both hands free, pulled on a pair of sturdy work gloves, and hauled himself up onto the rim of a dumpster. With his height, he had no trouble getting from there to the roof. It had rained in the last couple of hours and puddles dotted the flat surface. Declan masked the wide beam of his flashlight and surveyed the area. The roof peeled and sagged in places, but there were no holes. He still couldn't identify the bubbles he noticed on the satellite view; in the feeble light, they looked like marshmallow puffs.

As he approached, he saw they were domed skylights, but so covered with grime that not a single ray of light could reach inside. He kneeled by the dome belonging to MKA. The half globe was fastened to the roof by a rusty metal ring. The screws were as corroded as the ring and resisted the screwdriver. Declan went at them with a hammer and chisel. The screws popped. He removed the metal ring and found hard putty underneath. Whoever installed the skylights had done a prime job. The chisel was the right tool again. He didn't worry about leaving traces on the roof; he was concerned about debris falling into the office.

He brushed away the crumbs of metal and putty before trying to lift the plexiglass dome. He couldn't get a grip and resorted to pushing it to the side. So far, his travails had been discreet. Rap issued from the tattoo parlor and Tejano gushed from the pizza joint. The globe slid and dropped a shower of dust down the hole. Declan shone his flashlight through the opening.

Nobody would notice an extra speck of dirt in that mess. The office was cluttered and shabby. Under the skylight, a little to the right, was an old metal desk with a desktop computer and stacks of files. It would make a stable landing spot. Declan filled his pockets with the tools he might need for the job. The duffel bag with Bjorn's heavy equipment remained on the roof.

He let himself down, hung from his fingers, and found the desk without having to let go of the skylight's rim. Burglars should all be tall. Now he was faced with the impossible task of finding a pin in a crummy haystack.

One of the laptops looked new. It was docked and tethered with a thick metal cable. Dirksen Loomis's workstation? Declan sat in the desk chair and surveyed the office. He didn't bother to shield the flashlight. Its glare couldn't reach through the closed blinds on the barred windows.

He replaced his work gloves with a pair of thin leather ones and switched on the computer. Password prompt. Guessing was pointless. He preferred to rely on the innate laziness of human nature. He looked around the machine, under the mousepad and the flat screen monitor, in the mug holding pencils and paperclips. Nothing. He used his lock picks on the desk drawers. Loomis was a sloppy employee. Crushed cracker packages and peanuts cohabited with post-it notes and dull pencils. The password was stuck to a tray in the right-side drawer.

Declan scrolled through the files. There were too many. He called Leyla. "If I give you the IP, can you pump the thing?"

"It won't fit on a thumb drive?"

"I don't have time to cherry-pick, Leyla. I have an entire office to go through."

"On it," she said.

While she wielded her hacker magic, Declan tackled the filing cabinets. He ignored the unlocked ones and focused on a series of solid metal drawers that tested his thieving talents. They contained hanging files in alphabetical order. A quick scan clarified what business MKA Trading was in. They were data brokers. The names on the files were familiar. He pulled out a thick folder labeled H.G. Media. Hank Gerard's PI firm headquartered in Clear Lake. Declan often competed with them. At first sight, the cases weren't the kind Declan would have taken. Squeezing permits for construction in flood-prone areas. Declan closed the folder in disgust. He could have taken pictures but that would be stooping to these people's level. He pulled out Buddy Pagett's file. What kind of unsavory surveillance did MKA carry out for The Legendary Texas Investigator, Pagett's tagline? Bid rigging. It figured. Declan slammed the file cabinet close. He had seen enough. Bottom feeders feeding more bottom feeders from the deepest, smelliest pits.

Declan went around the room. The other computers were antiques. Nobody could possibly do a web job on those. Most filing cabinets were so dusty they must not have been accessed in months. Then, in a corner, he saw the safe.

Steel, with a dial. It brought back memories. He grabbed his phone.

"Leyla, you still there?"

"Almost done. I haven't scanned all the data yet but this is where the social media garbage comes from, Dek." She didn't ask what he was doing. Leyla kept secrets for a living.

"If you find anything about a murder in Tampa, ping me, okay? I'll stay on the line."

He put the phone on top of the safe. It had been a while but some things were hard-wired. His breathing slowed and so did his heartbeat. No thinking, no distraction, just the dial. One click after the other.

The safe's contents were impressive. Stacks of banded banknotes. Declan didn't try to guess how much was in there. He stared at the gun. Smith & Wesson and a box of cartridges. He stuck his gloved hands in his jeans pockets to keep them from reaching for the revolver. This kind of time warp belonged in the dream world. What were the odds he would encounter the same kind of gun twice, not in a shop or at a shooting range, but in the shady recesses of a safe? With piles of money to keep it company.

He was about to close the door of the safe when a large manila envelope propped against the side caught his eye. He opened the package and pulled out a dozen 8 by 10 color prints. The first photograph was of a couple walking in a park with a boy on a trike between them. The parents looked happy, the boy wore a Spiderman helmet that was too big for his head and for the speed he could hope to reach. The other pictures forced Declan to sit down. April talking to the man who was in the family shot with the boy on the trike. April with her head on his shoulder. With her arms around his neck. Leaning into an open car door, the man behind the wheel. More shots of the man with the woman and the kid, and with an older couple. The man was the main subject of the collection. He didn't look familiar. Declan hadn't seen him in any of April's group shots. Thirtyish, good-looking, clean-cut, a little bland.

"Declan, you're there?" Leyla said. "That Tampa stuff is nasty."

He took pictures of the photographs from the safe and asked Leyla to read him the posts. They used the same words as the anonymous caller 'the PI who should be locked up.' Either the trolls had a source at HPD or Tampa, or they were behind the calls to the police.

Declan put the photographs back, in order, in the envelope, and closed the safe.

"I'm going to email a series of pictures to you, Leyla. I need to know who the guy in the photos is. It's extremely important. Are you done with the hack?"

"Yeah. Send the stuff."

Declan waited for the 'sent' acknowledgment. He had spent too much time in this place. The back of his neck felt prickly. "Bye, Leyla. Thanks." He shone his flashlight on the floor, the desks, and the computers, checking for signs of intrusion. The safe and the drawers were closed and locked. Papers weren't more rumpled than before. He wiped off clumps of dirt from the carpet, blended them with the general shabbiness, and blew crumbs from the desk he landed on. The place was so dirty nobody would notice a break-in. He stepped on the desk again and hauled himself up through the skylight. The plexiglass dome was easy to move back in place and spreading dirt erased the traces. Nobody would come to work on that roof anytime soon.

Declan went down from the roof to the alley the same way he got up. As he approached the hubcap shop, police lights swept over the rows of wheel accessories. The Mexican restaurant was dark and his truck looked suspiciously lonely along the sidewalk. Declan watched the officer approach the pickup, flashlight in one hand, the other on his holster.

No problem, he was planning to turn himself in anyway, even if he would have preferred to walk into HPD headquarters without a chaperon. He had to get rid of compromising evidence. Bjorn's tools, his lock picking set, bugs and trackers, and the burner phone with the pictures of April and the mystery man. He trotted back toward MKA. Bjorn's tools went over fences into the no man's land of industrial refuse, never to be seen again. The rest of the gear ended in various garbage bins.

Before thrashing the burner phone, Declan called Moira. Her husband picked up.

"Declan?" Roger Perkins was very awake. "For fuck's sake, come in. Homicide issued an APB. The entire force is after you."

"There's a cop standing by my truck right now. I'll surrender to him. Is Moira awake?" Roger grunted in protest but Moira came on the line.

"How can I help?"

"Call Vince. He better be at HPD when I come in. It might get tense."

"Dek, this is ridiculous. Rog told me about that Tampa thing …"

"They'll want the details of my Florida trip. Make scans, don't give them the originals. Bye, sweetie."

Declan smashed the phone to pieces and dispersed the debris on sidewalks and into storm drains. At the rate he went through burners, the office would need to be resupplied. Only his tablet and the camera he used at the San Jacinto monument were left in the bag. He lit a cheroot and walked back to his truck.

TWENTY-ONE

Maybe the cop observed from a distance. Declan crossed the street. He expected to be stopped at any time.

The command rang out as he was reaching for his keys.

"Police. Both hands on the roof of the vehicle."

Declan let the bag slide off his shoulder and dropped the cigar. He obeyed the instructions. He turned his head to look behind him. The cop was young, Black, and nervous. His gun was out of its holster, pointed at the ground.

"ID?"

Declan broke eye contact and stared ahead. "In my back pocket."

"Take it out. Put it on the hood. Further. Now, get back to the driver's door, hands on the roof." The cop flipped the wallet open. The PI license was right there, in a plastic sleeve.

"There's a bulletin out for you."

"I was planning to go to HPD headquarters first thing in the morning. You gonna give me a ride? Where are you parked?"

"Smart mouth, eh? Hands behind your back."

The cop cuffed him. Too tight.

"Spread your legs."

A quick frisk. All it delivered was a set of keys, a cigar case, and a disposable lighter.

"Turn around. Sit down."

The cop checked the bag, dropped the wallet and other items recovered from Declan's pockets inside, then got on the radio to report his catch.

The radio squawked in response. A rapid-fire of police jargon stuffed with code numbers.

"Okay. I'll wait. Over."

The cop called for a tow to get Declan's truck impounded.

The driver of the unmarked sedan hadn't bothered with the police lights. As he passed by, Declan looked up and saw the bulky shape of Bogs in the passenger seat.

It didn't bode well.

Bogs's loud voice boomed through the car window. "You searched him?"

"Yes, sir. All he had on him was his wallet, keys, lighter, and a cigar case. Nothing suspicious in the bag."

Bogs's partner, the driver, came out of the sedan first. He was short, stringy, with a pointy rodent face. He ignored Declan, still sitting on the tarmac, handcuffed. He lifted the bag and emptied its contents in the street.

"I wonder what's on the camera," he said to Bogs who had extracted his bulk from the passenger seat. "You think he takes pics of his kills as souvenirs?"

The young officer remained a few steps to the side.

"Fucking pervert." Bogs bent at the waist in front of Declan as if to examine him, enormous gloved hands on his knees. Their faces were a foot apart. The big sergeant reeked of sweat. The glare of the streetlight at the corner of the garage drew deep shadows on his face, catching an ear, a wide nostril, a blunt chin, like a distorted Halloween mask.

Declan didn't see the fist coming. Nothing in Bogs's expression gave any warning. It was as if he'd been struck by a bowling ball. His nose exploded and his head banged into the door of the truck. Bogs grabbed him by the handcuffs and jerked him upright. Something gave way in his shoulder. He screamed in pain. Bogs turned him around and slammed his face against the bed of the pickup. Bogs had his own definition of extreme frisking. It involved punches to the ribs and the kidneys. When Declan's knees gave, Bogs helped him on the way down by kicking his legs from under him.

Through the fog of a partial blackout, Declan heard the voice of the young uniformed cop.

"Sir. This man isn't resisting."

Bogs answered: "The punk tried to run."

Declan had curled up, knees drawn to protect his head. It left his back and his cuffed hands exposed. A kick caught him in the small of the back and he rolled sideways. He wished for complete darkness, but the pain instead of knocking him out kept bringing him back in blinding flashes. He was dragged by the handcuffs, whirled around, and thrown in the back of a car.

There were brief images, overexposed, bursts of light, then searing pain, then darkness, the sequence playing in circles, like a nightmare carousel. When Declan regained semi consciousness, he was naked and tied to an armchair in what looked like a garage. Out of the thin slit of the eye that wasn't swollen shut, he saw a workbench with an open toolbox, stacks of discolored tires, and the carcass of a minivan. A twinkling fluorescent strip light hung from the ceiling.

"You're back, good." The voice came from behind Declan. It wasn't familiar.

A bald man came into view. He had the compact, thick-necked body of a professional wrestler. His flat face was blank, pale, with bleached eyebrows. The light in the watery blue eyes was a lantern swaying in a storm. Declan felt his skin crawl. The man wore gloves and a gun was shoved in the waistband of his dirty cargo shorts.

Declan strained against the nylon rope holding him and cried in pain.

"Let's see what we can do about this," the man said. He went to the workbench and rummaged in the toolbox. He came back with a hunting knife, a heavy hammer, and several wrenches. He put the tools on the floor by Declan's feet and pulled a rag from his back pocket. He forced it in Declan's mouth.

"Temporary," he said. "It soon won't be needed anymore."

He aimed the hammer at Declan's left hand. The blow broke the armrest.

Declan passed out. And came back.

"A few minutes this time. You're a good player," the man said. "I like that. I was promised a play date but when they brought you in, I was disappointed. You were in and out. And the heart … too fast. There are a few things one can do to amuse oneself but it's not the same. Participation makes everything much better. Let's see about that other hand. Then we'll do the rest of the work."

The man's monotone put Declan to sleep. He knew what this was. He was going into shock. Mercifully. Let it be over now. He felt the blissful cool of the air displacement when the hammer came down.

The hateful voice was at the edge of perception. Whatever shreds of perception were left. He knew he was dying.

TWENTY-TWO

"YOU'RE TAKING RISKS, BUDDY."

After much delay, Wade Benning was on his way to Colorado and Elida. There was no reason for him to stay in Houston any longer. And now Pagett was making his departure even sweeter. Well, sweet and sour. Benning would have liked to see if his Tampa trap panned out. He put enough money and effort into it.

"It's an opportunity I can't let go to waste," Pagett said.

"An opportunity you want to cash in on."

"A favor for my clients, a gesture of goodwill."

Benning didn't point out that goodwill by definition should not be monetized. "A donation, rather. What would be appropriate?" They went back and forth before settling on an amount Benning deemed reasonable. "I'm taking your word for it, Buddy."

"Would I spin you a tale?"

No, Pagett wouldn't dare, but Shaw was that rarest of commodities, a lucky Irishman. "I'll wire the money to the account of your choice when I get confirmation that you delivered."

Pagett protested and Benning hung up. He switched on

his computer. He would know in real-time if Pagett had succeeded. The last bug capture was the short phone conversation between Moira Perkins and Shaw that he had listened to earlier. Protesters were blocking the agency's office. She packed some items and left, presumably to go meet him. She didn't come back to the office and neither did he. Benning knew the bugs were working because they recorded the phone ringing and the air-conditioning kicking in.

When Benning left for the airport, the bugs were still silent.

TWENTY-THREE

FIVE IN THE MORNING. Vince Wallace had been at HPD headquarters for two hours already and he wasn't getting any answers. Moira said that Declan planned to surrender, and that was hours ago. There wasn't anybody Wallace could talk to. He had driven to the Joint Processing Center and been turned around. Declan hadn't been brought in. Frank Murphy didn't answer his phone. Where else could he go for help? He called Moira back.

"I can't find him, Moira."

"Vince?" She sounded drowsy.

"I'm at HQ getting nowhere. Murphy doesn't answer my calls and every officer in the building gives me the stink eye. You're sure he said he would let that cop take him in?"

"Have you tried Steve Robledo?" she said.

The Homicide detective investigating the Easton murder. "Why?"

"I'll text you his number. Declan's working April's case with him. Here's Rog."

Wallace didn't have time to absorb that stunning revelation.

"Wait for me by the front door," Roger said. "Don't worry.

Declan turned himself in to a precinct cop; they might not have brought him to HQ yet. He must be held in one of the stations."

That made sense. Except … "They should have given him his phone call."

"It was the middle of the night, Vince. I won't be long. Stay where you are."

Moira's text dinged with the promised phone number and Wallace called Robledo. He couldn't believe Declan had gone behind his back to collaborate with the police.

Robledo didn't sound sleepy. "What do you want, Wallace?"

"I don't know where Declan is."

"In bed, if he's sensible."

Wallace swallowed his irritation. He told Robledo Roger Perkins assumed Declan was held at one of the precincts.

"I'm five minutes away. Don't move."

Wallace paced in front of the door. His anxiety flared up again. Declan was stuck somewhere in the cracks of the system. There were so many layers, so many ways to lose somebody, in a maze of paperwork and procedures. Wallace fought the arthritic joints and inertia of the legal system every day of his life. His usual clients didn't look like Declan. He knew how they got in trouble and worked on ways to get them out of trouble. This tasted different; Declan was his friend.

Robledo arrived first. He was shaking with nervous energy and lack of sleep. He grabbed Wallace by an arm and pulled him inside.

"Rog wants me to wait here," Wallace protested.

"Whatever. I'll be up in Homicide."

Wallace watched him run to the elevators. Ten minutes later, Roger's car screeched to a halt in front of the building.

"My office," Roger said. "I'll get in the system."

"Robledo's already on it."

They found the Homicide detective hunched over a computer in a corner of the deserted squad room.

"You got the APB log?" Roger said.

The two officers had never met. This wasn't the time for polite introductions. Wallace dragged a chair from another desk and sat to the side. He was too far to read what was on the computer screen.

"Nothing in the log." Robledo resumed his typing. "Get the printouts." An hourglass popped on the screen. He cursed. He hit the enter key several times. It didn't do anything. Then rows of data appeared.

Roger dropped a couple of printed pages on the desk. "That's the fucking APB. What am I supposed to do with it?"

"The phone number," Robledo snapped. He scrolled down the data dump. A pop-up window appeared in the middle of the screen covering the lines of text.

"What about the damn phone number?" Roger said.

"Dead number." Robledo clicked on what looked like dialog boxes. "I didn't recognize it, so I called. Nothing."

"What does it mean?" Wallace looked at Roger who was as confused as he was.

"Don't know." Robledo pointed at the screen.

Roger leaned in closer to read. "'4:05 incoming call. APB suspect evading arrest. Officers in pursuit.' What the hell?" He looked at the printed bulletin. "Same reference. Why would Declan run?"

Robledo was on the phone. He raised a hand to silence Roger. "Hi, Sergeant Robledo, HPD Homicide." He rattled off his badge number. "Question for you. Did one of your constables notify you this morning they had an APB suspect in custody?" He grabbed a notepad. "How do you spell that? Okay. What time? Right. Where is Constable Boyer now?" He scribbled something undecipherable. "Thank you."

"Is Declan on the run?" Roger said. "What the fuck is going on? Answer me!"

Wallace had never seen Moira's husband angry.

Robledo was typing again. "He's not on the run." He dialed another number. "Admissions please." He leaned back in his chair and swiveled to turn his back on Roger and Wallace. "Yes, hi. My name is Steve Robledo. I'm a detective with the Houston Police Department. Did you recently admit a Declan Shaw, male, Caucasian, mid-thirties?" He straightened up. "What's he in for?" He blinked. "I understand. Can you tell me where he is? I see. Thank you."

When Robledo pushed away his chair and stood up, Wallace was shocked by the expression on his face.

"You mind driving?" Robledo turned to Roger. "I don't think I can." He grabbed his phone and his hand shook so much he almost missed his pants' pocket.

"Where're we going?" Roger said.

"Pasadena. St. Luke's."

They piled into Roger's car and he peeled out with lights pulsing. Wallace was in the back. He leaned between the front seats, quick-firing questions that both cops ignored.

"Seatbelt, Vince," Roger snapped.

Buckling up was recommended. Roger drove like a man possessed.

"Mind explaining how you figured it out?" Roger said.

Robledo pulled out a pack of cigarettes. "There was nothing in the APB log, but Declan's truck was towed in Pasadena around 3:00 this morning. That gave me the precinct. One of their constables called at 4:35 to report he was taking the *individual from the bulletin* to the hospital."

"Why didn't he call EMS?" Roger said.

"What's that 4:05 a.m. evading arrest call about?" Wallace said.

Robledo cranked his window open. The cigarette was steady in his mouth but the lighter wobbled. "You know what I know."

Roger sucked in air. "It stinks. Bad number on a bulletin and Declan on the run. And the timeline sucks. Dek calls us at 2:00, the truck is towed at 3:00, he runs from the cops at 4:00, and he's in the hospital half an hour later. Somebody's playing fucking games. What's he in St. Luke's for? Being shot full of lead?"

"They wouldn't tell me." Robledo puffed and blew smoke out of the window. It didn't help. The outside air was thick as mud. "He's critical."

Roger's hands on the wheel were white-knuckled in tension.

Wallace looked from one cop to the other. They were both on edge.

"What's that APB shit?" Roger said. "Declan is a suspect in a murder in Florida? You out of your mind?"

"Don't bite my head off. Another woman was raped and murdered last night in the Energy Corridor and Declan was in the wind. It's a shit storm. I told him to come in yesterday before the bulletin went out. He hung up on me."

Wallace was about to burst. "You're crazy. Declan's being railroaded."

"That's what Declan said when he decided he didn't want to talk to me anymore." Robledo turned in his seat. "You see where that got us."

"Your fucking bulletin got us here," Roger bit back.

They were silent for the remainder of the hair-raising ride. Wallace reviewed scenarios in his head and they were all nightmares.

At the hospital, Roger pulled behind the Pasadena prowler. The car was empty.

Robledo peered into the back-seat compartment and immediately stepped back. Wallace lurked behind him and he grabbed him by an arm. "There's nothing to see here."

Wallace was taller and heavier but he was propelled by a steely hand toward the emergency entrance.

Roger's credentials worked wonders. Say *terrorism* and flash a badge that shows the word and people scramble. Declan was in ICU. Wallace followed on auto-pilot a few steps behind the two cops who rushed down corridors, up elevators, and along hallways as if frenzied movement would solve all the world's problems. Men of action. Wallace fought the urge to puke.

As it turned out, the cops couldn't get to Declan's room.

Roger's credentials didn't sway the nurses upstairs and Robledo's Homicide badge was ignored. They healed people here. The morgue was the place to go for dead ones. The officers turned to the lawyer.

Wallace swallowed hard. "I'm Vincent Wallace. I'm Mr. Shaw's friend and lawyer."

The word *friend* did it. And the color of his skin. The head nurse signaled for him to follow her, and seared the two cops with an incinerating glare. Wallace felt a little better. He could count on a measure of sympathy on this floor.

"Call Dr. Shahin," the head nurse told her colleague behind the desk.

When they were out of earshot from the nurses' station, she turned to Wallace. "It's a clusterfuck, Mr. Lawyer."

"What happened to Declan?"

"The white boy got on the wrong side of somebody. Don't know what he did to deserve that, but the officer that brought him in insisted that he be cuffed at all times. I'm telling you, in the state he's in, he's not going anywhere." She pointed at the end of the corridor. A uniformed cop sat on a chair by a door. "The kid hasn't moved. Not even to go piss."

He *was* a kid. Wallace pegged him at early twenties. And he was terrified. He jumped to his feet, hand on the holstered gun on his hip, eyes focused behind Wallace and the nurse. Roger Perkins and Robledo were following.

Wallace turned to them. "Let me handle this."

Robledo raised both hands in surrender.

"I'm Vince Wallace. I'm Shaw's lawyer. I want to see him." He showed a business card and his ID to the young Black cop.

The kid refocused on him. "I'm not letting anybody in."

"You can't deny me, officer. He has the right to see his lawyer."

"I don't care." Tense, determined not to budge.

Hurried footsteps clacked in the corridor behind them. "What's going on?" The badge on the newcomer's breast said "Baraz Shahin."

"Doctor, I can't let these people into the room." The young cop was on the verge of tears.

"I'm a lawyer and I demand to see my client." Wallace showed his documents again. "These are Houston police officers." From the corner of his eye, he saw the kid pull his gun half out of the holster.

"Mr. Shaw is under heavy sedation. He's unresponsive," Shahin said.

"Please, Doctor. I need to know what happened to my friend."

Shahin locked eyes with him. Trying to decide if he could be trusted. "Very well, but just you, me, and the nurse. These gentlemen stay outside."

One of the beds in the double room was empty. The curtains around Declan's bed were open and he was surrounded by an array of equipment with tubes snaking in all directions. Wallace's eyes went to the screen with its colorful lines and pulsing numbers. The lines were undulating. That was supposed to be a reassuring sign. In this setting, the silvery cuff clasped to the bed railing was incongruous.

"Your friend was brought in around 4:30 this morning. He sustained a slew of injuries and I believe he was left for dead. Without that young officer, he would probably be dead by now."

Wallace approached the bed. He was relieved that he couldn't see much. Declan's head was wrapped in bandages, as was the part of his body visible above the blanket; one arm was in a flexible cast, from wrist to neck, the other was connected to a network of tubes and devices. Both hands were wrapped in thick bandages. The handcuff was on a taped wrist. Wallace cringed, afraid of what he couldn't see, under the sheet. "The two officers who came with me need to see this, Doctor. I'm going to let them in."

While Wallace was inside, the tension in the corridor had climbed several notches. The constable still had his hand on his gun. Roger was as rigid as a concrete pillar and Robledo was as fidgety as a cat on flooded pavement.

When Wallace opened the door, three pairs of burning eyes skewered him.

"Is he dead?" the kid said. He sounded like a scared six-year-old.

"I want you to come in and hear what Dr. Shahin has to say. I believe we're all on the same side here. Or close enough. These handcuffs are an obscenity. Keys, officer." Wallace held his hand out.

The young cop went to the bed instead, and released the restraints. He stood there, cuffs in hand, unsure what to do next.

"You want me to slap them on you, kid?" Roger said.

The young officer was paralyzed by fear. Wallace wanted to tell him he would be protected. He reminded him of his clients trapped in their broken lives.

They gathered around the bed. It looked like a wake and Wallace shivered. Nobody dared ask, so he did. "What's the prognosis, Doctor?"

Shahin stuck both hands in his pockets. He wasn't tall, the cops towered over him, and he raised himself to his full height. "The shot to the head bothers me the most. It grazed the skull and we're definitely looking at a concussion. There's a risk of cerebral edema. We'll know soon. If that happens, the damage might be significant. No skull fractures. The nose, one cheek-bone, and the jaw are broken. We'll reset the jaw and wire it shut once the swelling's gone down. The other major area of concern is the kidneys. Internal bleeding. No lung puncture from the broken ribs. The dislocated shoulder and the torn muscles and tendons will take time to heal and require rehab. We're looking at extensive bruising, contusions, and cuts. Somebody took a hammer to his hands. He's under sedation and a heavy course of antibiotics. To use non-medical language: your friend was tortured, Mr. Wallace."

Robledo blanched and Roger flushed. Wallace was speechless. The young cop sobbed. He crumbled on the visitor chair, head in his hands. They all watched him for what seemed an eternity.

"Doc, do you have an empty room or an office we can use?" Roger said.

Robledo brought coffee from the hospital cafeteria and they huddled in a room two doors down from Declan's. Robledo and Wallace were taking notes. They had the visitor chairs. Roger and the young constable sat on one of the beds.

"Pull yourself together, kid. My friend in there will wake up. You want to be in front of what he's gonna say because I'm more inclined to believe him than you." Roger had taken the lead. His long friendship with Declan gave him seniority.

Cedric Boyer, two years out of the police academy, was shaking but his fear had abated somewhat. "I was on patrol last night. I saw a pickup truck parked in front of a closed garage. There were no other vehicles nearby. I ran the tag and the APB came up. I parked the cruiser behind a restaurant nearby and waited to see if the driver would show up. It was 2:36 a.m."

"Did you call the bulletin number?" Roger said.

"I decided to wait a bit and if the driver didn't show up, I would call it in."

Roger motioned at him to continue.

"Ten minutes later, I saw Shaw turn the corner. I knew it was him, he matched the description. He was smoking, relaxed. He carried a bag. I watched him cross the street and I came behind him. I identified myself."

"How did he react?" Roger said.

"Compliant. I asked to see an ID and I searched him. He was aware of the bulletin, said he was about to turn himself in, and asked if I would give him a ride to HPD HQ."

"He'd joke on the guillotine," Robledo mumbled.

"He didn't resist, sir," Boyer said. "I cuffed him and told him to sit down. I took a look at his bag. Just a camera and a tablet." He looked at Roger. "I recovered the bag, sir. It's in my trunk. The admission desk has his wallet."

"No tools, phone, or electronic equipment?" Roger said. Boyer mouthed "no." "Okay. Keep going."

"I called the number on the APB."

"You got through?"

"Yes. They told me to wait. That a car would be along soon. They told me Shaw was a high-value target. While we waited, I called a tow, for the pickup. An unmarked came, fifteen minutes later." Boyer described the car. A brown four-door Chevy sedan, no lights, no siren. Two plainclothes inside. Boyer's trembling got worse and sweat coated his face.

Roger nudged him to continue. "They identified themselves?"

"Flashed badges, I couldn't read the names. The plaques looked real."

"Description?" Robledo stepped on Roger's leadership but everybody was too keyed up to complain.

"Both Caucasian. The driver was short, slender, with thin greasy blond hair, too long. I noticed his suit was kinda shabby, with one of these knit ties, ratty. He looked ... weird. Scary weird."

Robledo cursed under his breath. His pen hesitated on the notepad. Wallace could feel the tension emanating from his body, like static electricity.

"The other one ..." Boyer looked away. His young face was pinched in anguish.

Roger was on the ball. "We'll protect you, kid. There's no blue loyalty when lowlifes are concerned."

Boyer looked up.

Robledo was twitchy. Roger looked so tense he radiated. Wallace had never been that focused in his entire life. Every muscle in his body had turned to lead.

"He was a big guy. I mean, massive. Big shoulders, legs like tree trunks. Not fat, but strong." Tears streamed down Boyer's face. "The small guy took the bag. He said something about pictures on the camera. Then it went bad fast." He sobbed.

Roger wrapped an arm around his shoulders. "Get it out, kiddo, you'll feel better."

Boyer wiped his nose on his sleeve. Wallace's heart went out to him. "Shaw was still sitting where I told him to. The big guy went to him." Boyer took a deep breath. "He punched Shaw in the face, sir. Hard, just like that. The sound … Then he grabbed Shaw by the handcuffs and pulled him up. Shaw screamed. I'd never heard a scream like that. I think that's when his shoulder got torn."

It was quiet in the room, just this young terrified voice.

"The big guy threw him against the truck and punched him. Shaw fell to the ground. I told him to stop. The big guy said Shaw was trying to escape." Boyer clapped both hands on his face. "It wasn't true, sir!"

Roger let the emotions settle. Wallace had never seen Moira's husband in that light. He had misjudged him. Rog wasn't a laid-back cop stuck in a bureaucratic job. He was a sharp guy with a light touch and psychological savvy.

"Shaw was unconscious. They dragged him to the unmarked and threw him in the back. I tried to intervene. I said I would get him processed at the precinct. The small guy told me they had it covered and were taking Shaw to HQ." Boyer hiccupped. "I'm going to be sick."

He had turned green. Robledo grabbed a metal dustbin and

set it on the floor between Boyer's feet. The kid retched, but all that came out was a stream of bile mixed with coffee. Wallace got a wad of toilet paper from the bathroom and handed it to him.

"Thank you," Boyer said. "They left." He vomited again. Water and spittle.

"Then what?" Roger said.

"I … I didn't know what to do. It was wrong. What they did. I went to get my car and I saw the lights of the tow truck at the end of the street. That's when I decided to follow them."

Wallace exhaled. "Thank God."

Boyer turned to Roger. "I drove toward HQ and I didn't see them. I thought I'd lost them. Then I turned a corner and I spotted them between two warehouses. They weren't going to HQ, sir. I believe they went toward downtown in case I was behind them and when they didn't see me, they changed direction. They drove further east. It was all industrial sites. They went around an abandoned grocery store and stopped in front of an old gas station, all boarded up. I hung back. I hid the cruiser behind a row of dumpsters. I know I should have called it in but I didn't know what I was looking at."

"I understand," Roger said. "Keep going."

"They dragged Shaw out of the car. He was sort of stumbling. They took him into the garage, through a side door. I thought about going to investigate and I'm glad I waited because the small guy came out and got Shaw's bag. I left my position and went around the garage to find a window or a back door. I could hear noises and laughing." Boyer grabbed the dustbin. It was a false alarm and he pushed the bin to the side. "The place was all boarded up and I couldn't see inside. I don't know how long I stayed there. I heard the side door open and the two officers came out. Shaw was not with them. They got in the sedan and drove away. I waited a while to see if anybody else would come out, then I decided to go in. I was at the door, when I heard a voice and noises again, clanging, and a big crash. The person never stopped talking through all the racket. There was another crash. I was pushing the door open when I heard a gunshot."

"You still didn't call it in," Roger said.

"There was no time for that, sir."

"No, kid, you're right."

"I drew my gun, I identified myself, I tried to stay out of the line of fire. I heard a scramble in the back of the garage, running, things falling. It was the suspect escaping, sir. I didn't have a good look at him. Shaw was tied up in a broken chair. There was a lot of blood. I thought I was too late and he was dead."

"You went to check."

"Yes, sir. I found a pulse. Very weak. I got Shaw in the car and brought him here. I called my precinct to tell them where I was going. I didn't tell them what I saw. I ... was confused, sir."

"Nasty pinch, kid," Roger said. "I don't blame you for taking the time to think it over."

The young cop jolted upright. "I did nothing wrong!"

Robledo tapped his pen against the notepad. "You told your precinct you were taking the guy from the APB to the hospital."

"Yes, sir."

Robledo turned to Roger. "They didn't call it in."

"The number was off."

Robledo shook his head. "They would have tried another number."

Boyer cleared his throat. "I told my precinct I already called it in. I couldn't risk it, sir. These guys might come here and ..." He swallowed hard. "I almost didn't call the precinct. But they would know my position anyway."

"You didn't know who all was in on this," Roger said.

Robledo sneered. "Thanks for not shooting us on sight when we came down the corridor."

"It's pointless," Boyer said. "Maybe I should have let him die; he'll get the needle anyway."

"Declan didn't rape, beat, or kill anybody, kid," Roger said.

Robledo groaned. "Like it or not, we have to follow the evidence."

Roger jumped to his feet. "What evidence? My friend's in there because of you, sanctimonious prick!"

He was in Robledo's face who was also standing, quick and tense as a coiled rattler.

"You know who these animals are," Roger yelled. "You covering your department's collective ass? Fuck you."

Wallace was shocked by the hacksaw look on Robledo's face, the echo of the street-tough kid who decided at a young age he wouldn't take shit from anybody. Boyer's eyes were about to pop out of his skull. Roger's face was creased in fury.

"This mess is on *my* doorstep, not yours." Robledo spat out the words like cherry stones.

Wallace had to admire them. They were armed but none of them made a move to draw a gun. If it came to blows, it would be old-style. Even odds. Roger's range against Robledo's speed. "If you knock each other out, I'll call the nurses," he said. "And I'm pressing charges."

Robledo cooled off first. He turned away from Roger who was still purple in the face.

"I'll drive with the kid to HQ and get the cruiser processed," Robledo said. "I'll take down your statement, Boyer. And we'll send a team to that garage. You're welcome to join, Perkins, if you can keep your temper bolted. I'll get to the bottom of this. I suggest you stay here, Wallace. You have an in with the doctor and the nurses. I'll send a tech for DNA and photographs. Make sure he has access to Declan. This is attempted murder, understood?"

Wallace went back to Declan's room. The nurse was refilling pouches. Wallace told her he planned to stay for as long as it took. She asked if the police would be back and he said he had everything under control.

TWENTY-FOUR

THE RETURN TO CONSCIOUSNESS was a long slog through fog so thick Declan wished he could go at it with a weed whacker. He complained to nobody in particular. He trudged forward in what he was convinced was an inextricable maze. Till a clearing opened.

He saw the kind eyes of Vince Wallace. They were glossy with tears. The lawyer's smile wavered. He looked exhausted.

"Well hello there," Wallace said. "You've been making puppy noises for half an hour; we waited for you to come back." He pointed at a woman standing by a monitor. "This is Nurse Dionne, she runs the shop." The woman smiled.

Declan tried to answer but nothing came out. He could feel his lips moving, in a slow-motion mushy way. His tongue pushed against rough, gunky teeth.

"Your jaw is wired shut, but you should be able to get sounds out. You know who you are, right?"

Of course, he knew who he was. Jaw wired? He tried to speak again and gave up, stared hard at Wallace instead.

"Blink once if you know your name."

What an idiotic question! Blink.

"Do you remember what happened?"

Can't say I do. The B&E at MKA, then ... what?

"All right. No pressure. You're in a hospital."

I figured that out already, genius, where else are you surrounded by that much tubing, the space station? Declan let out a long sigh and felt a painful stab in his chest. Okay, shouldn't do that. He tried to move his arms and that was another fulcrum of hurt. He closed his eyes and tried to remember. MKA. The roof. The street. Police lights. His truck. How did he get to the hospital?

It was coming back to him.

The blade of pain struck from neck to tailbone, and he seized. It was uncontrollable, an electric quake; his back arched and his body lifted off the mattress, like something out of *The Exorcist*. The nurse sprang into action and grabbed an IV bag.

"No," Declan said. It came out raspy, but clear enough. It stopped the nurse. The pain vanished, and he lay flat again.

"Mr. Shaw," the nurse said. "There is no need to suffer through this. I'll adjust the drip."

"No."

"I better get Dr. Shahin." She was shaking her head as she walked to the door.

"She's right," Wallace said. "Pain management is critical to recovery."

God, his lawyer spoke like a book. Like a medical book. Declan went back to his memory dig. His truck. The cop would take him to HPD, because of the APB, that Tampa thing, a woman was raped and killed, April, no, not April, a woman he didn't know, but he didn't do it, he was cuffed, and then ... fuck. Bogs. Bogs and a weasel in a brown car.

The seizure struck again and he gasped. It was a conspiracy, to prevent him from remembering, and they planned to give him drugs so he would go to sleep and that would throw a thick blanket over the entire goddam thing. Not gonna happen … The pain relented and all was quiet again, the sheets smooth, the tubes gurgling, the monitor pinging.

"Tell. Them." Getting the words out.

Wallace had a haunted look; he gasped worse than Declan.

"No. Drugs."

The doctor and the nurse came in. They looked capable in their uniforms, with badges pinned to their white coats and dream-making candy in their pockets. They were here to help and they were the enemy. Declan had to make them understand that he was susceptible to the stuff. It would fix his body but turn his mind into goop.

"He spoke, Doctor," Dionne said. "He said *no* when I went to adjust the drip. He had a seizure."

"He said more than that," Wallace said. "He said, *no drugs*."

"That is laudable, Mr. Shaw," Shahin said, "but it isn't realistic. Without the painkillers, you'll be a mindless drone. Pain is totalitarian."

"Juss this leff …" It was a hard one to negotiate. He willed his mushy mouth to work around it. "Le-fel. Not more." Was talking that exhausting for babies? No wonder they took their time to get to it.

Shahin turned to the nurse. "Compromise. His mind is working fine. Do you know what happened to you, Mr. Shaw?"

"Wha day?" He was getting better at it. On the one-syllable words at least.

"Sunday. You were brought in Thursday morning."

Four days. He lost half a fucking week. He could have lost much more, but then there would be no reason to worry, right? He would be in the great wormhole in the sky, at one with the galaxy. RIP Declan Francis Philip Shaw.

"Whass wong with me?" That was sloppy. "What rong." The nurse smiled. Vince had said her name was Dionne.

Shahin leaned on the bed railing. "I've seen run over people that were in better shape."

Ah! That blasted spasm again! He gnashed his teeth. The crisis passed.

"Is a noy … in."

"I'd say. I'll ask the neurologist to swing by," Shahin said. "I'm an ER guy, I patch things up. I leave the fine-tuning to the smart ones."

"Will I haff, uh." The word was on the tip of his sluggish tongue. "Sea kwel."

"That's a subject for the specialists, but I'm sure you'll have headaches. A bullet came very close to being inside your head." Shahin sighed. "Then there's trauma, of course."

Trauma. The events of that night were coming back to him, in shards. Crude snapshots. Bogs punching him, dragging him. Pain. Darkness. Tearing. The monster in the garage. The hammer. He didn't remember being shot. Who was the crazy fuck with the hammer? He closed his eyes. Forget these pukes, he had work to do. Leyla Kareem, the MKA data dump, and the pictures from the safe. Who was the man in the pictures? The list of classes and seminars April attended. Amy Corrigan. Rowena Dowling. Carlyle and the building report. Daisy. So much work.

"Has he gone to sleep?" Wallace said.

"That would be a positive sign," Shahin said. "You should go home, Mr. Wallace, get some rest. The worst is over. I have to notify the police."

"I'll do it. He's serious about the drugs, Doctor. It's not out of some desire to appear tough. Declan had issues with painkillers after the accident that shattered his leg. He had a devilish time kicking the habit. He doesn't want to slip back."

"I'll let the nurses know. Thank you, Mr. Wallace."

The doctor and the nurse left. "I need Moira," Declan said.

Wallace jumped in his chair. "God, you scared me. I thought you were asleep."

"Moira."

"She'll be here soon. We've been working in shifts, with Rog helping out. You haven't been left alone more than a few minutes at a time."

"Bogs?"

"That's for Murphy and Robledo to handle. You were gone a long time. You gave us a bad scare."

"Sorry."

Wallace touched his wrist, the one that showed a little skin between the bandages. "Try to sleep until Moira gets here. I have calls to make."

Declan drifted. His sleep wasn't heavy, he had too much on his mind. The seizures took a break. Maybe they preferred to strike when he was awake.

When Declan woke up, Moira was sitting in the chair Wallace had vacated. The overhead lights were off, a small table lamp lit her face sideways. The glow of the e-reader illuminated her from below. The picture was timeless, suitable for a small Rembrandt study, intimate.

"Love," he said. "You been here long?"

She closed the reader and moved her chair closer. "A few hours. You were sleeping so soundly, I didn't have the heart to wake you." Her smile had a touch of shyness in it. "It's wonderful to hear your voice, even if it's molasses. I want to touch you and there isn't a square inch of you that isn't wrapped." She ran a finger on a cheekbone that was exposed. "Are you in pain?"

"In and out. Listen. The case."

"Oh no, you don't. No case. Your job is to heal."

Of course, she would say that. "Leyla. Tomorrow."

"The smear attacks are the least of your problems, Dek."

"Leyla. And the list. Events April went to."

"With everything that happened, I haven't started on it yet."

He breathed and it tore through his chest. "A party. April as Bonnie Parker. Who was there?"

The seizure came from deep in his gut this time and the pain traveled to his neck. The bed shook and Moira screamed. A nurse rushed in syringe at the ready. She had to wait for the shakes to subside to administer the drug.

"I know," the nurse said. "Light on the painkillers. This is a sedative to take the edge off. Give your heart a rest. You hear me?"

"Okay," Declan muttered. It was a bad one. 8.0 on the Richter scale.

"What was that," Moira whispered after the nurse left. "Scared the shit out of me."

"Bad plug. The party."

"I'm glad your brain is shipshape but, Jesus, Dek, can you lay off the job for a minute?"

He couldn't. April was fading from memory. He couldn't let that happen. "A phone. Contacts. Vince, Daisy, Rowena, Leyla, Amy Corrigan, Robledo, Murphy." He paused. Who else? "Stan Borelli."

"A word?" Moira said.

Declan would have waved her to go on but his movements were limited.

"The cops came with a search warrant for information on your Florida trip. They asked why you changed your flight. Why you left from Miami instead of Tampa. I didn't know. Did you spend the night with Daisy?"

"I wish I had. They said when the woman was killed?"

"When do cops ever tell you anything? Rog said Tampa filed for extradition. Murphy is stalling."

"What else?"

"Rowena and Daisy both wanted to come and I told them you were under. Should I call them?"

"I need a phone."

"You're a handful. Your truck is impounded. What the hell were you doing in Pasadena?"

"I hope Robledo comes."

Moira sighed. "The dashing detective. He'll be here soon. Now your eyes are closing. You're sleepy, very, very sleepy."

"You stay? Please."

Declan wondered what drug was supposed to take the edge off the seizures. Then he didn't wonder anymore.

Robledo came before Leyla. No surprise. She was a night owl.

"Pulling out, eh?"

"Wouldn't call it pulling." Declan felt gazillions better. His tongue wasn't occupying ninety percent of the space in his mouth, and Nurse Dionne brushed his teeth the best she could with the wiring.

"Bogs and Fisher are under arrest."

So that was the weasel's name, Fisher. "May they rot."

"Agreed. The organization went into damage control. I don't need to draw you a picture."

"I don't remember much, Steve. I kept blacking out. I remember Bogs's fist in my face. And the creep in the garage who talked and talked. I was dying and that voice freaked me out. I don't know when I was shot." Declan closed his eyes. "You know what I thought while all this was going on? What a shitty way to die. It takes too long."

Robledo leaned on the bedrail. "We have a witness. Cedric Boyer, the constable who saved your life." He gave Declan a summary of the events. "Boyer couldn't give us a description of the garage guy. He ran out the back and Boyer didn't go after him. You were the priority. And we have no prints or DNA."

"The freak wore gloves." Declan described the pale monster with the dead eyes. A squirmy thing that lived in a swamp. "He's got to have a record."

"We'll find him. Let's talk about Tampa."

"I didn't do it," Declan said.

"The simplest explanation is usually the best. It would have been almost impossible for you to swing it. I say *almost*. There lies the rub."

"When was the woman killed?"

Robledo settled in the chair. He leaned on the bed rail. "This is what we know. Some hard facts, some less so. A woman was assaulted and murdered a little after five a.m. behind a bar in North Tampa. Time of death is semi-solid. Somebody heard screams."

"The same somebody who gave a description of the attacker?"

"No. A neighbor. He was interviewed when the body was found. The description was part of the anonymous call to the Hillsborough County Sheriff's Office last Wednesday."

"I didn't go to Tampa Friday night," Declan said.

"And you have supporting evidence: the ticket from the gas station where you filled up before returning your rental car at Miami airport. You couldn't hit the girl in Tampa after five and be at the airport between six and seven."

"Why are we still talking about extradition?"

"Because of *almost*," Robledo said. "How do I know *you* drove that car to Miami?"

"You're nuts."

Robledo hiked his shoulders. "You could have taken the Tampa-Miami shuttle under an assumed identity. HCSO has requested security footage from both airports. Or the witness who heard the screams is mistaken, somebody else screamed at five, and the girl died closer to three than five." He slapped both hands on the bedrail. "Far-fetched, but possible. You're the smartest cookie in the tin, Declan. It's unfortunate."

A seizure decided an intermission was in order. It shocked Robledo as it had shocked Moira but he didn't scream and nobody came running.

"What was that hell show?"

"Shorts in the system," Declan said, out of breath.

"Can they do something about it?"

"Drug me." He closed his eyes, enjoyed the respite. "Where were we? Ah, my masterful alibi. I met Daisy Diamond at the Miami Airport Hilton after dropping my rental. It must have been before seven. We had coffee. She paid."

Robledo sighed. "Friend, occasional girlfriend, fellow PI. Would she lie for you?"

"She would, but she won't have to. People in the restaurant. Customers and staff."

"And they'll remember you." Robledo smiled. "Yeah, I bet they would remember you. How you can be a successful PI baffles me. Private dicks are supposed to be shades of neutral gray, be forgettable, merge with the tapestry. You stick out."

"I can disappear when I need to."

"All right, we'll check with Ms. Diamond and the hotel staff. That'll take care of the early morning slot. What about the rest of the night, can you account for your whereabouts?"

"Most of it. Thursday evening, I had dinner in Clearwater with Rowena Dowling, my client's lawyer. I didn't go back to the penthouse afterward. I drove north. I went past Tarpon Springs, found a place with a view, and had a smoke. You understand about having a smoke, don't you?"

"Don't remind me. Anybody saw you?"

"A cop."

"He identified himself?"

"No. White cruiser, Tarpon Springs Police decals. I have the tag number."

"You're shitting me."

"Memory dump." Declan gave him the number. "He checked my ID."

"When was that?"

"One thirty or so. I drove back to Clearwater Beach. I got home before two. I was too hyped to sleep. I decided to pack and hit the road. I didn't drive through Tampa. I went down to St. Petersburg."

"You should be all right. I'll follow up with the Tampa cops." Robledo gave Declan a sip of water. The straw gurgled. "What about last Wednesday? Another woman was attacked on the west side. Bogs was already hot for you and it sent him overboard. He got it in his big stupid head that you did another one and would get away with it again."

"I was in Pasadena all night."

"We have your camera. What the fuck were you doing at the San Jacinto Monument?"

"Killing time before going to MKA. You guessed that, didn't you?"

Robledo pocketed his notepad. "You got in? Off the record."

"'Nothing is ever off the record.' Who said that?"

"If you found something, it's useless. You know it. And everything we find afterwards is useless too. Fruit of the fucking poisoned tree."

"It will come down, Steve, and the fruits will be so ripe they'll rot. You'll smell them from the top of the Williams Tower."

"Nice line." Robledo sighed. "Will you share?"

"I thought you didn't want to know. Poisoned kumquats and other exotics."

Robledo twitched in his chair, impatient.

"In a day or two," Declan said.

"You're flat on your back in a fucking hospital, you idiot. What's the difference between now and two days from now? What can you do?"

By himself, not much. But he had help.

TWENTY-FIVE

LEYLA KAREEM IN A SUIT, WOW. She smiled at Declan's wide-open eyes and twirled. On the way out of the twirl, she flashed an imitation of a police badge.

"I passed the nurse's gauntlet with flying colors. You'll be amused to hear that the media is in total confusion. You are, check all that apply: A victim of police brutality, a rapist with police protection, a white man, the son of an immigrant. You have a Black lawyer. You're persecuted because you have a Black lawyer. And a Black cop saved your life. It's like a fireworks factory blowing up, blinding everybody. Imagine if they knew you work cheek to jowl with a brilliant Palestinian hacker from Lebanon. *Moi.*"

"*Tout et son contraire,*" Declan said.

"*Ouais.* With so many wild shots, somebody is bound to blow off their own foot."

"What about the MKA upload?"

"You're not missing a beat. *Mon chéri*, if I wanted, I could be the wealthiest blackmailer on the planet. These MKA people are unbelievable. They have dirt on everybody and they're in bed with everybody. It's hard to separate truth from lie. They specialize in the kind of disinformation campaign that splattered gunk on you."

"You know who hired them?"

"Their biggest and steadiest source of income is the notorious Buddy Pagett."

Not a surprise. The man's favorite methods were subterranean. And the entire scheme reeked personal. There was enough bad blood between Declan and Pagett to keep them going at each other for a couple of generations. "Any others?"

"Four firms for smaller amounts. Hounding you would have cost more than what these people paid for."

"The question is: who pays Pagett. He hates my guts but he hates spending money even more."

There was nothing on who Pagett's backer might be in the material Leyla retrieved. The details of April's case were uploaded without a source, then used to feed Dirksen Loomis's blog and the social media flood. Same for the Tampa-related posts.

"Buddy has ears and eyes in HPD," Declan said. "I was Bogs's wet dream. He decided I was the serial killer. A nudge would be enough to put him on Pagett's side."

"Looks like Pagett tried to get rid of you."

Declan was reluctant to go that far. Pagett wasn't a killer. Too squeamish. But using Bogs's rage, yeah, he could see that.

"Our New Orleans trap worked, by the way," Leyla said. "I had a bite from MKA. I watched them gobble up the drivel, and put it on Loomis's blog."

"You're still accessing their data?"

"My claws are in their hide. You want me to pull out?"

"Not yet, but focus on their relationship with Pagett. And my trip to Florida." The timing of the Tampa murder was so convenient. If he hadn't decided to drive to Miami, he would be in a world of trouble.

"I found a mention in one of the blogs that the inept cops

let you loose and the first thing you did was run to Florida to resume your nefarious activities. Did Pagett try to frame you?"

"If Buddy had me in the bag for Tampa, why sic Bogs on me?"

"Double tap? A case of the right hand not knowing what the left one is doing? A team sets you up for Tampa, the sneaky approach, while another one goes the more radical route in Pasadena."

Declan sighed. "What about the photographs from the safe?"

"Nothing yet."

"Moira will bring me a phone. Text me the photos. Can MKA find out that you have access to their system?"

"Who do you think I am?"

After Leyla left, Declan had a brutal seizure. The attack unplugged the IV and the connection to the monitor. The alarm rang and doctors and nurses came running convinced he was coding.

"Sorry," he said as Dionne reset the entire apparatus. "It's the first one this afternoon. I'm improving."

"That's not a valid medical opinion." She proceeded with the cleaning and maintenance ritual that took place when the curtains were drawn close. "Dr. Mulvaney, the neurologist, will be here around five. Be nice to her."

"I'm always nice to the ladies."

"Packaged like you are, you won't be able to ride on your looks, babe."

"My charm will shine through the bandages, like the sun between the clouds after a refreshing spring shower, lass."

"Don't try that with her or we'll have to reset your nose again. Tomorrow we start feeding you the regular way. Liquids only."

Dr. Mulvaney was in her fifties, petite, with a shock of black hair streaked with white. Her clear blue eyes stared at Declan through glasses that were too big for her delicate frame.

"You fell under a steam roller, Mr. Shaw?"

"More like a compactor," Declan said.

"You have control of the vocabulary. How's your recall?"

"Full of holes. I don't remember the gunshot. I was punched and kicked and my shoulder was torn. I thought my arm was being pulled off. After that it's flashes." He closed his eyes. "There was a hammer."

She stared at him. "A less healthy person would have collapsed sooner, but might not be here today. Your body will heal. Your mind might not be as resilient. I'm concerned about damage that is not psychological, yet difficult to pinpoint. Describe the seizures."

Declan did, as best he could. He was puzzled by the randomness of the fits and asked about triggers.

"If you were suffering from epilepsy, I would tell you that we don't know what causes the condition. Your seizures are trauma-related. We'll do another EEG and scans to look for lesions. We'll slice your brain. Fine slices. We'll find where it misfires." She smiled. "This is where I usually say 'Don't panic.' You don't strike me as being prone to panic."

"I've convinced myself that problems have solutions."

"Your line of work. Mine too." She touched his bandaged hand. "I'll see you tomorrow at ten." She gave him a little bow on the way out.

Dionne was back within five minutes. "What do you think?"

"She's a character."

"It takes one to know one. I'll turn off the lights now."

"Moira will be here later," Declan said.

"Yeah, why don't you marry that woman?"

"I like her husband."

Moira came but he was asleep. Dionne told him that she stayed an hour. She left an envelope on the nightstand. It contained a phone and a copy of the list of events April attended during her years at Sloats & Archer. Half the lines were crossed out. Moira scribbled: "Still searching."

Declan called Rowena Dowling and left his number.

He texted Leyla, "photos?" Then he tried Daisy who answered after two rings.

She was brief. "I'll be there tomorrow," she said.

Life in a hospital is as controlled as a mission to Mars. Maintenance, feeding, tests, visits. The patients have very little time to themselves. Maybe that was deliberate. Keep the poor bastards occupied. It irked Declan. He couldn't even pretend to be asleep to give himself the time to think because the moment he closed his eyes he drifted off.

Murphy visited and confirmed that the Florida extradition was history. Cedric Boyer came, to apologize for the handcuffs and for not intervening sooner. Declan had to comfort the kid.

The visits were heartwarming but didn't move the needle on anything. Rowena, on the phone, was more productive. She convinced Carlyle to sit tight for a few weeks, arguing more research was needed to solidify the case. She was a seasoned lawyer and bending the truth didn't faze her.

When Daisy appeared, so alive that she glowed, the monitor readings went wacko. Dionne happened to be in the room or the entire floor would have gone into alert mode.

"Is that a new seizure flavor, Declan?" Dionne said.

"Meet Daisy." He was delighted. She looked ready for a country picnic, tall and willowy in a flowery cotton dress a shade darker than her sun-touched blond hair. Her haircut was different, shorter. Her wedge sandals matched her tote bag. She brought the Sunshine State to his hospital room.

"Shall I close the curtains?" Dionne didn't wait for an answer. "I'll hang the 'Do Not Disturb' on the door. Don't tear anything, now." She winked at Daisy and stepped out.

"Have you seduced the entire staff?" Daisy said.

"I'm doing the best I can under the circumstances. Where are you staying?"

"Your place." She jiggled a key ring. "Moira gave me access to the sanctuary." She lowered the railing and sat on the side of the bed.

Declan winced. Daisy flinched and he took her hand before she could rise again. He had regained some mobility. "Stay right where you are. I love that dress."

She leaned over and kissed him on the lips. "This needs tender care." She searched in her tote and dug out a tube of lip balm. "Colorless."

"It feels good," Declan said.

"I'll have to reapply regularly for a couple of days." She kissed him again, deeper this time. "Are you all taped up?"

"They're revealing a little more skin every day. The suspense is killing me."

She lifted a corner of the bedsheet. "Nice colors. Mardi Gras."

She put a hand on his stomach. It felt cool against the heat generated by the healing bruises. He closed his eyes, enjoying the gentle touch and the soft feel of her hand. Definitely enjoying it.

"I don't want to start something I can't finish," she said.

"Leave the hand there. I'm glad the circuitry still works."

She gave him a sip of water and reapplied the lip balm. "I read they arrested these cop creeps. What did you do to cross them?"

"Bogs got stuck in his head that I killed April and a few others. He sees himself as the avenger of victimized women. He's got a few screws loose."

"You excuse him? He handed you over to a complete nutjob for final rites."

"He went off the deep end dead certain he was right."

Daisy held his hand, and told him about islands where the fishing was plentiful and the beaches sweet as sugar. By the end of hurricane season, he would be fully recovered and that was the best time to go south. She weaved her low, pleasant voice around tall tales of secret coves, sunken galleons, and colorful reefs. Declan drifted on the warm current of her voice.

Roger and Moira popped in later.

"Tremors top to bottom on the reporting line," Roger said. "The brass wanted to bury the whole thing, settle with Vince, pay you off. They talked about shipping Bogs to a mental facility and firing Fisher. Not gonna happen, not with Vince waving your medical chart in their faces, Cedric Boyer's testimony, and Murphy and Robledo making a stink. Fisher tried to dump everything on Bogs. It might have worked if they hadn't made a phony call pretending you tried to escape when Boyer knew you were in that garage. And Homicide arrested the garage goblin. Turns out Fisher promised to bring him a present, as the goblin said, 'a plaything.' The goblin is known to break his toys."

Plaything. Declan shivered and pain traveled up and down his spine. "Somebody's behind Fisher. No way Bogs planned it."

"Fisher lawyered up," Roger said. "There might be a deal in the works. It's far from over."

"Well, it's over for now," Moira said. "Enough of that crime stuff. I'm still working on your list, Dek. Event organizers have a huge turnover and short memories."

Declan was relieved she changed the subject. There was only so much he could take about garages, creeps, and hammers. "Has the news scared clients away?"

"Quite the opposite. I'm fielding calls from people worried you might be out of contention. I tell them I see you every day and you're better every day. You want to see the get-well cards?"

"Pass."

"You know I will respond to every single one of them," she said.

Declan didn't have a seizure that day. Maybe it had some-thing to do with Daisy's soothing touch. Or the lip balm.

In the morning, after Nurse Dionne's ministrations, Declan called Amy Corrigan. She said she would swing by in the afternoon.

He wasn't used to inactivity. He called Stanley Borelli because he didn't feel like taking a nap.

"I'm on my way to Colorado," Stan said. "After what hap-pened to you I decided to blow town for a few weeks."

Declan could hear road noises in the background. "I'm glad you did, Stan."

"The cops that beat you up are in league with the folks that came after me?"

"I don't know, but the end result is the same. I'm benched."

"When will they release you?"

"No idea. The dope in my IV would make you smile, Stan."

"Not at all envious. I'll let you know where we're staying when we get there. Maybe you could charter an ambulance and join us. There are ways to stay in the clouds in Colorado."

"I'll think about it. Take care, Stan."

Declan was wide awake when Amy Corrigan walked in. He waved at her. It looked formal, two stiff fingers sticking out, like the Pope dispensing benedictions.

"The news said you were beaten up but I didn't expect this," she said. "Did they come after you because you're investigating April's murder?"

"I'm a victim of misguided wrath. Did you look at your sou-venir pictures?"

"You're still working the case? You're one stubborn dude. I didn't find anything that looked like the party you described."

"I want to show you something." He plucked the phone off

the side table and scrolled to Leyla's text with the MKA photos. "Do you know this man?"

Amy enlarged the shot of the couple with the baby boy on the trike.

"Scroll, there's more."

She looked up from the phone. "I told you April gushed about her men. She never mentioned this one."

"Maybe because he's married with a kid."

"She avoided married men. Too much trouble and too much baggage. This guy is not her type. Too preppy." She swiped through the pics. "He looks familiar but I can't place him. Can I send one of these to myself?"

"It's delicate, Amy. I'm not supposed to have them."

"You stole them?"

"Sort of. I broke into a place and took pictures of these photographs."

She put the phone down. "Let's talk about something else. Maybe it'll come back to me if I let it sit. Can I get you something?"

"I'm dying for a cup of real coffee with tons of sugar. The nurses give me dishwater."

Amy brought back the genuine thing. The brew gave him a buzz. The smell alone brought tears to his eyes. His nerve endings were raw.

"Hey, it's just a cup of joe!"

"It tastes glorious. It'll rocket my heart rate into the red zone. How's life at S&A?"

Amy was in the middle of a vivid description of lawyers stabbing each other in the back when Daisy came in. Daisy didn't expect another woman in the visitor chair and couldn't hide that it troubled her.

"DD," Declan said, "meet Amy Corrigan. She's a friend of April's. Amy, this is Daisy Diamond, a PI colleague from Miami."

"A lady detective." Amy studied Daisy, with clear appreciation and a touch of intrigued speculation that made Declan smile.

"Detective, sure," Daisy said. "Lady? Not in your wildest dreams." She brought over the chair assigned to the other bed. "You know me, Dek. I'm not good at waiting doing nothing. I took over the party search." She raised an eyebrow. Could she talk in front of Amy Corrigan?

"Amy knows I'm looking for Bonnie Parker. She told me she didn't have the picture."

"I know when and where the party took place." Daisy pulled stapled sheets from her tote bag. "That's the list of attendees. Sixty-four. I've got the names and credentials of the speakers. Fifteen experts in tax havens and money laundering. A three-day seminar. The party was on the evening of the second day." She turned to Amy. "Your name ain't on the list, love."

"Help me sit up." Declan scanned the six-page list. No familiar names. He handed it to Amy who fished her glasses from her purse.

"I know this one," she said. "Casey Dillard. He was April's top guy for a few months. That was, oh … five or six years ago."

"The seminar was five years ago," Daisy said.

"They might have met there. April was full speed into him. When I asked her to go out with me on the weekend, she said, 'can't, I'm on a case!' and laughed her head off. Case Dillard. Handsome and unreliable. April's typical guy."

"Clyde to her Bonnie?" Declan said.

"High probability." Amy turned to Daisy. "You know why he's so obsessed with this photo?" Daisy shrugged. Amy swung back to Declan. "Tell us?"

"You have to keep this to yourselves. It's crime scene evidence." They were both hanging to his words. "I noticed the group photo on the fireplace. April with the Bonnie Parker beret. I asked April where her partner in crime was. She said

Clyde was long gone. When I went to the apartment again, with Robledo, that picture was gone. The cops didn't take it."

"The murderer did," Daisy said.

"Case. My God." Amy flushed and her freckles stood out more.

"I'm glad I didn't start calling the people on the list," Daisy said.

Declan leaned back on the pillow. "Wait … Oh, I'm an idiot. It isn't Clyde, it isn't Casey Dillard, of course not." The two women stared at him. "I asked April about Clyde because he wasn't in the picture."

Daisy got it first. "Why would he take the picture if he's not in it. Duh."

"You win the teddy bear, sweetie. It has to be somebody who's in the fucking photograph."

Amy still held the list. She ran a nail-bitten finger down the alphabetical roster. She turned a page, then the next. If Declan's hands hadn't been wrapped in bandages he would have been biting his nails too. She looked at him, over the top of her reading glasses. "Adam Leary."

Daisy grabbed the sheet of paper. "Based in San Antonio."

"Not anymore." Amy switched on Declan's phone. She selected the picture of the family. "He's an assistant DA in Fort Bend. That's why he looked familiar."

"An ADA, are you shitting me?" Daisy said.

Declan's mind was firing on all cylinders. Then it misfired.

Amy ran out to find a nurse and Daisy tried to hold Declan so he wouldn't hurt himself. She didn't know where to grab him and by the time Dionne arrived, she was frantic.

"It's going to be all right," Dionne said, stretching her syllables. "Declan and I know how this goes, don't we, babe, and Dr. Mulvaney knows where the little tear that causes all that misery is located. Nothing we can do about it except keep an eye on it and wait for nature to take its course. Now, your girlfriends here think I'm a babbling fool because they don't know that you can hear me and understand everything I say."

The tension went out of Declan and he relaxed in his previous sitting position. "You're a ham, Dionne. You hog the stage." His heart was running a steeplechase.

"I smell coffee on your breath," Dionne said.

"I had a cup. I want to start walking tomorrow, Dionne."

"I'll lend you an arm, babe. I added juice to your drip. You have about thirty minutes to do your business with these ladies." She nodded at Daisy and Amy. "The seizures are less frequent. It's his first today."

Amy was rattled. Daisy had recovered. She took her seat again. "Where did you get the pictures, Dek?"

"A collateral investigation."

MKA gathered dirt for its clients. If Adam Leary killed April, he was a prime extortion target. Was Buddy Pagett the client? MKA's business was information; they didn't carry out the physical shake-downs. That was more in Pagett's wheelhouse. But the Leary pictures were taken *before* April's murder. Why was the Fort Bend ADA under surveillance?

Amy Corrigan was swiping through the photos again. "This isn't right." She leaned over the side of the bed to show Declan the picture of April with her arms around her lover's neck.

"What am I supposed to look at?"

"She wears high heels and look where her head is. Right at the guy's chin. Adam Leary isn't that tall, Declan."

Why didn't he see it before? He should know, he had seen the woman at the funeral. "It isn't April in the photo, it's Jill."

He sank back on the pillow and closed his eyes. *Jill.*

He understood why Leyla hummed. White noise to blanket disruptions.

The odds that one sister would be involved in a blackmail scheme and the other would be murdered, and the two events unrelated … How did April get entangled in this? The target of the photos was Adam Leary. What the fuck did it mean?

"Who's Jill?" Daisy cut through Declan's mental churning.

"April's sister," Amy said. "She's this buttoned-up suburban housewife, and she looks a lot like April, but she's shorter and rounder."

"Not that buttoned up," Daisy said. "Why would the guy kill his lover's sister? Did she get in the way?"

"Not April. Jill misbehaving would have given her the giggles."

Declan looked at the pictures again. Now that he knew the woman was Jill, he noticed all the little differences. But at first sight … and in person too, at the funeral … The sisters were a lot alike. Robledo said April's murder was a hit. And Leary was being blackmailed. Could it be that simple?

"There's one explanation that checks all the boxes," Declan said. "It was a cold-blooded murder and it was stupid. A fucking mistake."

Amy was half out of her chair. "What do you mean?"

"The killers mistook April for Jill."

The silence in the room was broken by the regular ping of the monitor, an occasional gurgle in the IV bag, and the air conditioning kicking in.

"Jill has a key to April's apartment," Amy said. "She checks on the place when April is on tour."

April was often on tour, and Sam Koenig, Jill's husband, traveled a lot on business. Declan felt a surge of nausea. The coffee crept up his pipes.

"I can't square blackmail and murder," Daisy said. "Killing to pressure a mark is extreme. How loaded is that fellow, Leary?"

"Whatever an ADA makes in Fort Bend County."

"There are other reasons than money to put the screws on an ADA," Declan said.

"Important court cases," Daisy said.

"I can find out." Amy grabbed her purse, ready to go get the information right away.

"We're going after dangerous people, Amy," Declan said. "Be careful."

She straightened her jacket and walked to the door.

Daisy smiled. "There must be a name for that kind of triangle."

"Every silly boy's wet dream?"

"You're very young at heart." She perched in her previous spot on the bed. She ran a finger from his temple to his cheekbone and lifted a piece of band-aid from his nose. "They should ice that."

Leyla Kareem appeared after sunset, when bats go hunting. "I identified your guy."

"Adam Leary," Declan said.

"You have someone else on this?" She looked offended.

"The threads are coming together, Leyla. I feel like a spider in a web. Vibrations all around are getting stronger." He told her about the brainstorming session with Daisy and Amy.

"It's extreme. Killing a woman to put pressure on an ADA. And Buddy Pagett in the middle of it? I'd never thought he had the stones for it."

"He doesn't," Declan said. "It's whoever he's working for."

"Somebody with an interest in a big court case."

She crossed and uncrossed her legs, uncomfortable in the skirt suit. Leyla lived in jeans and t-shirts. She was out of her natural garb. All for him. Declan was moved. A tear formed and ran down his cheek to be captured by the bandages. Damn that sentimentality. It must be something in the drip.

"I wonder," she said. "You had these geeks on your back, fake protesters, and an attempt to frame you in Tampa, do you think you might have been bugged?"

Of course, her concerns would skew that way. Surveillance

was her specialty. "I worked the case outside of the office. Bugs wouldn't have delivered much. You're welcome to check. The office is due for a sweep anyway."

TWENTY-SIX

THE TRIAL WAS OVER. Temporarily. Hung jury. The DA announced he would retry the case. For Adam Leary, it was the end of the nightmare. He dared breathe again. The lives of those he held dear were spared. Their continued wellbeing depended on his silence. And it weighed on him.

Adam considered himself a good man and that belief was shaken to its foundations. He went to law school to seek justice for the wronged. He knew it was naïve but it drove him.

In this trial, he had failed the victims in the worst possible way. Sixteen innocents were thrown under the judicial bus because criminals with boatloads of money and less moral qualms than Beelzebub decided that they mattered less than the two morons that left them to die when their truck broke down in a Walmart parking lot.

They could have opened the doors.

Could that be called a *youthful mistake*, as the defense argued?

Adam didn't think so. The callousness of the act, the lack of a speck of empathy were beyond his comprehension, and the jury had to feel the same. The closing argument was branded in his brain. It would stay there forever because he could never use it.

The case was sheer horror. Two kids, eighteen and twenty-one, working for human traffickers, let sixteen people, seven children among them, die of dehydration and heatstroke in the back of their truck. They abandoned them in a parking lot when the vehicle blew a gasket.

Depraved indifference.

Adam had to hold back because he was terrified of what might happen if he won. He didn't do his sworn duty, he didn't do the victims justice, and it ate him alive. In the aftermath of the verdict, he wanted to resign but was scared of the questions he'd have to answer.

When the result of the lengthy jury deliberations became known, Adam's boss lost his legendary cool and released the ripest stream of obscenities ever uttered by a white-haired Texas aristocrat tracing his roots to Washington-on-the-Brazos. The jury, the prosecutorial team, the judge, the cocksuckers on the defense, and the clueless witnesses were all thrown in the same shit-reeking bag. When he had cooled off, with generous helpings of bourbon, he talked to Adam in private.

"Everybody can have a lousy day in court, but you chose a corker of a day to have yours, boy."

The DA told Adam he still had a job; he hadn't taken a torpedo below the line of flotation, but he would have to work triple-hard to get rid of all the water in the hold. The DA loved war movies with battleships.

The pat on the back didn't soothe Adam's conscience.

The entire mess had started with an invitation to lunch.

The DA wasn't in the habit of taking his subordinates out. He was too keen on his political connections to waste a networking opportunity on a lowly cog.

"I want you to prosecute the truck case, Adam," the DA said, before appetizers. "You're good and juries like you. I want you to take it to the bank for me."

"I thought you would do it yourself and I would be second chair." Adam was excited. He could feel sweat pooling in his armpits. He kept his hands in his lap. He didn't trust them to be steady.

"Optics matter in a courtroom. The defendants are young and so are you. It will be harder for the defense to paint the prosecutor as a symbol of the patriarchy. You'll have all the help you need. The cops did a solid job on the case. There is no doubt these punks are guilty. I wish we could prosecute their employers but that's pie in the sky." It came out *pah in the skah*.

"Wouldn't they plea?" Adam said. "Give us the upline to save their necks?"

"They're more scared of their hierarchy than they are of us, kid. They know that the first word they say, they're *bah-bah*."

"Who's on the defense side, sir?"

"The best money can buy. How do you feel going head to head with Chester Powys?"

Adam gulped down too much of his sparkling water too fast and it went down the wrong pipe. He coughed so hard it made him cry. "He must be doing it for the publicity. The cartels don't waste money on foot soldiers. Unless these guys are more important than they seem."

The DA shrugged. "If they knew anything important, they would be dead by now. Anyway, the cops looked everywhere. Nada. If there's anything, it's buried so deep it's in Australia. So, you're in?"

Adam could see the ladder, leaping up it three rungs at a time. He was thirty-three. Hell, he could be DA before he hit forty. He closed his eyes. He hadn't touched the pre-lunch drinks and he had a buzz.

"I'm your man, sir."

Adam dug into the case the moment he was back at the office. He went home on a cloud. He waltzed Clare across the dining room and threw little Colin in the air to the boy's utter delight. Adam was happier than he'd ever been.

The pressure was applied two weeks later. It was after work. Two men approached him in the parking lot. He couldn't see their faces. The lights were behind them, they wore ballcaps and dark clothes. One of them was big. The other was short and pudgy. The big guy didn't say anything. He slammed Adam against the side of his SUV. No punches were thrown but the hands of the giant were on his throat. Adam was petrified.

"We know everything about you, Adam Leary," the smaller man said.

He sounded just like Adam's neighbor. He went on to prove he wasn't boasting. He rattled off Adam's home address, the names of his wife and kid, the names and address of his parents. He knew that Adam had a lover, he knew when he fucked her at the westside apartment and how long he stayed. He made obscene comments about the sexual stamina of prosecutors.

"Not enough jerking off in court, Mister Assistant District Attorney?"

Adam freaked out. This couldn't be happening. How did they know?

Then the man got down to business.

A transaction. If Adam didn't help throw out the case, the people he loved would get hurt. The big guy grabbed his crotch and squeezed. Adam yelped.

"Much worse pain than this," the small man said. He slipped a cell phone in Adam's jacket pocket. "For instructions."

Then they were gone.

When Adam calmed down, he tried to look at it rationally. These people were trying to scare him. But what could they do?

This was the United States. This was Texas, and he was an officer of the court. It was crude intimidation. What kind of prosecutor would he be if he let himself be bullied in a parking lot by a couple of goons? The affair with Jill Koenig was the bigger danger. If it was exposed and Clare threatened to divorce him, it would become a distraction and the DA would pull him off the case. He should call Jill in the morning. He had to prepare for trial; he wouldn't have time for her anyway. She had to understand. He would make her understand.

Adam didn't go to the police or the DA. His fear had receded. The cops would laugh him out of the room. Did you throw a punch, Adam, did you kick the big guy in the nuts? He didn't do any of that. He was relieved he didn't piss his pants.

He went about his job. The worry at the back of his mind went dormant. The trial date approached.

One afternoon, the cheap cell phone he'd stuck in his desk drawer dinged. Text. "Your Mom is in the hospital."

Adam called his father and couldn't reach him. He left a message. "Hi, want to see if you're coming for dinner Saturday."

Later that night, his father called. Adam's mother had fallen down the steps at her doctor's office. She broke her wrists and would need surgery. Adam asked how it happened. Mom didn't know. A crowd had gathered near the door, she must have missed a step. Could she have been pushed? His father grumbled. What a ridiculous idea.

Maybe it was a coincidence and his mother just fell, but Adam couldn't risk it. He went to his boss and asked to be taken off the case. He was concerned about his mother's health and not sure he could take the load right now. The DA said he was throwing away a golden opportunity. For broken wrists? Or was there something else wrong with his mother?

"Family is important but think about your career. Go talk to your mom, sleep on it. If you still feel the same in the morning, we'll work out a solution. Baxter is briefed and can jump in, but you know he's not my first choice."

Adam dropped the cell phone in a dumpster. That night, he slept like the dead. On his way to a hearing the next morning, he ran into a crowd of people summoned for jury duty. He didn't pay attention to the incident until a buzz in his jacket pocket interrupted him in the middle of a conversation with a colleague. It was a cell phone, identical to the one he threw away.

"I have to take this," Adam blurted. "My mother's having surgery."

It was the voice from the parking lot.

"You can't get off that way, buddy. It's your case and you're stuck with it. Or we knock over your Pop. And it won't be broken bones. That was a gentle warning. To show you we mean what we say."

How did they know he asked to be taken off the case? They must have informants in the DA office. Adam didn't know where to turn for help. He couldn't trust anybody. He went to his boss and told him he changed his mind. He invented a story about his mother being tested for Alzheimer and the results coming back good. The DA said he was glad Adam's mother was fine.

All Adam could do was play for time. He could not throw the case. If he made obvious mistakes, he would face penalties. Winning the case for the prosecution was no longer in the cards. It was fortunate Chester Powys was on the opposing side. The man was brilliant. If Adam played his hand right, he could engineer an honorable loss. Justice would not be served but his family would be safe.

He received instructions the night before jury selection. "Don't object to the defense's choice of jurors." Easier said than done. There were a few potential jury members he could not possibly accept, and he used his peremptory challenges.

One day later, he paid for this show of professionalism. Clare texted him. He called her back during a brief recess. She was frantic. Colin was in the hospital with a severe case of food poisoning.

"How did it happen? What did he eat?"

"He said a kid gave him a snack. Now he's delirious, and I can't get a word that makes sense out of him. Adam, I'm so scared."

"I'll be there as soon as I can."

Adam had disregarded the instructions. They, whoever *they* were, showed him that his rebellious actions had consequences. A text message on the loathsome cell phone drove the point home: "Who will be next? Wanna guess?"

They struck at his mother and his son. If he told Clare she would demand he go to the police. That would be a disaster. He called Jill to tell her he would be busy for a couple of weeks. She didn't take it well. Did he still love her? He calmed her the only way he knew. They had sex, right there, on the phone. She was in her bedroom and he was in his desk chair at home. Was it less seedy when you didn't pay for it and your partner wasn't doing the dishes while you jacked off?

He couldn't fight these people. He needed more time. He should talk to these unsophisticated men and explain. Tell them to lay off. He had this. He would deliver the verdict they demanded. He sent a text. "Need to talk." The answer came. "Later."

While his son was in the hospital recovering, a jury was empaneled. Adam presented the prosecution case. He had no leeway; the facts were indisputable. The DA complimented him for his cold delivery that was more effective than the courtroom theatrics that got big playtime on TV. The case was gruesome enough by itself.

Adam was about to close the prosecution case when he received a large package at the office. He didn't have to open it. The cover said it all. He was looking at the defense team's trial strategy. If possession of this file was leaked—and it would be, that was the whole point—the case would be dismissed and he might be subject to disciplinary actions. He called for a meeting of the prosecutorial team in his office and showed them the package. It was clear it hadn't been opened. The police were called in, statements were taken, and the documents were shipped back to Chester Powys's office. The incident motivated the prosecution team. When the defense resorted to dirty tactics it meant they sensed defeat. Adam planned to get with the judge on Monday. This was grounds for mistrial.

The cell phone was silent on Friday night and Saturday. Adam and Clare spent time with Colin at the hospital. The boy was better, his fever was down. Sunday afternoon, the phone rang.

It was a different voice, flat, scarier than the other one. "That was a stupid move, Adam. We offer you an easy way out and you spit on it. What happened to your girlfriend is on you. She won't play the piano for you anymore." The line went dead.

Adam sat paralyzed, phone in hand, staring at the garden outside his window, not seeing anything. Jill didn't play the piano. She hated the instrument, couldn't listen to Chopin without wanting to puke. It reminded her of home recitals when her parents paraded April in front of their friends. Her talented sister, always the center of attention. One day she insisted Adam take her on the piano bench, at the apartment. She was wild and he couldn't have enough of her. He would have fucked her on top of the grand piano if she'd asked.

He called her, ready to apologize for dialing a wrong number if somebody else picked up.

"Hello?" Silence. "Who is it?"

"I … just wanted to hear your voice," Adam said, relief flooding. She was okay. It was all a bluff.

"Are you done with that trial?" Jill said. "Sam has travel coming up."

Her voice had dropped an octave, into that honeyed darkness he could not resist.

"Another week." He had imagined the worst. "I'll call you when it's over."

"April is leaving on tour Wednesday. We'll have all the time in the world. I want you so much." She made a kissing sound and hung up.

Adam felt lightheaded. A knock on the door kicked him out of his trance. Clare had a drink in her hand.

"I made you a scotch and soda," she said. "It's been a tough week." She smiled. "One drink won't numb your neurons, love."

It tasted wonderful. "It might help. Make me creative. How many drunk lawyers can you think of in literature?"

"You won't get drunk from one of these. It's loaded with ice. That's water, for you non-scientific types. Dinner in an hour."

She was the perfect lawyer spouse. Not upset by long hours, obsessive behavior, and piles of paper scattered around. Adam wished she was that easy-going in bed.

The trial files were spread out in front of him and he couldn't focus on them. All he saw was the grand piano in April's west-side apartment.

How did these men know about the piano? They must have been in there. Maybe they pretended to be maintenance people. Maybe they hid cameras inside and they had recordings of him and Jill.

She won't play for you anymore. The meaning was clear. But Jill wasn't dead. Up to then, none of the threats had been empty. His mother was hurt. His son was in the hospital. Adam grabbed his jacket and car keys.

"I need papers from the office," he called to Clare. "Don't wait for me. I'll get something to eat on the way."

"Adam, that's silly. Can't it wait till tomorrow?"

He didn't bother answering. He was already in the garage.

Traffic was light on a Sunday evening and he made it to April's apartment in less than thirty minutes. He had the key Jill made for him when they got wary of suburban motels. Neither of them intended to leave their spouse. The affair was a stand-alone chapter in their respective marriages. From the first night, they had been in agreement. Jill was bored with Sam, and Adam didn't get what he needed from Clare. After a year and a half, the relationship was showing signs of fatigue. The lust was still there but Adam wanted to disentangle himself. With his career on a fast track, there were risks he shouldn't take.

He parked near the pool. The complex was crowded. A loud party hopped nearby and fizzy pop music issued from open windows. He walked to April's apartment. There were no lights in the windows. If April was in, what would he say? They had met, years ago, that's how he hooked up with Jill. Would she remember him? He could say he was visiting a friend and got the wrong apartment. He went up the steps, knocked on the door. No answer. He rang the bell. Waited. Rang again.

She wasn't home.

He used his key.

He switched on the lights.

Signs of chaos. Adam peeked into the kitchen. The dish-washer door was open. He went to the main bedroom.

He knew right away what the stains on the comforter and the rugs were. He could feel his heartbeat in his throat. He took a few tentative steps toward the bathroom. The light from the bedroom bisected the naked body curled up on the tiled floor. Red blood on the white towels and the pale skin, a glossy puddle around the head. The smell with an undertone of salt, something from the sea. Adam had been to a few crime scenes. The blood hadn't congealed yet, the body was lifelike. It happened recently. Could she still be alive?

He switched on the bathroom lights. April's eyes were open and glassy, the cut on her throat wasn't bleeding anymore.

Adam stumbled, fumbled for light switches, banged his leg against the doorjamb on his way out of the bedroom, and fell on his knees in the living room.

He must have remained like that for a while because when he tried to stand he had lost all feeling in his feet. His eyes focused on the grand piano. It filled him with dread and grief. For April, for Jill, for the mess he was in. He went to the piano and its collection of pictures. April was the successful sister. More beautiful, more polished. Adam met her at a seminar in Chicago, years ago. She had hooked up with a friend of his, Case Dillard. Case who could always be relied upon to pluck the most interesting bloom in any bouquet. Adam met Jill later, through Case. It had amused Case to make an entrance with a sister on each arm, as if he'd scored a set of twins. It had amused April too, much less Jill. Nothing happened that night. He drove Jill home; April was otherwise engaged. He met Jill again. The attraction grew, shy at first, then passionate.

Now April was dead. Because of him. If he had gone to his boss after the incident in the parking lot, none of this would have happened.

Adam's first impulse was to call the police. Then he thought it over. It wouldn't change anything. The rats would still get what they wanted. The judge would declare a mistrial. Adam would be disgraced. No firm would ever hire him. His marriage would be history. Maybe he would be allowed to see Colin at Christmas.

Nothing connected him to the murder.

He did a quick survey of the apartment. He wiped off the light switches. His last date with Jill was three weeks ago. The apartment had been cleaned since then. On the way out, he stopped at the fireplace and glanced at the framed photographs. His heart skipped. Fuck. There he was. In a group photo from the party at the Chicago seminar. He looked rakish in a fedora. He took the frame and, tissue in hand, rearranged the display to hide the space he created.

He threw the apartment keys out of the car window, somewhere on the Katy Freeway, and stopped in a grocery parking lot to toss the picture frame. The photograph, torn up, went in another bin.

The cheap cell phone rang again Monday morning. Adam was at the office before heading to court. He almost screamed. His sanity held by hair-thin threads.

"You said you wanted to talk," the voice said. "What about?"

Adam wanted the thing to stop. "Let me handle it my way."

"You've finally decided to be incompetent, Adam?"

That summed it up, didn't it?

"Answer me."

"Yes."

The trial went the way Adam scripted it. His crosses were lackluster, his final summation was tame. He disguised his lack of bite behind respect for Chester Powys, the unbeatable defense attorney. He brought all the acting talent he didn't know he possessed into the courtroom. The jury stewed on a verdict then announced they couldn't come to a decision.

The DA had the final word. "Next time they won't have Powys and I will be there."

Adam planned to be miles away.

TWENTY-SEVEN

THE SPECIAL NUMBER Buddy Pagett reserved for sensitive clients hadn't stopped ringing. He wished he had an automated system that said "You are number X in line. Your call will be answered in the order it has been received." Not that he had dozens of callers, but they kept hanging up and trying again. By now, Pagett had his speech memorized. It was like a telemarketer script except the client questions were even more predictable.

They all reneged on their financial pledges.

Pagett had committed the ultimate sin. He overpromised and underdelivered. Declan Shaw was still alive. That the fucking private dick was injured, possibly in a terminal way, didn't make any difference to the pompous pricks that had jumped on his proposal with both feet. Pagett tried to negotiate. Half back, one-third back, two-thirds back. Because decking Shaw had to be worth something.

It wasn't worth anything.

Pagett bitterly regretted having succumbed to temptation, and he resented Fisher for creating the mood that made the temptation possible. The man was like a toxic cloud. And now

Fisher was under arrest. He would jettison Pagett to save his hide, no doubt about it.

Could Wade Benning help?

The millionaire was in Colorado. Pagett was put on hold for twenty minutes.

"You shouldn't have done it, Buddy," Benning said. "It's out of your field of expertise."

Pagett wanted to scream that the man hadn't objected when he thought the plan was promising.

"You were dead set, Buddy." A light chuckle. "And it might, it just might have worked. Why are you calling?"

Pagett held the phone in a hand that was getting sweatier by the second. "I thought … maybe you could help."

Silence, then, "Are you threatening me, Buddy?"

"No, no, it's just … you know people."

"We both know people. What does it have to do with anything?"

This wasn't going anywhere. "I thought, maybe, I could borrow …"

"What?" Benning snapped.

"Fisher knows …"

"You're not finishing your sentences, Buddy. If you want me to handle this, you should ask clearly. I'm not sure why I should help you get out of a problem you created."

"Well, there are some dealings …"

"You are in no position to put pressure on me, Buddy." A pause. "Very well, I'll see what I can do, and for God's sake stay put."

TWENTY-EIGHT

"YOU HAVE AN INFESTATION," LEYLA SAID.

Declan was up. Nurse Dionne gave him a crutch that he struggled to use. He still hurt all over and felt as limp as a dishrag.

"I found bugs in your office. Moira retrieved your truck from the pound and it had bugs and a tracker. Professional gear."

Declan shuffled back to the bed. Moira had brought him a robe, the plushy hotel kind, and it covered the humiliating hospital johnny.

Leyla described the high-tech gizmos hidden behind his plinths. "I left everything in place. I figured you may want to use the knowledge to your advantage."

"I didn't think the muck bloggers were that sophisticated."

"There were no surveillance transcripts or audio files on MKA's machines. I went through everything again to make sure."

"I'm dealing with two sets of snoops?"

She grinned. "You're in high demand. Any idea when they got into your place?"

"When I was in Florida, I guess." Declan tried to remember what he might have said about April's murder that was critical to the investigation. The conversation that came to mind was the long one with Robledo, that Sunday. "Were there bugs on the terrace?"

There were none. That limited the damage. The office surveillance wouldn't have told the watchers much. The truck showed that he was full bore into the investigation. His trips to see Stan and Murphy, the funeral, Amy Corrigan, Sloats & Archer.

Pensacola.

He parked near MKA. If the bloggers had known he was that close, they would have stopped him. He had to be dealing with two sets of snoops. The second group was more professional and more worrisome.

"April's killers were keeping tabs on me," Declan said.

Robledo texted he would pop in later. By then, Daisy had gotten news from Amy Corrigan and compiled a briefing that she delivered with buttery croissants and a large decaf coffee. The smell of freshly baked bread was so distracting that Declan begged her to wait with the case until he was finished eating. He had never tasted anything that good, even if he struggled to fit the pieces through the slit in his wired mouth.

"I didn't think you were ready for a cheeseburger," Daisy said.

"I'm tired of soups and yogurts."

"What about the freaky seizures?"

"Less freaky." She didn't need to know that dizzy spells had taken their place. Doc Mulvaney was pleased with the progress. She didn't seem concerned that he twice collapsed in the hallway. All she said was, "That's why I don't want you to wander alone."

"Adam Leary was lead prosecutor in a big case," Daisy said.

"Was? It's over?"

"As of yesterday. Hung jury." Daisy handed him her tablet. She had bookmarked a series of articles from the *Houston*

Chronicle. "They're a good summary. The reporter covers the facts leading to the trial, the fireworks in court, and the reactions to the jury deliberations."

As he read the articles, Declan forgot he was in an armchair, at the end of a hospital corridor, with the hesitant shuffle of patients, the roll of wheelchairs, and the voices of personnel and visitors all around him. He sipped his coffee, motioned for a refill, and didn't notice when Daisy left to get him one.

"This doesn't imply that the prosecution bungled the case," he said. "Chester Powys is a megastar. Why would a man of his reputation defend two despicable losers?"

"Amy's trying to find out if Powys did it pro bono. She said the prosecution missed opportunities, was weak on cross, lacked empathy for the victims, and made no attempt to connect with the jurors. She didn't call it bungling, but Adam Leary sure didn't shine."

Declan's college degree was history and pre-law. He could imagine what he would have done if he'd been prosecuting.

"Four jurors came out on the defense side," Daisy said. "They said that the young men were victims themselves, poor, uneducated, and disenfranchised. Not understanding the consequences of what they were doing. A couple of jurors said they didn't like the prosecutor, and that he didn't seem to care one way or the other."

"They voted eight to four," Declan said. "It wasn't a total disaster."

"The first vote was eleven to one," Daisy said.

"Was that one among the four holdouts at the end?"

"I don't know. Does it matter?"

"If the jury was tampered with, yes," Declan said.

"That goes against our Leary-being-blackmailed theory."

"Not necessarily." He closed his eyes, worried that an episode might be coming. "I need to get back to bed, DD."

She helped him up and guided him along the corridor. Dionne appeared a minute later as if she'd sensed he was in distress.

"Say goodbye, darlings. I have work to do here."

Declan couldn't focus on the case while Dionne performed the multiple tasks that he was used to by now. She asked the usual questions about pain and discomfort but he didn't feel like chatting and she didn't push. She left him alone with his thoughts.

The people who ordered April's—or rather Jill's—murder wanted to derail the trial. An acquittal was unlikely, no matter how talented Chester Powys was. The DA was bound to retry. Sixteen undocumented dead in an overheated truck. Nobody could get off on that. A delay bought time. To cut off relationships, close loopholes, bury evidence.

Castrating the head prosecutor didn't guarantee the final result. The sure way to deliver the goods was to buy the votes. When jury unanimity is required, one captive juror is enough. If the tampering attempt is discovered, you still get the mistrial. If Adam Leary goes to the judge to complain that he's being squeezed, again, mistrial. The logic was clear, not the brutality. Why did they have to kill? They knew of Leary's affair. Wasn't the threat of revelation enough? Declan couldn't put himself in the shoes of the murderers. The killers were more alien to him than the slugs that munched on the potted plants on his terrace.

"You look a hundred times better," Robledo said. "The nose is still a Chinese eggplant and the jaw is out of Hollywood special effects, but I can almost recognize you. How's the head?"

"Functioning. How's yours?"

"Now I'm sure you're back among the living and sneering."

"How's the investigation going?"

"We expect DNA results in a few days."

"I've done more from this bed than you from your perch at

HPD, Steve." Declan was gleeful. He was also crippled and that gave him prerogatives. "I know why April died."

Robledo dragged a chair closer.

"It's a tangled web. MKA is involved. And so is Buddy Pagett. They're bit players. I don't know who's pulling their strings. And my office and truck were bugged."

Robledo pulled out his cigarette pack, contemplated the cancer sticks. Smoking in a hospital …

"The window opens," Declan said.

Robledo pulled the window open and hung half out to light up. "I have no qualms about going after MKA and associates, they're scum, but I need more than your hospital bed drug-induced cogitations to get going. God knows I have enough to keep me busy. Bogs and Fisher suck up my time. Bogs admitted changing the phone number on the APB, to be told first if anybody picked you up. So he could get a jump on you."

"Wanna bet the phone was Fisher's idea?" Declan said.

Robledo took two long drags and crushed the butt of the cigarette on the windowsill. He waved his hands to clear the air before closing the window. "All right, what's that bright insight of yours?" He sat on the side of the bed, in the same spot as Daisy. He didn't put a soothing hand on Declan's tummy.

"It's all in here." Declan dropped his phone by Robledo's side who didn't make a move to take it. "Look, for fuck's sake!" The monitor pinged. Goddam spying robots ruled the world. "What I found at MKA."

Robledo scrolled through the photos. "April being naughty. Who's the guy?"

"It isn't April, Steve. It's Jill." Declan saw understanding dawn on Robledo. The detective's face went soft, the tense jaw loosened, and the focused eyes wavered. He looked ten years younger. "Adam Leary, Fort Bend County ADA. A major case that he should have bagged ended with a deadlocked jury. Human trafficking. Sixteen dead in the back of a truck."

Robledo pushed the phone away. He wiped his hands on his jeans as if he'd touched something slimy. "I know the case. Leary was pressured into holding off?"

"The pictures were in a safe, Steve, in the office of an outfit that makes money gathering dirt on people with the intent of gaining influence. I saw files on bids, permits, and crooked officials. They weren't deemed important enough to be in the safe."

"What else was in there?"

"Money and a gun."

"Who does MKA work for?"

"Buddy Pagett looms big on their balance sheet. They're scavengers that don't mind getting into the smelly stuff that nobody else will touch. They carried out the smear campaign against me."

"Pagett paid for the Leary assignment?"

"MKA worked mostly for him these past few months," Declan said. "I never thought he would get mixed up in murder."

"How did you connect Leary to April?"

Declan told him about the law seminar in Chicago where the Bonnie Parker pic was taken.

Robledo played with his pack of smokes. "You know how to follow a trail. Even crippled. When are they releasing you?"

"I keep hearing *next week*."

"It's weird going about regular business knowing spooks are listening to every word I say." Moira had brought clothes. She accounted for Declan's limited mobility and selected loose pants and ample tropical shirts.

"It's more cheerful than what they're used to around here," Declan said. "How's it going with Daisy?"

"I don't know where she is most of the day. Is she still doing research for you?"

"She has a business to run. I should tell her to go home." He sighed.

"She loves you."

"Like a bird with a broken wing. Once I start flapping around, she'll lose interest."

"Because you'll make sure she does. You're a prick, Shaw."

His love life was Moira's hobby. If he wasn't so easily bored, she would have managed to get him hitched a long time ago. Daisy was the leading current candidate. Moira didn't know they had a long history of volcanic passion and epic battles.

"What's the business news?" Safe subject.

"Churning," Moira said. "I closed one of the missing person's searches. And we got two new background checks on a short deadline."

"You're keeping us afloat."

Moira patted his hand. "If you didn't do the acrobatics, my floor exercises wouldn't be noticed. Is there revenue in your current obsession or should I write this off as advertising?"

Declan lifted his broken hands; one of the fingers stuck out. "You call this a PR campaign?"

"Name recognition is priceless."

The ordeal started with getting dressed. Declan got halfway through and had to sit to catch his breath. Dionne watched.

"You notice I'm not offering to help," she said.

Buttoning the shirt made him sweat. "I should stick to t-shirts."

"Wait till you try to open a toothpaste tube with no hands and a broken jaw."

"When will they remove the contraption? It makes me want to bite someone."

"As if you could," Dionne said. "What about going downstairs for a cup of coffee?"

With increased mobility came impatience with the numbing routine of hospital life. Declan was bored stiff. He didn't mince words with the two doctors that came to see him together, Shahin and the neurologist, Mulvaney.

"As far as I'm concerned you can be released," Shahin said. "Providing you have adequate support at home. The kidneys are healing nicely, the lesions are clean, and the bruises are fading. It's time to start rehab for that rotator cuff. It will be a long process before you get the full range of motion. Six months to a year. I'll send the physical therapist over. What's your take, Mulvaney?"

"It's counterproductive to keep him here. You need a quiet and relaxing environment, Mr. Shaw, and confinement stresses you out. I'm concerned about the fainting spells. I hoped they would be gone by now." She looked at his chart. "You had one this morning. Do you live with somebody?"

"I work out of my home. Moira, Ms. Perkins, comes in at nine and leaves around six." He smiled. "I can't ask her to suffer my presence on the weekends too. She needs a break." He thought of a solution. "Am I allowed to travel?"

"You can't drive a car, obviously, and flying isn't allowed. Otherwise, I can't see anything wrong with a change of scenery. If there are adequate medical facilities nearby."

Daisy had to go back to Florida, and Harold Carlyle and his sinking building couldn't be left dangling forever.

"What about my jaw?"

"That's a question for the surgeon who wired you shut," Shahin said. "I'll ask him to come have a look. It usually takes three to four weeks for the breakage to fix itself."

Declan stared down the calendar at months of struggle. Talk about being sidelined. What kind of investigation could he carry out from the depth of his den? He couldn't be tied to a computer screen for that long, it would drive him crazy.

"I can go home tomorrow?"

"After you see the surgeon," Shahin said. "I'll leave instructions for your prescriptions."

"I want a daily text telling me how many spells you had and how long they lasted," Mulvaney said. "I look forward to seeing a message that says *zero*. You can stop texting after a week of zeros."

Declan nodded. "Thank you, both."

TWENTY-NINE

DAISY HAD COME TO A DIFFICULT DECISION. The Miami agency limped in her absence. She delayed the visit to the hospital as long as possible knowing that it would be a heart-wrenching ordeal. The nursing staff was used to her sneaking in at all hours, but eleven at night was pushing it.

"This is not acceptable, Ms. Diamond," the night nurse said. "He needs all the sleep he can get."

"I apologize, Nurse. I'm leaving tomorrow and I'm not looking forward to telling him."

"Stop by the station when you leave. I'll adjust his sedatives."

They'd knock him out. Declan would be raving mad in the morning.

He wasn't sleeping. The only light in the room came from the glare of the traffic on the nearby freeway and a reading lamp clipped to the headboard. The bed was a protected nest in the diffuse circle of light. Declan was deep in a book, a pair of round spectacles balanced on his bandaged nose. Daisy paused in the door. The glasses made him look vulnerable.

"You're positively professorial. Where do these come from?"

He smiled, eyes twinkling, and her heart did a Texas two-step.

"Cheaters from the shop downstairs. I hate the neon tubes and the poor light gives me headaches. How come you're so late, sweetie?"

"Miami business." She sat on the bed and he shifted sideways to give her more room.

"You need to go back," he said.

She took off his glasses and tried them on. Why did he make it so easy for her? Maybe he was tired of her. "I can stay a few more days." She had promised herself she wouldn't say that.

"Mmmhh … no." He lifted a broken finger. "One more day."

Daisy's heart sank. She put the glasses and the paperback on the night table. When would she stop behaving like a lovestruck teenager around him? She was appalled at the exhausting nature of her feelings for him.

"I'll be released tomorrow. Will you take me home?"

"Oh, that's wonderful. Everything's all right then." Relief overwhelmed her.

"There are precautions, medications, but yes, it's increased degrees of freedom. I was starting to get a rash rubbing my hide against the cage doors." He let out a long breath, eyes closed. "I'm afraid to ask, DD."

She wiped off her eyes with the back of her hands and blew her nose. "What?"

"Can I go to Florida with you?"

She forgot her runny nose. Sat there, stunned, with a crumpled tissue in her hand.

"It's a chore, DD. I can't be left alone unless I'm seated or bedded because of these fainting fits, and I'm limited to a liquid diet for the next month. I can't fly, I can't drive, and there must be a hundred more complications that I can't even think of because the nurses are doing it all for me."

"You realize what you're saying?"

"I need a nanny." He grinned. It looked dangerous with the wiring. "A fantasy of a nanny."

"It's gonna cost you." She leaned over, careful not to touch anything damaged, and kissed him on the mouth.

"I can't even kiss you properly. My hugging capabilities are limited and as to the rest …"

"All that pales in comparison with the satisfaction of having you all mine for a few weeks." He did her the favor of looking worried. "There isn't much to feast on." She lifted the coverlet. "You're a scarecrow. How much weight have you lost?"

"I can hear my bones click when I walk. Seriously now, I have to work on the Carlyle case. We'll go full partnership on it. We might have to spend a few days in Tampa. Is that manageable for you?"

He was infuriating. "I wish you would stop doing that," she said.

"Doing what?"

Could he be unaware of the constant changes in temperature in their conversations? He could be tender and playful and within a minute be all business and efficiency, without missing a beat. His mood swings were so swift they gave her whiplash. Daisy tried to push away the doubt that gnawed in the back of her mind. They had gone through similar scenarios in the past, when he became restless and short-tempered after a few days of intimacy as if he couldn't sustain the closeness. This arrangement would last much longer than a few days. She could feel the tension creeping up already.

"Nothing. I was trying to imagine what it would be like to work together that close."

"I do it with Moira all the time. She hasn't shot me yet," Declan said.

You're not sleeping with Moira!

It took the medical professionals all morning to complete their visits and various recommendations. Daisy received a file of "dos and don'ts" covering what looked like every possible circumstance of Declan's care. Was she supposed to memorize that? Getting him into the car already broke half a dozen rules.

Declan said warm goodbyes to the people that took care of him for almost three weeks. He was drunk with the feeling of freedom reclaimed. It took years off his emaciated face. He looked like an excited kid about to board the bus for the trip to camp. He was too cute and Daisy felt so much older than him. A nanny. She mumbled a stream of curses. She should never have agreed to do this.

A squad of well-wishers waited at the loft. Moira and Roger Perkins, Robledo, Murphy and his wife, Vince Wallace, Bjorn-the-artist, Amy, and Leyla. For a couple of hours, Daisy could forget her chaperoning duties. Declan couldn't have any of the pizza or the booze but Moira made frothy smoothies that he sucked through a big straw, with deep sighs of gratitude.

"He's starting to fade," Daisy told Moira around nine.

Declan was stretched out on the sofa, drifting to sleep.

"I'll get the word out."

Robledo motioned for Daisy to follow him on the terrace, out of range from the spying bugs. "What time are you leaving tomorrow?"

"Late morning," Daisy said. "We'll have to stop often. He can't be stuck in the same position for long." She sighed. "I hope I can handle it."

"You have to keep him busy. He'll want to run and can barely walk." Robledo popped a cigarette out of a pack and lit it in one smooth move.

"Can I have one?" Daisy said.

"I didn't know you smoked."

"Only in extreme circumstances."

He gave her a light and grinned. "You better keep the pack."

"I'm busting my gut, I'm laughing so hard." She inhaled and stared at the city lights. "I'm scared, Steve. Declan and I have a bumpy history."

He leaned on the railing, blew smoke at the sky, and watched the little cloud hesitate and disappear. "Yeah, I know."

The cigarette felt funny between Daisy's fingers, like it belonged there and somehow didn't. "He told you about us?"

Robledo hummed. "'Should I stay or should I go.' 'With or without you.' 'Love me or leave me.' I wonder if April Easton ever took requests on that theme."

She took a deep drag of the cigarette and squashed it on the balustrade. "Declan said that?"

Robledo turned to face her. "He didn't. I'm adding the soundtrack. I haven't found one that fits his relationship with April."

"Try 'Strangers in the Night.'" She bit her lip and tasted blood. Tears welled. "I shouldn't say that. He's hurt." She thought he was hurt because April was taken from him before he could get tired of her. It was a despicable idea, but she couldn't erase it. What if April had been *the* one and was snatched away?

"You can't battle a dream, Daisy," Robledo said. "Be it love or something else. Last year, I went to Chichén Itzá. I'd always wanted to see the temple. I had that image in my mind. Big. And the place was impressive. But not as big as I'd made it. It's the dreamer's curse. Reality tends to disappoint." He smiled. "Declan keeps coming back to you. It can't be that bad."

She punched his shoulder, hard, and he staggered, playful. "You have a crush on him, Steve. I know that look on your face. I have one exactly like that. Declan has that thing. A gap, a crack. He hides it well but we can smell it, you and I. It triggers something in us that makes us want to fill the gap, fix the crack, slap Bondo on it. Our repairs hold for a while and then …" She held her hands up, palm to palm, and slowly pulled them apart. "And instead of saying 'what the fuck forget it,' we get our trowels from the shed and get to work again. Change the formulation a tad, less spackle, more glue." She shrugged. "He's not doing it on purpose."

Robledo reached for her and wrapped an arm around her shoulders, pulling her near. Her arm found his waist. It felt comfortable, warm, reassuring.

"We make a fine pair of suckers," he said.

His laughter was contagious.

THIRTY

"LET'S TAKE MKA DOWN," ROBLEDO SAID.

Frank Murphy tore himself away from the monthly budget report he was sweating over. "On what charges?"

"Criminal conspiracy."

"To do what?"

"Disturb the peace. I have three rabble-rousers in holding that confessed to having been paid by MKA to start a riot in front of Declan's office. They admitted to recruiting others and bringing baseball bats and Molotov cocktails. The gear didn't come into play because we broke up the gathering. I need a search warrant, boss. I want the photos from the safe at MKA."

"Then you'll go after Leary?"

"I haven't decided yet. You have a minute?"

A young cop in uniform was taping pictures to a whiteboard in one of the interview rooms as Robledo walked in with Murphy.

"Meet Lou Braxton," Robledo said. "I drafted him. I'm wary of seasoned veterans."

The cop saluted. It made Murphy smile. "At ease, kid. When did you graduate?"

"Six months ago, sir."

"Nice. What have you got?"

Braxton's ears turned bright red. "The Fort Bend County trial started on June 3. On June 1, ADA Leary's mother had an accident. She fell down the steps at her doctor's office. Two broken wrists. She needed surgery. A week later, during voir dire, Leary's son, Colin, came down with a severe case of food poisoning. Burning fever. He was hospitalized. June 11, there's an incident at the Fort Bend DA's office. A box containing copies of documents from the defense team is delivered to Leary's office. Nobody opens it and it's sent back to Chester Powys, the defense attorney. June 14, April Easton is murdered."

Murphy whistled. "They went at this guy with a cannon. How do we know it's MKA?"

"Well, because of …" Braxton started.

"Stop," Robledo said. "We don't know that it's MKA. Officially. We know they were digging dirt on Declan because Stanley Borelli was harassed by two individuals that tried to pump him for information. One of them gave his name as Dirksen Loomis. Declan noticed the other one spying on him and Amy Corrigan at April's funeral. He described the man's vehicle to me and we traced the registration to MKA. Then the social media and blog barrage against Declan started. Blogs penned by Dirksen Loomis. Ergo, we know MKA is involved in the smear campaign. Leyla Kareem set bait in a chat room and they jumped on it, with a blog authored by Loomis. Moira Perkins and Bjorn Gonzalez took pictures of the protesters in front of the building. We identified three professional troublemakers. They gave us MKA. That ties up the harassment campaign against Declan. Notice that I did not mention Adam Leary."

"Fishing with a juicy worm is still fishing, Steve," Murphy

said. "Bolster the search warrant or you'll be restricted to their computers."

"The blogs used confidential information from a police interview. At best it's a leak, at worst it's corruption. We'll be looking for related documents."

"Okay, do it," Murphy said.

Robledo hoisted himself on the table and lit a cigarette. Against the rules. Nobody stopped him. "What I want is the lowlifes that hired MKA. Declan thinks Buddy Pagett's mixed up in it. I'll make sure the warrant includes financial records. Then we follow the money."

"Pagett." Murphy sighed. "I wish he'd keel over from a coronary. It's whack-a-mole, Steve. Why would Pagett be interested in the trial of human traffickers?"

Robledo lit a fresh cigarette from the half-smoked butt of the previous one. "First we get MKA."

The search warrant wasn't an issue. It helped that the judge was a technophobe. "Online trash," he growled. "When people stopped writing letters, civilization started walking backwards."

Robledo handpicked officers from various HPD departments and kept the objective under wraps until they were at destination. The red Ford Explorer was parked in front of MKA. They would find the birds in the nest. One of the police cars went to the back, Robledo's unmarked parked in front, and a prowler stopped by the pizza place. Robledo knocked on the door. He was concerned about giving people inside time to destroy the documents in the safe.

The small, bald man who opened the door matched Declan's description from the funeral home. Another man sat in front of a computer.

"Police." Robledo flashed his badge. "We have a search warrant." He shoved the document in the guy's chest and pushed in. Three other officers were right behind him. One of them opened the back door to let in two more. With the two MKA employees, the place was sardine-packed.

Robledo contemplated the mess. "Haul off the computers." He turned to the two men who were frozen in open-mouthed surprise. "IDs please." They complied. "Keith Morell." That was the bald one. "What's your job?"

"Lead researcher."

"Ronald Gavin. You're the writer, Dirksen Loomis?"

Gavin nodded. "What's this all about?"

"Read the warrant. You engineered protests leading to public disturbance."

"This is a democracy. Free speech …"

"We can debate the First Amendment later." Robledo went to the file cabinets. He pulled on a pair of latex gloves. "We're boxing the contents of these." He grabbed the handle of a locked cabinet. "Please open it."

"I don't have the key," Morell said. "I have to call the boss."

"We sent a car to pick up the honorable Preston Macaulay Derring." Robledo acknowledged the pretentious name with a smirk. "He'll be here soon. The key, sir, or we take a crowbar to it."

The key appeared. The officers carried equipment away. Morell and Gavin stared glumly. Robledo paced the room. Time to *discover* the safe.

"Open it," Robledo said.

The two men exchanged a glance and Gavin shrugged. Morell went to the safe and turned the dial. He went to pull the handle.

"Step away from it," Robledo said. The contents were as Declan described, with the gun on top of the stack of banknotes, and the box of ammo. "Who does this belong to?"

"It's mine," Morell said. "I have a permit."

"Is the money yours too?" No answer. "Officer Braxton, count this in front of these two gentlemen and give them a receipt for the amount. Same for the gun and ammo." He waited for Braxton to empty the safe. The manila envelope was left inside. He opened it on one of the desks that were now computer-less. He held the picture that showed Jill's face. "Who is this woman?"

Morell didn't react. Gavin studied the patch of linoleum between his feet.

"I read your blogs, this woman is front and center. You're telling me you don't know her?" Keeping the pretense that the woman in the picture was April, not Jill.

Preston Macaulay Derring appeared at the door. "What's going on here?" The man was short, fat, and dripping sweat. He rolled on his heels in a ludicrous imitation of some fourth-rate fighter in a seedy boxing gym.

Robledo could smell him over the funk of the office. He wrinkled his nose. "We have a search warrant for these premises, as the officer that drove you here told you." He still held the picture. "How do you explain this?"

Derring's head went down in the folds of his neck, turtle-like. He was smart enough to keep his mouth shut.

"All right," Robledo said. "Braxton, you're in charge here. You go back in the car that brought you, Derring." He turned to a tall Black officer. "Mboya, you come with me and we haul these two. You're not under arrest, gentlemen, but we have questions. I would advise you to accept my invitation." The pictures went back in the envelope. Robledo kept it.

"How's Florida?" Robledo said.

"Hot," Declan said. "How's Houston?"

"Hotter. You're in Clearwater? How's it going?"

"We're getting organized. Daisy is out shopping, and I'm confined to the couch. I hope to have my daily fainting fit soon, so I can start moving around without being afraid to land on my head. Entertain me, Steve, please."

Robledo described the events at MKA and the interviews at HPD. Derring and company acknowledged that they took assignments from clients and that their field of expertise was information gathering and communications.

"They claim they were never involved in any act of violence," Robledo said. "I tend to believe them. They're these kids that whisper in your ear 'Donny says your dick is crooked' and then stand back to watch the fight."

"Makes you respect the true brawlers."

"They work a lot for Buddy Pagett. He paid for the online campaign and placard-waving at your place. Adam Leary was a Pagett assignment too. Just the pics, nothing else."

"They sure didn't kill April," Declan said.

Robledo said they didn't push Ms. Leary off the steps, or poison little Colin either. The incidents were news to Declan.

"I'm starting to sympathize with Adam Leary. Will you interview him?"

"Not looking forward to it," Robledo said. "I think I'll talk to him in private. I don't believe in kicking a man who's already down. We're going after Pagett. He's under surveillance."

"He's made of impervious material despite his blubbery appearance."

"Hard to nail, eh?"

"Buddy Pagett learned filing from J. Edgar, Steve. His 'Who's Who' is 'Who Will Pay for What.' He's been shoveling dirt for forty plus years and still smells of lilac. What more can I tell you?"

"How to do it." Silence stretched on the line. Robledo wondered if Declan had slipped into one of his freaky mental blanks.

"The bugs," Declan said. "They're still in my loft listening to Moira hammering on a computer keyboard. You could use them to stir the ant pile."

Robledo chuckled. "I'll visit with her. Tell her about MKA,

the money, and the pics in the safe. Hint at bank transfers leading to Pagett."

"Before you do that, hack Buddy's network and tap his phones. Don't involve any law enforcement, unless it's federal, or a remote Maine or Vermont Sheriff. Buddy's tendrils cover the geography. He's slippery as fuck, Steve."

"Sounds like fun."

Declan's grunt came through the phone loud and clear.

"What's the hitch?" Robledo said. "Pagett will have to go back to his client if we apply pressure, won't he? Or is he so loyal he'll take a fall for a sponsor?"

"Buddy knows how to cut fraying cords. He didn't survive that long by being loyal."

Silence again. Robledo wished he could read Declan's body language.

"Buddy's client employs killers," Declan said. "He thinks murder is justified. Buddy isn't capable of that kind of total warfare. Have you questioned Fisher?"

Robledo was taken aback. "He's a freak."

"Isn't it what we're dealing with? A psychopath who orders the murder of a woman to engineer a mistrial. Who wants to delay reckoning for two punks responsible for the death of sixteen people. This isn't about Buddy Pagett."

Robledo had friends and family south of the border. He was familiar with insane cruelty. The unbridled violence, the choking hold of the powerful cartels, the constant fear. Some of his relatives crawled across the border. Their stories were the stuff of nightmares.

"Go do some policing, Steve."

Robledo was left holding a dead phone. Declan had hung up. Damn, he wasn't done with what he had to tell. He called back. "Don't hang up. I have the DNA."

"Why didn't you say so. You have a match?"

Robledo could picture Declan on the edge of his seat. "Two different strands on top of April's."

Declan grumbled. "We've known for weeks there were two attackers."

Robledo had to smile. That impatience. "A man and a woman."

"What?"

"We got two hits on CODIS on the man. A rape murder in Detroit a year ago and another in L.A. that's three years old. Similar MO. No ID. The cases are still open. No match on the woman."

A beat. "I heard a couple, Saturday night," Declan said.

"I remember you telling us that. Maybe they were waiting for April to come home. It doesn't matter. You can't identify them. I contacted Detroit and L.A. It's a long shot."

"Okay, thanks, Steve. I hoped the lab would get us further."

"Me too. Take care, amigo."

"Before you go, who's in charge of the Tampa murder?"

"You want to say hello? Sal Fuentes, Hillsborough County Sheriff's Office. I'll text you the phone number. Don't go messing them up, now."

DECLAN CALLED HCSO and made an appointment with Sal Fuentes for the following morning at nine. Then he had a fainting spell. Relieved that this had come to pass, he prepared dinner for Daisy. He was still limited to soups and milkshakes.

While the pot simmered, he went through the Carlyle file again. This time, he read it from Ricardo Cassino's perspective. What would the big man do if confronted by the owners of Artemis? Dismiss, deny, fulminate, intimidate … none of that was productive. Could Cassino be brought to the negotiation table *before* being forced into a defensive position? Declan called Evan Hollander to test an idea. Hollander had experience dealing with Cassino.

Hollander said it would help if the girl was part of it. The girl. Daisy. Cassino expected the men he dealt with to sport sex candy on their arms. Accessorize. Like an elegant pocket square or expensive cufflinks.

Declan doubted he could sell it to Daisy as a strategic move. Things were getting rocky between them. It always turned that way after a while. Close proximity meant friction and Declan's dependence on her forced them to be much closer than they ever were.

The road trip to Tampa had been uneventful. They were both on their best behavior. Daisy by choice, Declan by necessity. They stopped twice underway at forgettable hotels. Both times they booked a double room. Declan didn't need help with dressing, undressing, or showering. If it hadn't been for the random spells he could have taken care of himself. He took his pills on schedule and exercised the rotator cuff. The other injuries didn't bother him, as long as he didn't test the limits. Daisy circled him, undressing in the bathroom, and kissing him on the cheek before bed. It was the ultimate tease. He caught himself watching her, hungering for a glance or errant brush of a hand, hip, or strand of hair.

The dynamic would change in Clearwater, or so he thought. They stopped by Rowena Dowling's office to get the penthouse keys. Declan dropped his bag in the same guest room as before expecting Daisy to join him, but she claimed the master suite. Then she said she needed to get supplies and he shouldn't wander far from the couch while she was away. Smoothies on the coffee table and a pot to piss in.

He was in the kitchen when she walked in.

"I've had my episode sitting on the couch, so we're good," he said without turning to look at her. "I made korma. From a jar in the pantry." He heard her drop her bag and kick off her shoes and smelled her perfume as she approached.

She wrapped both arms around his waist and put her head on the shoulder that wasn't damaged. "I'm sorry I was gone so long. I needed time by myself. I don't know how to manage this, Dek."

"You're doing fine. I wish I could kiss you and carry you to bed." He turned around, not dislodging the arms circling him. He leaned down to kiss her. "Even that is not the same."

"Restraints are supposed to enhance desire."

"I'm a stick in the mud, sweetie. Ropes, chains, and buckles, nah. Never cottoned to that dungeon stuff." He unfastened the sling holding his injured arm. "It's in my instructions, I have to let this loose from time to time."

"Shouldn't we talk before we rut?"

"Nope. We're overdue."

There was some pain, a solid dose of physical awkwardness, and a fair amount of irrepressible laughter, but they managed to get to that ledge on the rock face with a breathtaking view of the landscape, both short of breath from the journey, heat-flushed, and relieved that it turned out as well as they hoped it would.

"Unusual," Daisy said. "You have to bulk up. I like to have a little more to hold on to."

"You know what I miss most? I can't yawn. I want to yawn right now, and roll in a ball with you, but if I do, we'll hear a big crack and it will reset the clock for another six weeks."

She adjusted herself around him and pulled up the comforter.

"Thank you for agreeing to do this, DD. You knew it would be tough." He felt her breath against his neck and expected her to say something, but she just pressed closer. He sighed. "I'm hobbled. It doesn't change the way my mind works."

"You're a scatterbrain," she whispered, "but I can stay focused on you for a long time."

Declan chuckled. "That's the problem right there. I suffer from emotional attention deficit disorder."

She unwrapped herself, leaned on her elbows to look him straight in the eye. "You need constant mental stimulation. It's an addiction. What are you thinking, right now?"

"Uh, the crime scene DNA, Steve going after Buddy Pagett, tomorrow's appointment at the Sheriff's Office, the Carlyle file, Artemis …"

Daisy flopped on her back, moaning, with an arm slung over her eyes.

"What? You wanted to know."

"You didn't have to be so honest. Any consideration for me?"

Declan smiled. "I hate that you'll spend the night in the master bedroom."

Daisy rolled back against his side. "If you'd said that without having to be prompted."

"But I'm thinking of all that stuff at the same time."

"Stuff? If you weren't already mangled I could kick you. Women in love want to be top of mind, not bundled up with crime scenes and crumbling buildings. Stuff. It's all the same to you, isn't it?"

"No, it isn't. A little while ago, I was only thinking about you." He raised a hand to her face, pushed hair away from her eyes. "Right now, I am." He closed his eyes. "I don't know how to do this any other way."

He felt her getting up. The shower splashed. A faint herbal scent drifted from the bathroom. Soon she was back, wrapped in a robe, her hair wet and mussed.

"I'll fix you something to eat," she said. "You must be starving. I love korma." She was at the door when she called. "We have an appointment at the Sheriff's Office?"

Sal Fuentes of HCSO was on the phone and they waited in a noisy corridor. Fifteen minutes later, an officer came along and led them to an interview room.

"There's a coffee machine right outside the door."

Daisy got coffee for both of them. "Do you wish you hadn't left Houston?"

"I would be a bystander and a nervous wreck. I'm happy to be away. I know what to do about the Carlyle case. Let's talk about it after this."

"What are we doing here, Dek?"

"Tying loose ends."

The door opened and a woman walked in. She emitted energy and purpose. "Sal Fuentes. Why are you here, Mr. Shaw? You have a problem with us?"

She was refreshingly direct. "Not at all. DNA analysis for the Houston murder just came in. It matched two cases with a similar MO. I understand no DNA was recovered in Tampa."

Fuentes stared at him. "He used a condom and the victim was incapacitated too fast to fight her aggressor."

"No fibers, nothing?" Declan said.

"We recovered a long blond hair, black roots. The victim was a working girl. We haven't been able to identify the person the hair belonged to."

"DNA analysis of the hair?"

Fuentes frowned, irritated by his brusque questions. "Mr. Shaw, I am extending a courtesy to you."

"I apologize. I'm not here in any official capacity. My work with Houston PD is on an informal basis. April Easton faced two aggressors. One of them was female."

Fuentes leaned back in her chair. "Is there female DNA from the other cases you mentioned?"

"No. The match in CODIS is for the male only. That's why I'm interested in that blond hair. It might be irrelevant, of course."

Fuentes pondered. "It's worth checking. All right. You got yourself a DNA test, Shaw."

"It's not his test," Daisy said.

Fuentes turned to her. "Daisy Diamond. Related to Kevin Diamond?"

"He's my uncle. I'm the Shaw agency's correspondent in Florida. We're working a case together. Declan was in the area at the time of the crime because of that case."

"I see. You've been cleared, Mr. Shaw. Why are you still concerned with this?"

"Somebody tried to pin the Tampa murder on me."

Fuentes squared her shoulders. "Right. I'll get in touch with Houston PD."

"Steve Robledo's in charge."

Fuentes stood up. She held out her hand. "I'll tell him about the hair. Thank you for swinging by, Mr. Shaw, Ms. Diamond." She smiled. "A bullet grazes your head, you want to know who shot the gun."

"That is an apt analogy," Declan said.

On the way back to Clearwater Beach, Declan texted Robledo. Not that he didn't trust Fuentes.

"Now what?" Daisy said.

"We wrap up the Carlyle case. Ricardo Cassino is on his yacht in Miami Beach."

She kept her eyes on the road. "How do you know?"

"Evan Z. Hollander. Z for Zachary. Of Hollander Properties. He has his wily ways. *Bayamo* is a thirty-meter, two-decker beauty that accommodates eight lucky guests. Evan is trying to get us an audience with Cassino. Dust off your dancing shoes, darling. We're running a sweet con."

"I thought you'd never ask."

Declan sighed. "You might not like the role you have to play."

She placed both hands on the steering wheel, at ten and two o'clock. "Floozie?"

"Elegant ornament?"

"Thank you, dear."

They locked the penthouse and drove to Miami.

Declan spent the evening and most of the night on Daisy's laptop typing a report that described in excruciating detail the multiple acts of bribery and corruption that made building Artemis possible. Names, transaction amounts, transcripts of phone conversations, graphs and drawings, with footnotes and references. He then wrote a two-page management summary and printed four copies of the entire package. He emailed the file to Rowena Dowling, with Moira and Vince Wallace in blind copy.

It was his first day without a fainting spell. He texted Dr. Mulvaney. Daisy was asleep. He slipped in next to her and reached for her hand under the pillow. Her fingers closed on his. The reflex didn't mean anything but it made him feel good.

In the morning, Evan Hollander texted that they were on for 2:00 p.m. and that Cassino was "suitably curious."

"You should wear light colors more often," Daisy said. "It's a cotton linen mix, it won't look like you slept in the suit by the time we get to the yacht club."

Declan would have gone to the meeting with Ricardo Cassino in his usual black jeans and a t-shirt, but Daisy insisted he should look the part. What part? Conman, wiseguy? She used one of her silk scarves for the arm sling.

"Nice contrast," he said. "They'll think I have a gun or a knife hidden in there. What about a panama?"

"You said Cassino was used to a certain kind of business meeting. We have to ride the cliché all the way. I'm the bling, you're the smooth operator in a tropical suit. You're going to hit him hard; you want him in familiar territory before you strike. I'll dress for the occasion, harmonize with you."

And harmonize she did, in a pale green clingy wraparound dress that drew the eye where it mattered and high-heeled gold sandals that gave an extra lift to her long legs. The look went well with her BMW convertible.

The *Bayamo* was a sight to behold. Bigger boats were tied up at the marina but few had sleeker lines or glossier brass. An athletic young man in a blinding white t-shirt and blue cargo shorts leaned on the railing by the gangway.

"Can I help you?"

"We have an appointment with Mr. Cassino. Declan Shaw and Daisy Diamond." It sounded like a tap-dancing duet.

They were told to wait dockside. The young man came back with a big fellow. A muscular security type in yellow shorts and a pink fishing shirt. The color clash hurt the eyes.

"Come on up," the bodyguard said. "Barefoot on deck. Leave your shoes here."

Declan kicked off his slip-ons and Daisy unstrapped her sandals. She handed the footwear to the guy who held the delicate shoes in a bear-sized paw.

"I need to check you," he rumbled. He didn't have much to check on Daisy. He peeked at her clutch that held her phone, keys, and lipstick. He patted down Declan, had a quick look at the folder with the documents, and pointed at the arm sling. "Can you remove that?"

Ricardo Cassino was on the top deck, forward. Two sun-tanned women in skimpy thong bikinis and a middle-aged bearded fellow in shorts were with him. The man with the beard stood next to a bar mixing drinks, the women were spread out on lounge chairs. Cassino was late sixties and well-preserved, hawk-faced, and gifted with abundant white hair. Tufts emerged from his shirt. His outfit was more subdued than that of his bodyguard. He sported dark sunglasses that he removed to welcome his visitors. Old Peppe might have been a quasi-gangster but this man was sophisticated. Which didn't mean he couldn't dispose of inconveniences in cold blood.

"Mr. Shaw, Ms. Diamond. Evan was mysterious on the phone. I had to know more." He had a pleasant, deep voice, devoid of any regional accent. Peppe sent him to the proper schools. How young Ricardo navigated the hallowed halls of the elite was anybody's guess. Declan doubted he was bullied. "Please have a seat. Bruno makes excellent cocktails. What can I offer you? Ms. Diamond?"

"I'll have some champagne."

"Water for me," Declan said.

"Really? That is so sad."

"Doctor's orders."

Cassino examined him, head tilted to the side. "That must have been a serious accident. I never had my mouth wired. It must be terribly uncomfortable."

"Some people do it voluntarily, for weight loss."

"Hear that, Cindy?" Cassino addressed the curvy blonde on the nearest chair. "Something to try, eh?"

Cindy, languidly, shot him the finger. "I'll have another Mai Tai, Bruno. Fuck the calories." She sounded Chicago.

"Well said, baby. What did you want to see me about, Mr. Shaw?"

Declan extracted the two-page summary from the folder and handed it to Cassino. He could feel the eyes of the bodyguard on the back of his head. "This will tell you everything faster than I can explain."

Cassino took reading glasses from his shirt pocket and leaned back to examine the documents. The expression on his face was benign. A patient and condescending mien.

The attitude soon hardened. Cassino looked at Declan over the glasses but said nothing. He read to the end. He put the pages down on a small table and used a coaster as a paperweight. He did all this slowly.

"Bruno, girls, leave us alone. You too, Ray."

"You sure?" The bodyguard had moved closer to Declan's chair.

"Nobody on this deck."

Cassino waited for his familiars to disappear down the stairs. "What's this about, Shaw? People have tried to shake me down before. No amount of wiring could hold *their* bones together."

Declan smiled. This was more like it. He handed the full report to Cassino. "I have a ton of supporting documents. I didn't bring them but I'll get them to you if my proposal interests you. Artemis is a big problem. There's a section in the file about how much it would cost to stabilize and reinforce it. Bank-breaking expensive and no guarantee it would work."

Cassino opened a cigar case and pushed it toward Declan who declined. "What's the proposal? Dynamite?"

"Before you do that, it would be smart to refund the owners."

"You know how much that'd cost?"

"Eighty million, thereabout. A lawsuit—multiple suits—will set you back way more. Not to mention agencies smelling fraud."

"I knew it was a shakedown." Cassino leaned so far forward, the smoldering tip of his cigar was a couple of inches from Declan's eyes. "You, presumptuous Irish punk. I'll have you thrown overboard, watch you swim with a clipped wing."

"It's not just the lawsuits," Declan said, unmoved. "It's your contracts in the Caribbean, the developments on the West Coast, your reputation as a reliable builder, your position in the business community." He had a sip of water and noticed Daisy's champagne flute was empty. He went to the bar to get her a refill. The broken fingers made the maneuver dicey but he didn't spill a drop.

"Scotch on ice for me," Cassino said.

Declan set the drink on the table, on a coaster. "I'm working with a lawyer who represents the Artemis owners. She doesn't want to go to court. It would take forever and nobody would see a cent."

"And even if I won, I would still be cut at the knees." Cassino raised his glass in salute.

"Keep it simple," Declan said. "Buy back the condos. The owners will praise your decisiveness and hands-on approach. Leadership and all that. Going the extra mile. Your PR team can supply appropriate platitudes."

Cassino took the full report and leafed through it. He read a paragraph here and there.

Declan could feel Daisy by his side, attentive. He should

find out what perfume she wore and get her a bottle. It complemented the salty sea breeze.

"All right, I'm convinced. I don't have a choice, do I? What about the bastards that lined their pockets?"

"You have something on them, they have something on you," Declan said. "Call it a standoff or a partnership. You're bigger than they are. They'll kiss the ring. You never know when you might need them."

Cassino puffed on his cigar. "Never did business with the Irish before. Lucky me. Tell you what, I'll throw in their moving expenses. Tell these suckers they have a gold-plated deal."

"I'll talk to the lawyer. I believe it would work better if you contacted the owners. It would make an impression. And you can frame the situation the way you like."

The reading glasses went back in the pocket. Cassino looked Declan hard in the eye. "They have no fucking idea that pile is kaput, do they? You have some balls, boy. Apologies, Ms. Diamond." He tapped the report with his cigar, ashes fell on it and he wiped them off, leaving gray streaks. "How much do you want for this?"

"It's yours. I've been paid already."

Cassino sneered. "People who refuse money. Downright icky."

Declan stood up. "I'll never be rich." He offered his hand to Daisy who took it daintily. "I look at your boat, Mr. Cassino, and I dream a little." He contemplated the elegant lines, the polished deck, the gleaming railing. "That's it. Done dreaming."

"Just curious, who beat you up?"

"A deranged individual."

"Don't you want a piece of paper, something that says I agree to this?" Cassino said.

"A handshake is enough."

Cassino pressed too hard on the mangled hand. Declan blinked. He could let the man have that small victory.

"I'll walk down with you. You know how my father would have handled this?"

"Simpler times," Declan said. "Less long-range technology." He winked at Cassino who had the good grace to smile.

Daisy was putting her sandals back on, leaning on Declan, when Cassino spoke. "I could use you, Irish."

"Shaw Investigations. We're in the book. Give us a call."

"I know you're not supposed to drink on the meds, but this deserves a shot of something strong." Daisy hadn't bothered with a scarf and her hair flew every which way. She was driving too fast.

"Slow down, we're not running from the law. You can make me a Bloody Mary. I'll write it down as tomato soup."

Declan called Rowena from the car. She was in charge now. The Carlyle case was closed. She reminded him to send his invoice and hinted there would be a bonus.

"Light me a cigarette, will you?" Daisy said. "There's a pack in the glove box."

Declan knew she smoked when she needed a prop or a pause in the conversation.

"What I want to know," she said after she had let enough time lapse, "is what we're going to do now."

"My creaky rehab requires three more weeks of nanny support."

"And after that?"

"What about the boat and these islands you keep tempting me with? Being on that yacht tickled my interest."

THIRTY-TWO

COLORADO WASN'T WHAT WADE BENNING hoped for and Elida hadn't welcomed him with the warmth he expected. Her activities kept her busy. Horse riding in the early hours of the morning, golf in the afternoon. He could have accompanied her. She suggested it a couple of times, but he demurred, and she gave up asking. He was preoccupied. His involvement in the trial was over but it wasn't the end of the Houston troubles. Listening to Buddy Pagett's plan to eliminate Shaw had been a mistake. Pagett must have sucked other eager clients into the scheme, no doubt, but when it came to fixing what went wrong, Pagett came to him.

Because Benning was good at remediation, and because the Shaw mishap was tied to that other blunder, the murder of the Easton woman.

Pagett believed he had leverage on Benning. He didn't. There were no witnesses to their conversations and no recordings. The payments had gone through so many intermediaries they couldn't be traced. If an investigation ever took place, it would be Pagett's word against Benning's. Underestimating the crooked PI was risky, however. Pagett had enough dirt in his files on a lot of people to negotiate a deal. Where would that leave Benning? Even more concerning was Gonzago's reaction. The man had radical ways to deal with anything that looked remotely messy.

If Gonzago was in Benning's shoes, what would he do?

Pagett's cop acolyte, Fisher, had to go. He would implicate Pagett in the attempt against Shaw. Then Pagett had to be taken care of. It was long overdue. There was too much festering history between them.

Shaw was a survivor and Benning was wary of survivors. They came back from the netherworld with dangerous knowledge about the nature of life. They had glimpsed the other side and emerged with traces of the unknowable attached to them. He would stay away from Shaw. He was crippled anyway.

Wade Benning felt better now that he had made a decision. The rest was operational. Pull those levers. The kind of thing he had done all his life.

Before placing the calls, he checked his computer. He still looked at the feed from the bugs that recorded the activity, or lack thereof, in Shaw's office.

The bugs had told Benning Pagett's plan misfired. He had listened to a teary Moira Perkins informing friends that Shaw was in the hospital, in critical condition. Then Shaw regained consciousness. Daisy Diamond, the Miami PI, moved in. Benning liked her voice. He knew what she looked like, from her website. A knockout blonde. Shaw knew how to pick them. She was in love with the man, no doubt about it. There was heartfelt dialogue between Moira and Daisy. They worried about Shaw. Affection poured. Benning was jealous. Would anybody talk like that about him if his life was on the line?

There was very little data. Still, it was intoxicating. Benning was addicted to the recordings. Soothed by the soft sound of the women's voices. He vicariously enjoyed the party Shaw's friends organized to welcome him home from the hospital. He couldn't catch the conversations, it was too noisy. Shaw and Daisy left the day after the party. To Florida. Not much happened after that.

There was a new file on the server. Fresh from early this morning.

The Latino cop, Steve Robledo, had come to see Moira. He was close to Shaw. They worked together on the Easton case and kept at it even with Shaw in the hospital.

Benning clutched his headphones.

MKA. Pagett's contractors. The internet bloggers that went after Shaw. The cops raided their office. They found pictures in a safe. Pictures of Adam Leary with his lover. April Easton's sister. The Bonnie Parker picture. Adam Leary was in it. He was the ADA involved in a notorious case in Fort Bend County that ended in a mistrial. Leary was blackmailed.

Shaw and Robledo knew everything.

Benning reached for his phone.

It wasn't the end of the recording. He heard Robledo say: "Fisher's lawyer told us his client was ready to make a deal. He'll give us Buddy Pagett for the attempt on Declan's life. That's conspiracy to commit murder. We'll put the screws on Pagett. We'll know who gave him the Leary assignment. April's killers."

Benning dialed the number he knew too well.

THIRTY-THREE

ROBLEDO WAS IN AN UPTOWN parking lot, in his car, focused on the entrance of Marquesas, a seafood restaurant. He had been there for almost two hours. He paced his smoking because he didn't want to run out. The passenger side door opened and he jumped.

"Boss, what are you doing here?"

Frank Murphy lowered himself in the passenger seat of the old Ford. "Tired of waiting at the office. What's new?"

"Nothing. Where's your car?"

"A driver dropped me. Who do you have here?"

"Lou Braxton is in the restaurant. Gomatam and Mboya are parked in front of the furniture store, to the right. We have a couple of cruisers patrolling in the area. We can use them if the tracking gets complicated." He shrugged. "So far, Pagett's been easy. Home to work, work to lunch, lunch to work, work to home, home to dinner, dinner to home. The guy eats out twice a day, no wonder he's the size of a hippo. He's more predictable than a Greyhound bus."

"What matters is who he eats with," Murphy said.

"In the past two days, he's broken bread with three City Council members, two attorneys, and the chairman of the Galveston Chamber of Commerce. None of these people behaved as if they had a fire under their ass. It's a big nada."

Robledo had gone to Declan's office as planned and told Moira of the raid on MKA. He blabbed about the pictures from the safe, Adam Leary, and the blackmail scheme, April's murder, and added that the investigation focused on MKA's clients. Buddy Pagett chief among them. He even added that Fisher was ready to roll on Pagett. He was so loose-mouthed it was a firing offense.

Pagett had been under surveillance before Robledo went to see Moira. The MKA sidekicks were muzzled by a plea deal. Fisher was due at HPD HQ later that afternoon for an in-depth interview that Murphy planned to attend.

Robledo expected Pagett to at least give a few phone calls, but there had been none. Pagett carried out his regular activities as if he wasn't about to step on a mine.

"I don't get it," Robledo said. "Even if Pagett suspects a trap, he should at least appear worried. We should bring him in and work him over."

"Leyla said the bugs were live?" Murphy asked.

"We checked." Robledo was annoyed. Why was Murphy hassling him?

"MKA was listening and we dismantled MKA. The bugs are transmitting into the void," Murphy said.

Robledo groaned. "Leyla Kareem didn't find recordings on MKA's computers. They didn't bug Declan's office and truck."

"You assume Pagett paid somebody else to surveil Declan," Murphy said.

"Obviously."

Murphy slapped both hands on his knees. "We're watching the great nothing. You know why Pagett isn't nervous? Because he has no fucking idea Declan was bugged. He doesn't know we raided MKA. As far as he's concerned, Fisher is his biggest problem and until last night Fisher was mute."

Robledo was struck dumb. "Pagett has sources at HPD."

"Bogs Sorensen and Fisher are locked up. Internal Affairs is on the hunt. Who do you think is talking to the outside right now? Damn, Steve, cops aren't even saying hi to each other in the elevator."

Robledo cursed under his breath. "If Pagett didn't bug Declan's office, who the hell did?"

"We're in the fucking dark. Recall the team. We'll bring Pagett in and try to shake something other than suet out of that tub of lard."

Robledo shook a cigarette out of the pack. The last one. He looked up. "There he is."

Pagett appeared at the restaurant's front door. They watched the fat man in the light blue suit with matching bolo tie and oversized belt buckle hand his ticket to a scrawny kid in shiny black pants.

"He's still driving that piss yellow 1970 Chevelle?" Murphy said.

"I've never tailed an easier mark," Robledo said. "It makes me queasy, like I know I'm being conned and I don't know how. You still want me to call it off?"

"We gonna bring him in, right? Why not now? He's fed and boozed. I love to rain on a hog's parade." Murphy pushed the door open. "You coming?"

Robledo dropped his cigarette, grabbed the mike, and gave the call. "Let's go get him."

The yellow Chevelle came from the left and cut in front of Murphy and Robledo, forcing them to stop and partially blocking their view of Pagett who now had a white Stetson glued to his head.

Two muffled shots popped from the right and a scream of

pain rang from the front of the restaurant. Murphy ran left of the yellow car, Robledo went right. He drew his gun.

"Get the shooter," Murphy screamed.

Officer Lou Braxton was in the swinging door of the restaurant. He raised his gun. Another shot made a swishing sound and Braxton collapsed on the pavement. It happened in Robledo's peripheral vision. He spotted the shooter. A tall, dark-haired man dressed in black. He was fast. Before Robledo could get a bead on him, he had turned the corner of the restaurant and was running across the parking lot. It was midday traffic with shoppers, restaurant-goers, office workers on their lunch break. Robledo yelled. "Police, get down!"

Cops ran between the vehicles. Robledo saw the tall lanky frame of Mboya to his right, the smaller shape of Sally Gomatam to his left. They were both in uniform and screaming the same warning. "Get down. Get down." Coming from them, it made a bigger impression.

The shooter zigzagged between cars and SUVs. A blond woman appeared in front of Robledo. The gun she held looked enormous. He fell to the ground between two cars as a shot, not suppressed, tore through his eardrums. He let off a flurry of rounds in the woman's direction before his body reacted to being hit.

He couldn't move for what seemed like the longest time but was, maybe, a couple of seconds. He rolled onto his knees. His right side was sticky with blood. He felt sick.

"Don't move."

He looked up at Mboya, an officer he selected for the case because he was new to HPD and a recent Academy graduate, like Braxton.

Mboya kneeled by his side, looked at the wound. "Medical support is on the way. It looks like it grazed the ribs. You'll be okay, I think. But Lou was hit. And the guy got Pagett."

"The woman?" Robledo mumbled.

"Oh, you plugged her good. Sally downed the guy. Fireworks, sir."

Buddy Pagett was in surgery with two slugs in his ample gut. Robledo needed stitches, a blood transfusion, and antibiotics. Lou Braxton took one close to the heart and was touch and go for a while. The shooters, male and female, were at the morgue.

"Fucking rad," Sally Gomatam said, and got stares from everybody in the squad room. She clamped her mouth shut. She had transferred from Precinct 5 three days ago. Many officers didn't know her name. All they knew was that she was a damn good shot.

"How do you want to handle this, Steve?" Murphy said.

His supervisor's tone was a little too sweet for Robledo's taste. He hurt, head swimming from the medication. "We protect Buddy Pagett with everything we got. He's our most valuable resource and somebody else's worst nightmare. If we have to lock him up in a bunker, we do it."

"What about the shooters?" Mboya said.

"DNA on fast track. My hunch is that we got April Easton's killers." Rumbles in the room. "And some. The Sheriff's Office in Tampa has a blond hair from their case. Buddy Pagett knows who hired these fuckers. We guard Pagett like the Holy Grail, folks."

Robledo thought that was it and he could go lie down and sleep.

Then the news came that Fisher had been stabbed during the short ride from the Joint Processing Center to HPD HQ. He was dead before the ambulance arrived. His attacker was a kid high on speed. Nobody knew how he got the dope or the blade.

"I appreciate the irony, Steve," Declan said, on the phone. "I'm sure Pagett does too. Even in his wildest dreams, I doubt he pictured himself under police protection."

"It's never going the way we want it to go."

"Ain't that a fact. How are you?"

"Tight. Stiff," Robledo said. "How's your love life?"

"Careful now, lover boy."

"Are you getting hitched? Because I might have something to say about that. You being removed from the dating pool and such."

"That's funny," Declan said. "Are you bound ankle and foot to HPD, Steve?"

"Because your lifestyle is so much better? Crushed and pounded? You are in a more life-threatening quadrant than me, amigo. I'll hang on to the badge for now, if you don't mind."

"Suit yourself. Freedom. Just saying. You want to know where I am right now, what I see from my window?"

"Go to hell."

THIRTY-FOUR

DECLAN TRAVELED BACK TO HOUSTON to have the jaw restraints removed. This time, he flew. He hadn't had any episode since before the meeting with Ricardo Cassino, and Dr. Mulvaney had given him permission.

He was on time to witness the aftermath of Buddy Pagett's disintegration.

The investigators stuck to the web of corruption surrounding the April Easton murder case. Other avenues of research could have waylaid them. Pagett had been involved in so many scandals over the past fifty years that following those threads would have mired the investigators in a labyrinth of mythical proportions. The sheer complexity of Pagett's dealings protected him and his clients. Declan had to tip his nonexistent hat to his rival's business acumen. Pagett's clients did what submarines were designed to do. They sealed the breached compartments and kept beneath the surface.

Wade Benning drowned.

Elida came back from her afternoon golf outing, a little later than usual because one of her girlfriends had a birthday party at the clubhouse. The gardener told her he saw her husband by the lake talking to another man. The man carried fishing poles. When the gardener rounded the corner of the house on his riding lawnmower, both men were gone. By dinner time, Elida was concerned. She went down to the lake and checked the boathouse. Their small bass boat was gone and two fishing pole slots were empty. Benning used to be an avid angler, going out daily at the crack of dawn. He still took the boat out from time to time, more to give it a good run than to fish. Elida was glad he went for a spin. He had been cooped up in the house, glued to his computer, since he came up from Houston. It wasn't healthy.

By 8:30 p.m. Elida was worried. Benning knew the lake but the sun was setting. At 9:00 p.m. she called the police.

The boat was found the next morning by a kayaker. The keys were in the ignition, there was gas in the tank, and the two fishing poles were in the boat. There was no trace of Wade Benning.

"I went up there," Robledo said. "Grand Lake. Beautiful area. The local cops were still looking for him. I talked to the wife, the housekeeper, the gardener. No trace of the man Benning talked to."

"A convenient disappearance," Declan said.

They were at a little café across from HPD Headquarters. A sulking waiter had brought two steaming hot espressos. He glared at Robledo puffing on his cigarette and rolled his eyes at Declan who had lit a cheroot. Two minutes later, the guy produced an ashtray that he ceremoniously centered on the bistro table.

"That's what I thought initially," Robledo said, "but the body was found three days ago. Drowning. No bruises. It was done skillfully."

"Somebody's cleaning house. South of the border?"

"Whoever had an interest in the Fort Bend trial. The financial guys are looking at Benning's business dealings. He had ties with firms in Latin America. Benning's wife has relatives in Mexico. I believe he got sucked in too deep."

"The Fort Bend DA will retry the case," Declan said. "He'll get a conviction this time. I can't wrap my head around it. All they managed to get out of this misery is a delay. And for two clueless kids. Talk about going overboard. Literally."

"The two kids are second or third cousins of a big Sinaloa cartel honcho," Robledo said. "No connection with Elida Benning. It's that old Mob thing. Trading favors."

"It's Texas, the kids are doomed."

"Do you sometimes feel we're just going through the motions?" Robledo said.

"That's what I don't like about police work." Declan's voice sounded much better without the wires and his nose was back to normal. The rotator cuff was still sluggish but he was working on it. "The repetitive nature of crime. Catch a punk, oh, wait, there's this other one and another. Every single one of them doing the same dumb thing with little variation. It's exhausting and you never see the end of it. Crime never takes a breather. I tackle it piecemeal. Find this person. Retrieve this object. In the big hoopla, my contribution is small, but it matters a lot to the people I work for. I'm incremental. Sometimes I hit a big one." He grinned. "When I hit a big one, it's always accidental."

"It would frustrate me." Robledo crumpled his cigarette pack. Gone. No more.

Declan handed him his cigar case. "Try one."

Robledo played with the cigarillo then leaned over for the offered light. He took an experimental drag. "I could get used to these."

"You can't chain-smoke them." Declan had a sip of coffee. His jaw felt weird. "So many people got hurt. We know who did it and it doesn't make anything right."

Robledo puffed too fast and Declan told him to slow down.

"Adam Leary resigned," Robledo said. "His wife has family in

New Mexico. They'll try to make it there. I'm glad we didn't drag him into this publicly. Not condoning what he did but he was under a ton of pressure. I'm not sure what I would have done."

"You talked to him," Declan said.

"It was the most awkward conversation. I felt like I knew this guy's life better than he did. He threw me for a loop, though, when he said he took the Bonnie Parker picture from April's apartment."

"Makes you wonder what would have happened if he hadn't. What did you tell the Eastons?"

Robledo ran a hand through his hair. He had stopped using the gel and it took a couple of years off him. "Murphy handled it. Told them it was a cartel hit and that April was mistaken for another woman. The parents took it as coldly as everything else. Jill must suspect she was the intended target. I can't imagine what she's going through. She wasn't stable to begin with. I wouldn't be surprised if Sam Koenig cornered me one day to give me the third degree."

"I saw MKA got off with a fine," Declan said. "You know they'll start again, somewhere else, under another name. There's a market for the filth they peddle."

"Pagett is going out of business." Robledo chuckled. "One less competitor for you."

"His accounts can never be fumigated to my satisfaction."

"What are you on now?"

"August is always sluggish. It's hot and hurricanes loom. Daisy asked me to help with her cases, and I'm flying back to Miami at the end of the week."

The relationship with Daisy was far from perfect. When tension reached a peak and they started barking at each other, one of them went for a drive. Some part of an investigation always required a field trip. It might forever be like that between them, passion and irritation in equal measure. They didn't seem designed for smooth sailing on an even keel.

"I have to ask you for a favor," Declan said.

"Ask away."

"I met a cop in New Orleans, twenty years ago. He impressed me."

"Some kind of mentor?" Robledo smiled. "An early days Frank Murphy?"

"More a guy I couldn't bullshit. He could have set me on a dark trajectory but he let me go. He said he would like to see me again sometime. I'm thinking of paying him a visit but I have no idea where he might be, or if he's even still alive."

"What prompted that? The fact you almost croaked?"

"Spending time with Stan Borelli. It brought back memories. Thompson Elijah Cross. He was a detective with NOPD. His partner's name was Alvin Compton. Compton was older, he must be retired by now. Cross might still be on active duty."

"I'll look him up."

"You didn't like me much when we first met," Declan said.

"What makes you think I like you more now?" Robledo grinned. "I didn't have a high opinion of private investigators and I thought your reputation was overblown. Like, okay, he got a few lucky breaks and he's riding on them."

"All hat, no cattle," Declan said.

Robledo nodded. "I changed my mind. I still believe you should switch your business cards. From Shaw Investigations to Shaw Private Dick. In all caps. So people aren't misled." He laughed and swallowed his espresso sideways.

"Serves you right," Declan said.

Thompson Cross had joined an anti-terrorism unit and recently retired from the FBI. He and his wife lived in Islamorada and he helped part-time at the Monroe County Sheriff's office. Robledo texted his address and phone number.

"What about going to the Keys for a couple of days?" Declan

had been back in Miami for a week and just completed a background check for one of Daisy's clients. It had been online research and phone interviews and he was getting antsy.

"It's blistering hot down there," Daisy said, "and teeming with sun-crazed tourists. Can we go to Canada instead?"

"There's somebody in Islamorada I want to see."

Daisy begged him to wait. The crowds would be smaller once school started, and a storm churned in the Atlantic.

The hurricane took a turn to the left and made landfall near the Texas-Mexico border. Another one was on the way and Daisy suggested they go the week before Labor Day and the holiday onslaught.

"We could look at boats," she said, packing their gear. "I haven't given up on a charter to the islands. With the Carlyle fee, remember?"

Declan had to be back in Houston in September. He had the distinct feeling they missed a window of opportunity somehow.

The BMW was loaded and the weather was perfect. Daisy drove. Soon, she left Highway 1 and wandered down rough and dusty trails.

"You have a treasure buried in the swamps somewhere that you want to retrieve?"

"I'm due for a little practice," she said.

If the practice involved testing the shock absorbers of her convertible, she had chosen the right place. It rained overnight and the potholes were full to capacity. When they were away from any civilized and less civilized habitations, she stopped.

"There's a duffel bag in the trunk." Daisy reached behind her seat and traded her sandals for a pair of scuffed sneakers.

Declan lifted the bag. Objects shifted inside. He had a fair idea what they were. "I don't like guns, DD."

"Sometimes they're needed and I haven't shot at anything in a while. Gotta stay limber. Bring the bag over here."

She walked around a magnificent tree bursting with red

flowers and unzipped the duffel. It contained two handguns, ammo, and a plastic bag full of empty cans.

"I don't use glass bottles. They make a mess that I can't pick up."

Litter-conscious, good for her. Declan didn't know if he should scold her. He found a fallen trunk to sit on—after checking that he wasn't encroaching on some nasty critter's territory—and watched her set up. Soda cans at different distances and heights, standing or sideways. She had designed a custom firing range and went through the motions with an ease born from habit.

"You come here often?" He lit a cigarillo.

"Once a month, on average. With the Houston trip and you around, I haven't been able to practice since June."

"There are ranges."

"When I go to a range, there's always a dozen guys watching me and hitting on me. I have to fight off so many groping hands, it's like I fell in an octopus nest."

Declan could see why. She was appetizing in her ragged t-shirt, cotton shorts, white sneakers, and a red bandana to keep hair and sweat out of her eyes.

She selected a Glock 9mm and assumed a classical two-hand stance. She knocked off all but one of the soda cans. She reset the targets and repeated the routine with a revolver. She missed twice this time and cursed.

"I'm damn rusty."

"You want me to throw a few in the air, Calamity Jane?" Declan said.

She looked dubious. "I don't know if I can hit that."

"Try. I'll throw them high in front of you. Wait till they reach full height."

She didn't get anything on the first three throws, then got used to the trajectories and whooped in joy when she hit two cans in a row.

"Maybe I should get one of these machines like they use for

tennis balls. What about you?" Her smile was challenging. She was flushed and excited. And exciting. Declan could think of more interesting ways to spend the time than pop at cans.

"I told you. I don't like guns."

She grinned. "You're a PI and you're nervous about guns, what kind of shit is that?" She nudged him with the barrel of the revolver. "Come on, don't be chicken. I'll load them for you. Which one do you want? The Glock is easy. Very little recoil."

Declan sighed. No way out. It was a game for her. A way to say, look at me, slugger, see what I can do. A sexual taunt. "All right, set the cans."

She righted one can, the closest one, and handed him the 9mm. "Now you don't have to close one eye. Just ..."

Boom. The can flew.

"Wow, that's good." She ran to set up more cans.

Declan was tempted to knock them off as she put them down but his better angel prevailed. And you never knew. The can could hit her, a splinter could nick her. He waited with the gun pointing down till she was back a safe distance behind him. He knocked the cans down in quick succession, the smell of gunpowder thick in the air. The 9mm was empty. He took the revolver and loaded it.

"Throw a can up, high and forward."

He hit the thing three times before it touched the ground and lodged a bullet in it when it rebounded.

"Jesus! And you don't like guns?" Her eyes were wide, her mouth open.

"I never said I didn't know how to use them. Let's go, DD." He made sure the guns were empty, picked up the casings, and stashed everything in the duffel. Daisy went around in silence, gathering the mangled cans.

Declan slid behind the wheel and they went back to the main road. When they left the mainland and were on the island stretch, Daisy spoke again.

"Is it because you were shot?" she said.

"No."

"Somebody you know was shot."

"Can we get off the subject? I don't want to talk about it."

She rested a hand on his leg, gave it a light squeeze. "You can trust me, you know."

He smiled. "I know. You have the hotel address handy?"

An hour later, they were checked in with the guns in the safe. Declan called the sheriff's office and was told that Cross wasn't on duty till the next morning. He didn't want to wait that long. Daisy was content poolside with an ice-packed cocktail and a book. She had been very quiet and subdued since the firing range. Declan kissed her sunscreen-coated nose and said he'd be back before dinner.

The house was a two-story white villa, oceanside, at the end of a crushed shell driveway that set it well back from the road. Palm trees and mimosas further screened it from traffic sight and noise. Declan stopped to let two tail-wagging iguanas cross in front of him. A white pickup truck and a blue Toyota were parked under an awning. The family was at home. Cane chairs were clustered on the patio. A red bougainvillea climbed the façade. The main entrance was up a staircase. Declan glanced at the sandy backyard. A small pool with lounge chairs, the sea beyond it, and a dock jutting out. A small cabin cruiser bobbed by the dock.

Declan rang the bell. He was in jeans with a short-sleeved white shirt, canvas shoes, no hat. His aviator sunglasses were on top of his head. He stood at a reassuring distance from the door.

A tall, good-looking woman in a sundress appeared behind the door. She opened a crack.

"Yes?"

"Good afternoon. I was hoping to find Mr. Cross at home."

"Excuse me, who are you?"

The Louisiana flavor of her speech was familiar and brought back memories. Some of them pleasant.

Declan pulled out his wallet and gave her his PI license. "Declan Shaw. I met Mr. Cross many years ago in New Orleans. He was Detective Cross then and I was a kid. He told me to stay out of trouble."

"Have you?"

He smiled. "Mostly."

"How did you get this address, Mr. Shaw?"

"A friend in Houston PD gave it to me."

"I see. Do you carry a gun?"

Declan patted his jeans pockets and lifted his untucked shirt. She stared and he dropped the shirt. "Sorry. I lost a lot of weight recently."

She gave him his license back. "Wait here." She closed the door and he heard the lock click. She was soon back with a basket and a small cooler that she gave him to carry. They went down the stairs.

"Thom is on the boat," she said. "Tinkering with the engine. Again. You know what they say about boats, Mr. Shaw?"

"About happiness and grief? And the length of each?"

"Something like that. I'm Kayla."

"Pleased to meet you."

Their steps rattled on the dock and a head appeared from the depths of the boat. Declan recognized Thompson Cross immediately. The hair was sprinkled with white and he wore bifocals, but he was the same tall, athletic man he met so long ago. He doubted Cross would recognize him but he was mistaken.

"I'll be damned. Didn't expect you, kid." Cross grabbed a rag to wipe his hands. "You got a busy track record. Come on board."

"You looked me up?"

"I check on you regularly. To make sure I haven't let a

dangerous sociopath loose on the unsuspecting world. What did you bring, love?"

"Sandwiches and cold beer. You boys dig in." Kayla Cross handed over the basket and was on her way back to the house. No fuss.

"You wrapped her around your little finger, eh? No surprise there." Cross fished two cans of beer out of the cooler. "There's lean and then there's too lean. What gives?"

"Broken jaw. If you're looking for a crash diet, that's the ticket."

Cross frowned at Declan's limp arm. "I doubt you fell out of bed."

"Sometimes it's hard to stay out of trouble, Mr. Cross."

"Thom, for God's sake. Your choice of career gave me pause, Declan. Can I see your license? Just curious." He studied the document. "Nice and official. Current. Are you working a case in Florida?"

"On and off. I'm helping a friend in Miami. Daisy Diamond."

"Miss Double D. She's good. A true professional." Cross nodded, thoughtful. "Is she around?"

Declan wolfed down the crab salad sandwich. "Relaxing at the hotel."

"You think she'd like to come over for barbecue, later?"

"If you don't mind shop talk," Declan said. "She's a very focused woman."

"Come over at five for drinks."

There would be more talking after the sun went down. Some topics shouldn't be discussed in broad daylight. Ghosts shouldn't be summoned at two in the afternoon. They talked about boats and fishing.

Daisy and Kayla fell into each other's arms like long-lost friends.

"Penny for your thoughts," Cross said. He handed Declan a bright green mojito. Lots of vitamins, salad in a glass.

"Some things I don't talk about with the police."

"I'm retired."

Coming from the guy who said *once a cop, always a cop.* "What's on the grill?"

The ribs and burgers were excellent and Declan regretted that his shrunken stomach couldn't absorb more. He had to take solid food slowly. Liquids were easier and he was getting a buzz. He suspected Cross planned it that way. Tough luck, friend. The body might go limp but the mind never closes shop.

Cross made his move. "The girls are cleaning up. Let's take the boat out for a little cruise. Take your drink and the jug for refills."

The move wasn't subtle and Declan told him. "You were less lead-footed in New Orleans, copper."

"I'm older and less patient. Untie her. We won't go far."

They chugged away. Far enough to escape the swarms of mosquitoes that hung around the mangrove.

"I could have shaken the truth out of you, boy, and it wouldn't have been pretty."

Declan felt mellow. "I did nothing wrong. You can't break somebody who did nothing wrong." He shrugged. "Well, you could, but not in any way that would stand in court."

"I sniffed that lawyer aroma on you. Why become a PI?"

"I needed money for law school. I helped a few people out and they paid me for it, and I realized I liked the streets." Declan lit a cheroot and put his legs up on the railing. The sky was all stars, snowflakes in reverse. Cross lit a couple of citronella candles. The skeeters would find them soon, now that they were stationary.

"You said something about the streets of New Orleans, I recall," Cross said. "They weren't too friendly."

Declan remained silent. They didn't need to disturb the old dust of the Colvin house. He wondered if Cross remembered the name of the place.

"Did you come to confess, Declan?"

"You suspected what happened when you questioned me. There isn't anything more to say. I did what I had to do to keep us alive. There's no shame or guilt in that."

"Then why cover it up?"

"I didn't leave any evidence and I didn't remove any. Does that count as a cover-up?"

Cross smiled. "You haven't changed one bit. It worried me that a sixteen-year-old kid could have so much control. The normal response to death and violence is fear, not intellectual disputation."

"The correct sequence was fear, fight, think," Declan said. "Twenty years later, I try to think before I rush in. It isn't always possible. It wasn't then. It wouldn't have made a difference for Maury. He died because of the choices I made."

"That is so arrogant. We all make choices all the time. Maury did. And the other two. I've forgotten their names. Any preacher would tell you that you lack humility. Even your guilt is full of pride."

Declan refilled their glasses. He moved the candles closer. The bugs were homing in. "I guess that's why I came. To be reminded of cardinal sins. And for tasty barbecue. Why did you let me off the hook, Thom?"

Cross slapped at a skeeter on his thigh. "I liked the way your mind worked. It made me think of a beautiful watch. A piece of art. I couldn't take a hammer to that. And I felt your love for Stanley. Hapless damaged Stanley, way more damaged than you could ever be."

Was he damaged? Bruised or tainted by the proximity of evil, maybe. Evil was never far away. The garage goblin and the killers for hire that destroyed April and the unknown Tampa girl, Wade Benning who paid them, the invisible boss in Mexico that gave the orders. The monsters in the old family house in New Orleans. Monsters Declan would have to face someday.

EPILOGUE

THE BEACH WAS ONE LONG SINUOUS STRETCH of pale sand, its span interrupted by leaning coconut trees and rivulets of running water from the rain that had fallen overnight. Declan walked past the palapas and the lounge chairs, past the kids playing in the surf, past the elderly couples looking for sand dollars and elusive unbroken shells. Soon the footprints stopped. And the hooves' prints from the early morning horse excursions. He was well past the boundaries of the resort and the beach wasn't as pristine, as *curated*. Another word for sanitized. *We deliver the unspoiled beauty of the Caribbean.* Was that promise printed on the leaflets and the mailers, or was it better left unsaid? Even the suggestion that the real world with its ugly warts was a few minutes' walk away could trouble the anxious tourist.

Declan stepped over brown algae, the black trunks of fallen trees, and the plastic remnants of a civilization that could be reached in an hour by diesel-stinking bus or noisy motorboat.

The bartender had been helpful. "The tall blond lady from Miami? Yes, sir, I know her. She always orders a Paloma. She went to the beach, over there." A finger pointing east, distance unspecified.

Of course, she wanted to be alone. After the Islamorada excursion and two days of sexual bliss, Declan had packed his bags and flown back to Houston. It had been a headless flight. He could have stayed longer and eased the pain of separation. He could have promised to come back, offered her to join him in Houston, proposed an agency merger, whatever. But he wasn't ready. The conversation with Cross raised questions that he couldn't ponder with Daisy nearby. He needed the shadows and she was too sunny. He hadn't remained long in Houston either. Moira pampered him and his patience with her cocooning frayed fast. It had taken two weeks in Colorado with Stan and strenuous hiking to reset the counters. By then, of course, Daisy had gone incommunicado. Pissed off at him for being so dense. It took him two weeks to track her down to this remote resort in the Dominican Republic.

Declan climbed over a felled coconut tree, got wet to his knees walking around a big boulder that had no business being there, and there she was, flat on her back on her resort-issued green beach towel, in a small cove of soft, clean sand with sandpipers and hermit crabs for sole company.

He sat on his heels by her side and pushed his sunglasses down his nose.

"I found you."

She didn't raise her head or open her eyes. "Took you a while. I expected you sooner."

"You did an expert job muddling the trail. I missed you by a hair in Costa Rica. I must have talked to every bartender in San José."

She giggled. "I didn't want to make it too easy. How long are you staying?"

"How long will you have me?"

ACKNOWLEDGMENTS

WITHOUT JIM there would be no Declan Shaw, PI If my husband had been a science-fiction fan, I might never have dipped my keyboard in crime fiction. I wanted him to read my work, and he didn't like aliens, androids, and far away planets. I told him I would write something he would read—a crime story.

The character's name existed before I knew what he did for a living. Declan Shaw: a hard start followed by a whisper and an exhale. I heard a woman's voice say his name, in a dark doorway, in a city at night. He became a private investigator with an office in Houston, a city I called home for twenty years.

So many words later, I can confirm Jim read all of them. He's my first and toughest critic. Our debates are spirited. We don't always agree, but he makes the stories infinitely better.

I also want to thank a group of writers who were incredibly generous with their comments and advice. They read this manuscript in various stages of development. Craig reminded me to be kind to the reader and provide markers in a complex plot. Mark pointed out long chunks of dialogue that needed to be broken up. Steve, who writes gritty retro noir that doesn't pull punches, had questions about a nasty scene two thirds down the book. I decided to rewrite it. I'm glad I did.

Massive thanks to Ron Earl Phillips who made this book a reality. It was (it always is) a long journey. Ron's leadership at Shotgun Honey, his passion for indie publishing, his support for writers are invaluable. I am honored to have been invited to join a group of authors whose work I love and admire. Their talent bowls me over.

I'll close with a tip of the hat to the family members, the friends, and all the magazine and anthology editors and publishers that have supported my work over the years. Writing a book is a road trip. Short fiction is the refreshing pause on the journey. Let's keep the stories coming!

M.E. PROCTOR is the author of four dystopian science fiction novels, The Savage Crown Series, and a short story collection, *Family and Other Ailments – Crime Stories Close to Home* (Wordwooze Publishing). *Love You Till Tuesday* is her first crime novel and introduces Houston private detective, Declan Shaw. Proctor is a Derringer nominee. Her fiction has appeared in various anthologies and magazines: Vautrin, Stone's Throw, Mystery Tribune, Black Cat Weekly, Thriller Magazine, Cowboy Jamboree, and Shotgun Honey among others. Even if she mostly writes crime fiction these days, she still enjoys an occasional foray into horror or science fiction.

Proctor was a freelance journalist for a music magazine, and worked as an advertising account executive, before becoming a corporate communications advisor. She prefers writing fiction.

Born in Brussels, and a long time Houston resident, she now lives in Livingston, Texas, with her husband James Lee Proctor, also a writer. After all these years, she still counts in French and struggles with the Imperial system. Find her online at www. shawmystery.com, and on Substack at The Roll Top Desk: https://meproctor.substack.com

ABOUT
SHOTGUN HONEY BOOKS

THANK YOU for reading *Love You Till Tuesday* a Mountaineer Mystery, by M.E. Proctor.

Shotgun Honey began as a crime genre flash fiction webzine in 2011 created as a venue for new and established writers to experiment in the confines of a mere 700 words. More than a decade later, Shotgun Honey still challenges writers with that storytelling task, but also provides opportunities to expand beyond through our book imprint and has since published anthologies, collections, novellas and novels by new and emerging authors.

We hope you have enjoyed this book. That you will share your experience, review and rate this title positively on your favorite book review sites and with your social media family and friends.

Visit ShotgunHoneyBooks.com

SHOTGUN HONEY
FICTION WITH A KICK
shotgunhoneybooks.com